FENIAN'S TRACE

BY
SEAN P. MAHONEY

For Josh –
All the best!
Sean P Mahoney

Published by Fenian Productions
Sonoma, California

Cover Photography from Rachel Rothstein

ISBN 978-0-9983207-0-0

www.fenianstrace.com

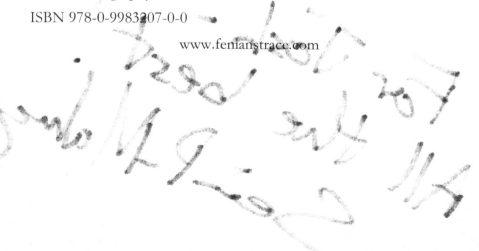

For my darling girl from Clare…
and our two boys

Chapter One

Captain Dinny's Horn

Could there be a grander place in all the world? When the sun is splittin' the stones across the whole west of Ireland, and yer lolling atop a cask of the black stuff set on the bow of a barge floating softly into the heart of Limerick, with near the whole of the city going mad for yer arrival?

If one's better, I'd trade it for there. For it was in that very spot I first saw the lads, the two of them basking in the youthful glories of a summer adventure.

I'd say the faint melody from the distance that delivered them there was nearly all they'd talked of since that poor mucky horse had her swim in the winter. Every day after, whether in the hot murk of the forge or off on the high meadow, the two kept a keen ear out for the deckmen's shrill horns sounding their warning for the lock-keeper: hold her open or get her that way. They learned well enough which calls belonged to which boats, but they knew only one could trumpet a song just for them. Just one that carried the promise-maker. It was that boat they waited on.

They both swore to Christ they heard their clarion call on a late April morning, even over the rain lashing the roof of the small McCabe forge. Even over the unfortunate fullering of an axehead.

Only but twelve, Rory was already strong enough to hoist the smaller sledgehammers and deliver a blow bang on, at least on the more simple jobs they took in. He was a ginger bull of a boy, the spit of Liam at the same age, but a real messer as well, all bold energy and

1

cheek. Nevertheless, and much to his father's gratification, he was indeed showing a precocious feel for the subtle rhythms and tempo crucial to becoming an adept striker. Liam held his hopes for his son right alongside his patience.

Also twelve his own self, and the chalk to Rory's cheese in nearly every way, Conor had a dextrous and steady hand for the iron, with a faculty for the finer bends and subtle twists that might someday produce true artwork, if there was any call for such niceties. There was not. Most needed horseshoes or hoes. Nails and bolts and the routine repairs of the bent axle or the bockety wheel. But Conor's crafty promise was unique to Liam's experience. The lads had their days in the forge since they were walking, but certainly Liam had never taught them anything of finesse... and he couldn't credit his own good stock as the source of it. Conor O'Neill was only his son in every other way but birth.

Liam McCabe shaped his iron better than any smithy in the parish. You wouldn't get a debate on that. At near fifteen stone, he wielded the hammer and tongs on the heavy metal without a bother and deftly worked the more intricate settings with equal prowess. He'd shown a knack for innovation in his younger days, some had even accused him of a wanton flourish, but he rarely conceded due cause anymore and by all accounts had managed to stifle it well down into naught. Deliberation was his first rule - one of few, all steadfast. If the lads were to glean anything from him, whether off his gruff instructions or through daily observations alone, that would be his wish. Never a blind alley.

On that wet and regretful April morn, Conor held a yellow-hot chunk of metal steady against the anvil in the clench of his tongs while Rory stood with an eight-pound sledge held aloft and ready, feet slightly apart to steady the weight, just as he'd been taught, and eyes on the top fuller. Ears to the tap, mostly. Liam adjusted the bottom fuller so to squeeze a bit more iron for the length of it, then double-tapped the precise spot where he wanted Rory to deliver the blow. It was in that split of silence, between the tap and Rory's coming hammer, that the hopeful horn may have sounded off the canal.

Rory stole a glance at Conor and was suddenly sure of it. Jaysus!

Trouble was, Liam's good training already had Rory on a reflex to his taps and with his eyes adrift with his excitement he brought the hammer down just off the mark, flinging the tools arseways and propelling the fiery axehead upward and just past Conor's chin on its way into an innocent ceiling beam.

Liam's displeasure was only betrayed by his thunderous silence. His anger had its own volumes. He simply stood upon the great anvil, wrenched the scorched chopper from the wood with a bare hand and held it out for the tongs. Conor jabbed it back into the fire to bring it again to forging heat.

Rory collected the scattered tools. "Sorry, Da."

As Liam reassembled the job, Rory checked Conor's face again, alight off the blazing flames. Every day of a life together, albeit only a brief one to then, and language needs no words. Conor's eyes said two things: yes, it was and no, we can't. He set the tongs back to the anvil.

But wasn't that glorious melody still echoing in Rory's ears? He chanced his arm. "We're after hearing Captain Dinny's horn, Da."

As Liam reset the top fuller, Rory raised the sledgehammer aloft and at the ready again, straight off practiced instinct, but his head was already well away on George's Street.

Liam double-tapped for the redemptive blow.

Rory balked. "Will we go then, Da?"

Now easy never knew anything of Liam McCabe, neither coming nor going. He'd take any interruptions only when he was good and ready to be interrupted. He tapped the metal again. Rory held the hammer stock-still.

Another tap-tap. Rory held fast.

The weight started to bear in on his young shoulders, yet he grew even more resolute. He was rapidly losing track of what he was after, but he knew right well he'd hold that hammer up 'til doomsday if he didn't see it come.

All eyes were fixed at the anvil. More taps. Deliberate. The three watched the ripe iron's glowing heat fading in the tongs. Its colors cooled from a pale yellow to a cherry red and through to a duller crimson as it yearned to regain its essential blackness.

Conor waited on tenterhooks for Liam's tap on the anvil's side, every smithy's signal to cease the work. The sullied axehead was too cooled now for fullering, a blow at such heat would only ruin its strength. Still, Liam tapped the top fuller once more. No blow came.

Conor's eyes finally moved up to Rory's. Tears dripped. His arms were quivering.

Tap-tap.

Conor didn't even wait. He pulled the axehead off the anvil.

As Liam turned to Rory and rose up his mighty hand, Conor leapt between them. "Da, please!" But Liam simply reached over him and grasped the head of the sledgehammer. He gently pulled it from Rory's grip, and then cast it hard against the door, jolting it wide open. The rain was bucketing.

"Go on then. Away with ye!"

Rory shuffled to the door, his legs suddenly exhausted. His arms still shook. Somehow he felt he'd won something significant, something big and mighty and final, yet lost something dear and delicate, both at the same time.

He looked out at the dark sky, then back inside. Liam was resetting his tools to the job. Rory picked up the sledgehammer and returned to the anvil. He took up a good striker's position, hammer high and at the ready, legs steady and balanced, the exact same stance his father had taught him. Then he spread his feet a touch wider.

Neither dared say it aloud for fears that it may make it true, but for the next three months both Conor and Rory fretted that the friendly horn music might never come again.

When it finally did, and on a late Sunday afternoon during the grand auld evening stretch of the summer weeks, it was all the more splendid. They were just finishing the last of their chores under a well-obliging sky when they heard the long buoyant bellow, trailed out by several jovial bursts. The sweetest music they'd ever heard. For the forge would be quiet. Holy hour was just past and the pub would be open again; the men's afternoon penance paid in full. The stars had aligned, all for them.

They quickly set the last of the fallen stones back into the old wall. The jaunty sheep secured once more, they bolted to find Liam. "Let me do the askin'," Conor said.

They ran down the hillside to their cottage. "Will we go then, Da?" Rory had the question out before he had the door open. "Will we?" No answer came. No one was inside.

Conor dashed across the laneway and ducked into the dark forge. Empty just the same.

"He'll be down the pub, lads." Mother Fiona and their sisters, Katy and Brigid, were in the small field around the corner, hanging the washing out under the sunshine.

"Did ya hear it, Mam?" Conor asked, as Rory tore off for the lower village. "Did ya hear Captain Dinny's horn there?"

"We did, of course," she called after. "Sure, we thought a parade was after arriving."

But Conor was away before he could hear her answer. If he gave Rory any more of a headstart he wouldn't catch him before he reached the pub. He couldn't let him bollocks this up.

Conor could run like a cutting wind and he caught Rory near the post office just past the church, but well in sight of the one pub Cloonlara has on offer. At a comfortable squeeze of just forty men, Brogan's is no rival to a proper city pub, but on a scald of a day a man could do worse than take a draught of Beamish to accompany him for a spell at the big open hearth. Indeed, it was Liam McCabe himself who fashioned the hobs and crane yoke that auld Francie Brogan used to wield the pots and kettle over his fire.

"Let me do the askin'," Conor repeated as the lads burst inside, dashing to the rear of the premises to find Liam, well into a fine session.

"Da!" Rory shouted. "We're after hearing Captain Dinny's horn." He was near dancing with the excitement.

"Bejaysus. Are ye feckin' serious?" Liam teased them. He had his pints on a Sunday, and this was a Sunday.

Conor stepped in front and made their case. "The wall's back up. The horses are fed. The wagon's clear."

"And now ye want to go off on the doss?"

"The nails are boxed," Conor added.

"Go'way. Ye boxed the nails as well?"

"We did."

"Ta."

"We'll go then Da, won't we?" Rory implored.

Toward Limerick, Cloonlara held the third of the six locks on that section of canal, the narrowest, but still nearly eighty feet in length, mitre to sill. The deck men would usually blow horns for the gates when they came in view of Paddy's Hedge, so the lads knew exactly how much time they had before they'd miss their opportunity.

As did Liam. And he'd employ every second.

"Will we, Da?" Conor asked as he fidgeted with the pendant that hung from the leather cord around his neck, which he was in the habit of doing whenever he was excited, or a bit flustered, or just generally restless… nearly all the time for a lad his age.

Liam finished his pint in a long swallow, peering down at the lads over his glass. Then he strolled to the front of the pub and leaned outside, his massive shoulders testing the doorway, and took a long study of the sky.

His youngest daughter was only just now catching up with her brothers. Liam smiled wide at her tottering run. "Well hello there, little one. Let me ask ya now. Is it a fine day, Brigid?"

"T'is, Da."

"Is it even a day for an auld cruise would you say?"

"T'is, Da."

"Then let's take us a walk, my dear," he said, taking her tiny hand in his. "And see these lads off."

The boys dashed ahead to the canal.

The cuts must have been a hundred years in by them days, the product of an elaborate scheme devised to circumnavigate the Shannon's often perilous Falls of Doonass. That vital bypass allowed Limerick vessels to access Lough Derg via Killaloe, and from there reach the Grand Canal and run it all the way to find the Liffey at Dublin. It took over forty years just to dredge the canals that branch the twelve-mile route between Limerick City and Killaloe, and to then build some ten locks to accommodate a fall in the river of near one hundred feet, but at the end of the day a man can float clear across the guts of Ireland and never set a foot on its dear green grass.

A good buzz of activity attended the canals, both the work and play usually centered around the locks. Each one needed constant tending and the Limerick Navigation Company afforded every lockkeeper a cottage. Some locks were stuck out next to nowhere but those that got situated near a village brought brand new life to its residents. Nearly every good worth trading in Ireland would go by on the regular. You'd want to be a dolt of a merchant to not take advantage of the passing commerce.

Of course, the villagers enjoyed the waterways to no end. Children would fish for eels off the lock walls, and there's no doubt many a romance bloomed on a leisurely boat ride within its intimate banks. Conor and Rory themselves learned their swimming in the canal, doubling their dares from a swift dive under the width of a passing boat to a bold, breathless stretch under the full length of the longest barges.

At their slightest, the canal locks gave just thirteen feet, so any boat needing to pass Cloonlara would want to be a narrow one. Still, the barges would come by spanning well past fifty feet of length and sure every inch was bursting with freight when times were high. Loads of turf and sand and gravel and grain were ferried all across Ireland. I was just a wee lad meself in 1860, sure a lifetime ago, but I still can remember watching the huge bell for St. Patrick's come in by way of those canals. Same bell you'll hear ring today.

Another glorious sight to behold was those barges carrying the finest black marble from the quarries of Ballysimon, heading east to Dublin. Giant, rough-hewn blocks glistening wet with the rain. Mountains on the move they were.

But nothing else compared with the boats weighed down with the casks from St. James's Gate. Every man knew what glistened wet inside, well on its way to the public houses of Limerick City. As the proud proprietor of one of the same (Clancy's it is - at the meeting of Patrick and Francis Streets, if you've a thirst) I can affirm that the four-day voyage in those tranquil waterways soothes the stout to its most perfect maturity, furnishing Limerick with the best pints in the whole of Ireland, and Clancy's by God still pulls the cream of them all.

It was that same precious cargo that made Captain Dinny McGrath the most welcomed man in Limerick. With over two hundred barrels of Guinness covering his decks, there was no mistaking his payload. Ah yes, upon the sight of those fine, white American oak casks spread atop that auld black barge floating over dark shimmering waters, it wasn't just a thirsty man might be reminded of a pint of the goodness itself.

Miles on end, whistles and shouts would ring out from the banks when his barge came in sight.

"God bless, God bless!"

"Alright Boyo, take her handy now!"

"Oh for the love of Jaysus!"

"Fair play to ye, Cap!"

Wee culchie children from the riverbank villages would skip alongside them, peppering questions: "Where ye coming from? Where ye off to? When ye passing back?" "What d'ye carry?" "Who's getting it?" "Give us some?"

At least twice a summer, some eejit would dive right in and swim up for a proper greeting. "How-ye lads. Any chance of a jar?"

Passing boatmen would enquire for the "leakage" rumoured to occur every so often on the longer journeys, though never on Dinny's watch. Might even offer to drill the hole…

Sure, it was a rare man in Ireland indeed wouldn't at least offer an appreciative tip of his cap to acknowledge the sacred freight. With his full, ruddy beard and long, wild hair, Dinny himself was quite a sight to see and he'd always acknowledge the gestures with the same proud but gracious nod, maybe send an extra thick puff of smoke up from that old dudeen that never left his lips. He knew well he was floating atop a treasure trove of the dark delight and was by no means above adding a dash of fanfare to affirm it.

The barges owned by Sir Arthur Guinness himself never left the Grand Canal, but sure a bad case of the dryness wouldn't be unknown beyond those waters and the black cure was in high demand. The Grand Canal Company supplied the barges to deliver it and Dinny skippered many a deck-full of hogsheads to the far reaches of Ireland along its waterways, each brimming with fifty-four measured gallons of fine stout. He took great pride in his charge and ran a right tight ship as they say. He aimed for smooth, uneventful journeys so to always make his schedules, and he quickly earned a reputation as a man to brook no nonsense.

T'was the brilliance of Sir Arthur's plan for mass distribution on the canals, dependent on the low-cost efficiency of men like Dinny, that allowed him to undercut the price of every brewery in Ireland and drive most of the competition to ruin. Indeed, some once fine brewers no longer local to Limerick still loathe the sight of the Guinness floating into town.

In 1913, it was still the steamships that towed the barges through Lough Derg to Killaloe - the Bolinder's engine had yet to be seen - but the steamers couldn't fit the Limerick navigation, so it was a horse that did the hauling. Linked by towropes of near a hundred feet, a good nag could pull the over fifty tonnes load of a full barge at four or five miles an hour, ambling steady along the tow-paths that lined the waterways. They got funneled off the Shannon beside the canal just below O'Briensbridge and lugged the cargo right by the lads' village before dispatching back into the river again at Plassey.

Dinny's trusty old Clydesdale went steady as they came. They called her Miss Hops because, just like that fine flavouring flower, if you hold your patience and treat her right, she'll eventually beget the stout. But when the hard rains of winter couple up with the more treacherous tides, the tow-paths often flood in their low spots and maybe give-way over their higher reaches. At the worst of times, even the most sure-footed of horses have been known to get so clattered up in the muck as to miss a step and topple from the bank. And so it was on a fierce spilling day of the prior February, along an especially precarious stretch of that pinched tow-path near Cloonlara, that Miss Hops took to the water and Conor and Rory first encountered Captain Dinny.

Word ran out that week that Con McNamara was on the lash again. To this day, Old Con mans both the lock and the post office at Cloonlara. He has for as long as anyone can recall. He also manned a small *poitín* still back then, well before he took the pledge and re-dedicated himself to his civic responsibilities after the occasion of the Rising in '16. Irish destinies or not, no man was going to assail *his* post office. The old fella dry was constant as the Rock of Gibraltar, but in them days, at those very rare times he'd get well-scuttered sampling his wares, the lockkeeping duties were simply abandoned to his faithful villagers.

The two lads were always eager volunteers for the chore, even in the most frightful weather. They loved to work the lock: to shoulder the heft of the gates against the water and bestow a sweeping welcome to visitors from near and far... to work the racks controlling the chamber depths - making the levels rise and fall like the moon in the skies above - then to open the gates again, releasing the momentarily trapped vessels to continue on their journeys. Both lads knew their little village upside down by then and I expect they already had a tinge of longing for further fields, a yearning heightened with every boat that passed them by.

Conor relished the opportunities to meet the various boat crews that would move through, always intrigued by those who spoke in odd tones and forever keen to hear the traveling tales they would tell. He was a fervent audience for his temporary captives.

Rory was simply helpless to stay away from anything that might have even a hope of resembling action or excitement, even the slow-moving barge traffic on the canals, but to be sure it was the power that was in it all that truly caught his fancy, one he wouldn't feel elsewhere. Indeed, if he'd catch Conor hanging off the words of a particularly entertaining boatman, he'd deliberately slow the lock machinations to dally the craft's exit. Of course, Captain Dinny wasn't one to stand for any of those shenanigans. His business was in transport and you couldn't move anything without moving.

A heavy blanket of rain covered Ireland most of that February, as it does, and Dinny's barge had been under assault since taking on his Guinness casks where the Grand Canal ends at Tullamore. He kept a limited crew, just himself to skipper, a deckmate to handle Miss Hops and maybe steer in relief, and then a greaser to clean and cook and do whatever else he was feckin' told to do. When they approached the Cloonlara lock they were all three huddled at the turf-fire in the small cabin. Just past Paddy's Hedge, Captain Dinny's deck-mate blew his horn.

Off the sound of it Conor and Rory hopped onto Oscar, the McCabe's loyal old draught horse, and galloped out into the rain to snatch the lock key waiting ready just behind the counter at the post office. That in hand, they rode to the canal to see what was coming.

They could tell immediately. "It's the Guinness!" Rory shouted. They knew damn well that was something special.

They watched Miss Hops splashing toward them on the muddy tow-path and got the gates pushed open just as she reached the lock. Conor gave her cold, wet mane a rub as she passed by, but she knew the routine well enough and didn't stop until the barge was in and past the gate. When it was, she didn't need to be told.

The greaser emerged from his dry shelter at the last possible moment.

Conor waved to him. "Well now. How's she cuttin'?"

The greaser didn't answer. A lad well short of whiskers his own self, he just grabbed the mooring ropes off the timberhead and tossed them up.

"Where's the lockkeep?"

Conor looped them around the bollards. "In the pub. We'll get you through."

"Ye best hurry on, boyo. Been pissin' all the way since Dublin." He looked about at the countryside, off toward the mountains of East Clare. "Arse enda beyond," he sneered.

Rory shut the breast gate while Conor closed down the sluices. "We'll have ye out in no time."

Rory quickly cranked open the land racks on either side and the waters rushed in to fill the lock. The barge slowly started to rise.

"All this Guinness for Limerick?" Conor asked.

The greaser ignored him and retreated back into the smoky warmth of the cabin.

Rory looked to Conor, imitating the lad's Dublin accent, "... 'Been pissin' all the way since Dooblin.' Feckin' jackeen."

They stood in the rain, watching the level rise until it finally reached equilibrium with the next reach. Conor tossed back the mooring ropes and Rory pushed open the deep gates, re-opening the lock.

The greaser trudged back outside.

Conor pointed up toward a high bank of the tow-path, not too far ahead. "There's a stretch on the higher path there that washed out last week. Been murder on the horses."

The greaser ignored them still. He gave two tugs on the tow-rope and whistled for Miss Hops to start off again. She had a spot of trouble getting started in the slip but eventually got a foothold.

"Bit pinchy now, might test her hooves. We could lead her through if ye like."

The young greaser made his way back and stood under the cabin overhang, out of the rain. He glared at the lads as the barge started moving. "Bog-off, ya bleedin' culchies."

Conor and Rory climbed back onto Oscar and walked him slowly along the tow-path. They kept him even with the barge as it moved ahead down the canal, trailing Miss Hops by a hundred feet as she ascended toward the spot Conor warned of.

They weren't saying it, but by Jaysus if they weren't hoping to Heaven for it with every leery step she took.

Sure enough, just before she reached the top end of the tow-path, Miss Hops lost her footing in the muck and slipped right down into the canal. T'was a great splash.

Rory's laugh was almost as loud as the greaser's cry for help.

Captain Dinny and the deck-mate burst out of the cabin. They saw Miss Hops sloshing about in the water. "For fuck's sake! What's after happening here?"

"She slipped right off the path," the greaser said.

Miss Hops swam to the edge and tried to climb back ashore but the near banks were too steep and too slippery.

"We offered to lead her through the muck!" Rory yelled.

"Then why didn't ye?" shouted the deck-mate.

"Ask that feckin' gobshite," Rory answered.

"Fuck off!" yelled the greaser.

They all watched the poor horse as the barge drifted closer with its momentum, waiting for her to find a way to gain the edge. She kept trying... but there wasn't a hope.

"No bother now," the greaser said. He pointed to a low spot on the tow-path about thirty yards ahead. "She'll be grand once she gets there."

12

Finally Miss Hops gave up on the edge and started to swim in circles, but she was struggling with the tow-line still attached at her neck. As the boat neared her it went to slack and started tangling around her legs, making her all the more frantic.

"She's gettin' all bollocksed-up in the rope," Conor said, hopping off Oscar.

The greaser leaned over the deck rail and started pulling the rope tight.

"She's in trouble," Rory said, reaching out his hand. "Here. Give us the rope."

The greaser kept tugging on it. "I've got it!"

But he was only making it worse. The rope was twisted about her legs and with his every pull they got more restricted. She couldn't move them to swim. She started jerking her head higher, straining for breath as she began to sink.

"Stop pulling and give us the feckin' rope!" Rory shouted.

Conor yanked off his boots. He called to Captain Dinny. "Mister. If he doesn't give him that rope yer horse is gonna drown."

The greaser kept pulling. Miss Hops could barely keep her muzzle above the water.

Captain Dinny grabbed a hatchet and chopped the rope free of the massive eye bolt securing it to the deck. He tore the rest of it from the greaser's hands and threw it all to Rory.

"Give it slack 'til I get to her." Conor yelled to him. Then he dove into the canal and swam toward Miss Hops.

Rory fed the excess rope back into the water as he steered Oscar ahead and past the low spot. He tied its end to his horse collar and faced him away from the canal, ready for a mighty pull at the right moment, if it was ever to come. He looked back to the water.

Miss Hops' went full under before Conor could reach her. He followed her down.

He got hold of her as she sank and quickly got atop her back to find his bearings, groping below for the rope. He felt a rush of water and just avoided a wallop to his hand, so he knew her left legs were still free, albeit wildly kicking. It was her right legs were ensnared, but still straining hard against the rope. Even if he could find where it was tangled, it was so taut he wouldn't be able to get it free. He wished to God he had a knife.

When they touched bottom, probably about eleven feet at that reach, Conor knew he had to let her go. His breath was nearly gone. He found her mane and gave it a tender rub. But with it, she suddenly quieted. The fight left her legs and the tension released. He bolted astride her, pulled her right hooves together and yanked the rope down with the last of his strength. It freed.

As soon as she felt the bind come loose, Miss Hops pushed off the canal floor, surging upward. Conor just grasped her mane in time, clinging to the great Clydesdale as she shot for the surface.

When at last they burst through, Rory kicked auld Oscar with all his strength, plunging him forward through the muck. The rope tautened, pulling Miss Hops toward the bank and finally hurtling her up and out of the canal, with Conor still hanging on. Neither any worse than wet.

As a child, Dinny McGrath fancied himself a future rogue sailor of the Seven Seas. But alas, a quare queasy stomach on even the mildest swells limited his skippering career to our tame inland waterways, far from the adventurous oceans of his young dreams. Though he never got to sail the world's blue, in Dinny's mind, he was still a warrior of wild waves and a conqueror of violent squalls.

No matter the weather, when he neared his next destination, he'd hoist a bold boot upon the foremost cask like it was a glorious dragon's head on a Viking ship, and he a High King of Ireland returning to harbour after a triumphant campaign of plunder and pillage. With his head thrust high at the fore, pipe clenched in his jutting jaw, he cut quite an impressive sight that was well-recognised at every quay he passed. Of course, none were wise to the fact that deep in the heart of the great Captain Dinny, he knew indeed that he was just a hopelessly whimsical fella being towed across peacefully flat waters by a clumsy horse.

It was the desperate need to protect his precious reputation that eventually prompted his renowned promise to the lads. See, Dinny was tight as a duck's arse and one day it dawned on him that he hadn't had to buy a pint for himself since he began hauling the Guinness. He realised that every publican in Ireland, meself included, knew well where his product came from and knew well that his livelihood depended on its prompt and regular arrival. For many, it was only Dinny's well-known prowess and pluck on the canals that ensured that schedule would be met. For that, he surely deserved just recognition and due reward. Nothing less than free jars in every pub within sight of a dock.

Sure, he couldn't risk all that just because his clumsy feckin' horse took a slip and got soaked. He'd be the laughingstock of the waterways.

Once the excitement was over and they determined Miss Hops to be sound and the barge to be ready for continuing on, Dinny offered up a firm handshake. "Thanks a million, lads. Sure, I know you'll be keeping this between us now."

Rory laughed. "I will in me hole."

"C'mere to me now, there's no call to be cuttin' da back off anyone." Dinny jangled the coins in his pocket. "A little something for yer assistance."

"We don't want it," Conor said.

"We don't?" Rory asked.

"No. We want a lift to Limerick. Any time yer passing."

"Not a chance," Dinny replied. "Only boatmen on board. Now, that's in stone."

Rory pointed at the poor greaser. "Then what's he doin' there?"

"Feck off, ye feckin' bogtrotter!"

"Now, now, lads." Dinny countered. "T'is down to Con McNamara to maintain these tow-paths and clearly he's been derelict in that duty. We wouldn't want him hearing trouble from the Company on account of a little misadventure."

Rory pointed to the greaser again. "It was that eejit caused the trouble."

"Well if it brings ya comfort, that eejit will be seein' no passage back to Dublin on this barge." Dinny turned to the greaser. "Ah lad, truth be told now, yer thick as a ditch. You can go ashore here or Limerick City, your choice. From there you can feck off, ya useless git." He turned back to Rory. "Now. There ya are. Sorted. Now, let's have your word as men that this stays our little secret and we can all get ourselves in outta the rain."

A few years older and surely they'd have negotiated a cask of Guinness for their troubles, but they were still just boys then and hard after adventure. Conor stood fast. "You'll take us on any time you pass. Either direction, 'til we want to get off."

"Or we spill yer story to every boat that passes," Rory added.

Dinny knew he was beaten. "If I hear word of this back from anyone, you'll never set foot -"

"How will we know when he comes?" Rory asked Conor.

"You'll hear me auld horn," said Dinny.

"We hear loads of horns," Rory said.

"Ah fer fuck's sake. I'll play ye a grand auld tune. You can jig yer ways right on deck."

"Play it now." Rory said. "So we know it."

"Are ye takin' the piss?"

The lads didn't bother to answer, wasn't an inch of budge or wither in them. Finally, Captain Dinny trudged back to the cabin. He returned horn in hand, an old curved bronze trumpet, about a good foot or so in length.

"Do ye know *Dublin Daisies*?" he asked. Both lads shook their heads.

"Well then, it's a treat you're in for, isn't it?"

And didn't auld Captain Dinny McGrath proceed to play a surprisingly tuneful chorus of *Dublin Daisies*? And sure he wasn't half bad at that.

Indeed, he was a fair sight better on it when they finally heard it again on that summer Sunday afternoon. They told him as much as they climbed aboard, much to Con McNamara's surprise. He'd never known Dinny to take on passengers, let alone young lads.

The barge was out of the lock and moving on when Liam and little Brigid reached the bridge over the canal. She waved to her brothers before they passed underneath, then skipped to the other side to see them reappear, just below the tawdry old *sheela-na-gig* carved into the face of the bridge to ward away the gray lady ghost.

"Couple a wee chancers," Liam said to Dinny, when his end came out from under.

"Ah, stop," says Dinny. "You know yerself." He had a smile for Liam, but at the same time he was carefully studying him for any hint that Miss Hops' mishap had been divulged. He could detect nothing, but that didn't quite allay his worry. Liam McCabe was one hard man to read.

The lads said hello to Dinny's loyal deck-mate and his new greaser, then perched themselves on two fine casks right up at the beak of the bow. They set their flat caps askance to the warm sun and settled in for the journey, without even a bother trying to contain their gratified smiles.

The first stretch covered the long, near straight run of the canal, through the lower locks at Newtown and then Gilloge, where the horses crossed over to the east-side tow-path. The lads chatted amiably with the befuddled lockkeepers.

"Ya taking on passengers now, Dinny?"

"Only royalty... The High Kings of Limerick they are," Dinny replied, through teeth sore from clenching his pipe.

When the chat ebbed, the only sounds to mar the silence were the ripplings of the water and the knock of Miss Hops' hooves, ever-trudging the tow-path. Over that expanse, Captain Dinny would hardly need hold his tiller, just set the rudder ahead middle and split the water. He could never resist looking back to watch the crests of the lazy wake drifting wide to gently splash the canal walls. Dead even they'd be.

Just past Gully's Quarry, the canal found the Shannon again at the Black Bridge, where at mid-river a horse would leave Clare behind for Limerick with just one step, and where the pinching canal broadened out into wider waters for the last mile of river before taking the final short canal into Limerick City.

They passed many fishermen, chasing pike and perch in their nobbies or paired up for snap-netting the salmon, drifting by in their flat-bottomed angling cots. T'was all before the motor-lorries about now, so merchant traffic was already well-harried. Add all the sailboats and rowing punts out under the rare sun and good Captain Dinny was suddenly faced with tricky summertime vessel navigations after their sleepy canal voyage. A bit of steering to keep him awake.

The lads needed no such inspiration. It was all there for the watching.

Under the afternoon sun the suddenly vast water took on a magnificently shimmering silver hue and splashed a gentle shiver upon the green reeds at the river's edge. They saw gray herons and water hens and black coots paddling against the high yellow water lilies. They spied the makeshift fishermen's huts hidden in amongst the alder trees and white willows towering just beyond the shoreline and agreed they glimpsed the remains of Peg's Height, the infamous old shebeen for thirsty anglers. They watched the cormorants diving for fish, trailing the sounds of their deep guttural cries to their quick striking splashes. They watched the big birds land on posts or buoys and spread their wet wings to the sun for drying, noting the snooty indifference with which they regarded the posh white swans drifting in the currents.

Miss Hops eventually pulled them into the short Park Canal, a shortcut avoiding another treacherous length of the Shannon that looped through the rapids of Corbally, and made way for the last reach into the city, to the giant Guinness storehouse on the south bank at Lock Quay, nearly at Baal's Bridge. From there, it was but a quick jaunt to the adventures of George's Street or the great walls of King John's Castle, but it was this last stretch on the barge that the lads would always remember.

For there was glorious bustle all along those quays. Crusty fishermen unloaded their catch to bickering merchants. Salty sailors tended to their ships as the dock-workers unloaded prized goods from the world over. Warehousemen guided giant cranes over the cargos, hoisting great crates over the canal walls. Gentlemen escorted fine ladies along the footpaths, observing the spirited endeavors of commerce firsthand.

Yet, to one and all, there was no finer spectacle, no greater cause for celebration, than the sight of a barge stuffed full of Guinness parting the last of the waters to reach its final destination. Every worker in view gave a wave or sounded a cheer and didn't Conor and Rory return each one of them.

Ye can rest easy, lads. The stout it's in, safe and sound.

Chapter Two

Jam Tarts With Custard

But all the fanfare and gawking in Ireland won't get the barrels off the barge and into the pubs. Unloading well over two hundred hogsheads takes hard work from strong men for long hours. An impatient Guinness agent awaits even the earliest barge and if a Guinness agent isn't fussy, demanding, meticulous and altogether a right bollocks, he isn't a Guinness agent for long. The most powerful dockmen on the quays scurry like frightened hare under his orders, barking his mandate, simple and clear: waste not a minute and spill not a drop. Every barrel weighed and logged and immediately sent on its way, into the depot or off to the road. It's a sobering business that gets out the drink.

Your man was not at all impressed to see the two lads perched so pleased atop his very own profit drums, right up at the front of the barge, proud as fuckin' peacocks. Captain Dinny got his ears filled even before he could toss up a mooring line.

"This sort of indulgence has no place in the Guinness distribution system!" hollers the agent, all high and mighty like he's addressing Parliament itself. "If it's ferryin' lads ye fancy, go fill yer decks with manure. Let 'em ride on shite. It won't be the black stuff."

He jutted his fat nose toward the lads. "Feck off with ye now."

Left not a thimble of hope for even the most affable protest or offer to help. Not a chance. Conor and Rory nodded their thanks to Captain Dinny and got themselves swiftly ashore just as an army of dockmen wheeled out their massive mobile cranes and descended onto the casks at hand. They divided the barge into sections and worked in groups of five: one on the crane and one on the chain, the sturdiest two men down on deck to lug each barrel into position for the lift, and a good hands man to roll it away. Each team quickly found its rhythm, buoyed it with a song, and kept a keen eye on the others for a bit of the competition that was in it.

The lads stood at the quay for a spell and watched them unburden Dinny's barge, relentlessly emptying that proud provider of liquid salvation back into a barren old raft of rust and rot… a coming eyesore under the rare summer sun. It didn't take long 'til they stopped watching.

They turned toward Limerick City, all the fun and messin' they could get up to, there for the taking. All that was between them and it was meself. How might our days be different if I'd already been off and on me way?

Rather, two men had just secured four barrels up onto the dray and I was climbing into the seat to get them heading back to my pub. Clancy's, that is.

"Sorry, sir?" Rory asked me, "Would ya be knowing the way to George's Street?" Sure, they knew the way well enough already. Enough to know a lift was handier than a walk.

"I do know the way," says I, never being one to eschew company. "Hop on up and you will too." They hurried aboard for their second free jaunt of the afternoon and off we went.

Wasn't long down the lane and I had them placed as Liam McCabe's lads from Cloonlara. Of course, I already knew well of Liam. Near all of Limerick did. His story held that kind of legendary secret that no one can bear to keep, at least until everyone is quite sure everyone else knows it, and then no one speaks of it ever again because it's such an especially private matter and must be rightly hushed as such. Amongst the Irish, a good secret is always at its safest once everyone's whispered it.

Certainly no one ever spoke a word of it to Liam himself. T'would take a fool.

The young lads wouldn't have known a thing about any old secret and by God I wouldn't be the one to divulge it. That was well back in the past, like history was then. Not like today, with it all around and right up on top of us.

I prefer the sort of history that stays old. It can bend and twist and stretch and swell, but it shouldn't ever come back at us. It ought to leave us be. Just leave well enough alone and not ever come back at us, like it did on the lads. Like a sly thief in the dread of dusk. It's the fucking secrets that keep it coming back. They are the shadows that beget the night.

There was a waft in the air from Geary's Biscuit Factory and the conversation along our journey quickly landed on jam tarts, as it will. Rory spoke quite keenly of the necessity for a dollop of custard alongside, insisting for the duration that the accompaniment wasn't just his personal preference, but simply the only way a jam tart should ever be eaten. Only a daft man would pass on his custard. Conor eventually agreed on the general principal, but he was after a slice of sweet seed cake loaf and couldn't be troubled in the least whether it came with any mushy old custard.

A sweet shop was first on their agenda. Then they were on the hunt for a game of hurlin' or maybe some rounders if they came across it first. Sure, they'd take on any city lads, no bother. Mostly rubbish them…

Upon Clancy's, I steered my horse close in to ease the unloading of the barrels. "Now, lads," I says, pointing my shillelagh further down the lane to the east. "Only a wee skip ahead to George's Street."

I lit up my pipe as they jumped off, looking about for the bustle and buzz. "Thanks a million!"

"My pleasure. Enjoy that custard, now."

They started off, then stopped again. "We'll help ya with the barrels first."

"Ta, but these are a might hefty. Off with ye now."

"How will ya get them off?" Conor asked me.

"No bother."

"Not alone you won't," says Rory.

"Won't be me at all."

"How?" they pressed.

"Well, I'll enjoy this smoke until two able-bodied men pass by, and if they look at all thirsty, I'll offer to stand them each a pint if they get them off and in."

"What if none come?"

"I haven't left them in the lane yet."

"We'll take 'em in," says Conor.

"Ah now lads, that's a lovely gesture, but these here take a man's arms. And I believe ye have custard waiting."

With that, they were right back up before I knew it. It took all of Rory's strength but sure he had enough to shift and shove and shuffle the barrels as needed, and together didn't they manage to get four full hogsheads off the dray and into the pub and even up onto the counter.

Then they sat themselves at the bar. "We're waitin' on those two pints, Mr. Clancy," Rory says.

Back then I was still bottling the Guinness (today Clancy's Public House draws it direct from the barrel - the best pint in Ireland!) and there was no chore worse than filling the bottles. Washing, sterilising, filling and capping, a right royal pain in me tired auld bollocks.

I poured two nice lemonades and set them on the bar. "I'll propose a deal with ye," I says. "Fill the bottles for me and you get as much lemonade as ye can drink. And, I'll even put a bit of grub in ye, and a few pence in yer pockets as well and still have ye off to the sweet shop for your custard before they're closed."

They tasted their lemonades and looked at each other.

"Now, are ye men or are ye mice?" I asked. Sure, it's the best lemonade in Limerick City. I had them.

"Deal," they says.

I explained them the process, each tedious, painstaking step, then gave them the shortest possible demonstration of the task and let them at it. I was sure, once they realised the misery they were in for, they'd leg it at the first opportunity that came, so I knew I couldn't turn my back to them for even a moment. I poured me a ball of malt, innocently set my chair in just such a way as to thwart an easy escape, and re-lit me pipe. I then endeavored to captivate them with long tales of times past.

There was once a great tradition among our peoples of the *seanchaí*, the designated storyteller of the clan, the guardian of the history, responsible for keeping it alive and for passing it on. Now, I'm no *seanchaí*, but I served a few years teaching in the national school before the dear wife passed and I made a good long study of the Irish Annals in my days there. When she took her leave of me and I found I could now spend my full days and nights in a pub and arrive home without quarrel or consequence, I promptly opened Clancy's... but I still know my way around our past.

Today, I'm just a humble publican who likes a bit of chat. I can lend the long ear now and again but I'll generally favor the sound of my own voice to yours, especially when it's recounting the grand history of auld Ireland. I've a fond nostalgia in me for times I never knew... times better than ours.

These days there's a clamor all about for the Irish history, but in my teaching days our schoolbooks were still written in England, by English politicians, with all their "sun never sets on the bloody empire" of Magna Cartas and Hundred Year Wars of Roses and other manner of such shite. When the texts omit the entire history of Ireland, from its proud ancient days and through seven hundred years of brutal subjugation, it beseeches the amateur historian to convey a bit of the past to the young ones when he gets a chance, especially if it might distract them from the relentless boredom of the bottling.

And didn't I have grand stories for the lads?

Where else to start but with the legendary Fionn Mac Cumhaill and his brave band of Fianna of ancient Ireland? The Fianna were the fiercest of warriors, sworn to defend Ireland against all enemies and be at all times at the ready for battle. They lived off in the forests, well apart from the peaceable common folk, but they kept a keen ear out for when danger was afoot, they could be summoned with three calls of a hunting horn.

"Just like Captain Dinny called us," Conor said.

"Ah yes, the grand call to action," I says. "Petitioning lads far and wide to come out for their jam tarts."

Fionn Mac Cumhaill was their greatest leader. As a young boy, he had caught and eaten the Salmon of Knowledge and so gained all the wisdom of the world. He grew to be a giant, and his doings and travels helped shape this island to what it is today.

"Giants my arse," Rory says. "Giant gobshites more like."

"Ah, yer just a prick," Conor says. "Let him tell the story."

Rory stood to go. "The feckin' Salmon of Knowledge? Let's get to the sweet shop."

"No." Conor wasn't budging. "How did he shape Ireland?"

"Well," I continued, "on his way to Scotland he didn't want to get his feet wet and so he made the great Giant's Causeway as stepping stones."

"Feckin' nonsense," Rory muttered, but he did sit back down to the bottles all the same.

"He once even tore free a piece of our land to throw at an enemy," I added. "But alas, he missed. And that lads, is how the Isle of Man came to be."

"He missed?" Rory says. "The great giant missed? Feck's sake!"

"What happened to him?" asked Conor.

"He's never died. He only sleeps, in a great secret cave hidden somewhere under the green grass of Ireland, along with the men of his trusted Fianna, waiting still for those three calls of the horn. He'll come when Ireland needs him most. When there is no other hope."

"Well there's no hope of me listening to more of this shite," says Rory, up again and away from the bottles. "Ye can lap up all the feckin' fairytales. I'll be lapping up that jam tart. With custard."

I couldn't have that. They weren't half through the bottles yet.

"Ah, ye prefer the more proper histories, do you lad?" I asked him. "A man for facts. Truths and realities? Blood and guts maybe?"

Rory didn't take the bait. "Come on will ya, Conor."

"If not Fionn Mac Cumhaill" I asked him, "then who is the greatest hero of Ireland?"

Rory didn't hesitate. "Parnell."

"Ah yes, Parnell, the uncrowned King of Ireland. Founder of the Land League and creator of the moral Coventry…" I raised my shillelagh high to signify the man's great heights. Then I let it drop. "… when he wasn't too busy romancing another man's wife."

Rory's face fell like the news was fresh with the day. It was no surprise he wouldn't know of the disappointment Parnell wrought on

Ireland. Liam McCabe wouldn't be one to relate another man's failures.

"Yes, yes, Parnell was almost great," I conceded, "but did he ever even raise a fist for Ireland? Did he risk his very own blood and guts? No, he didn't, and he gave everything away for a woman. Scandalous. Now Rory, is he really your best hero?"

"No." Rory looked at Conor, but this was his own challenge. "Daniel O'Connell is."

I stood for another bit of show. "Ah, now. The Great Liberator himself. Another of Ireland's greatest politicians. Catholic Emancipation, indeed. He gave his lifetime to it. Well, almost."

I sat back down. "He died actually in Italy, not Ireland. Fionn Mac Cumhaill sleeps forever in Irish soil but in the end O'Connell gave up on us and left. Another almost, I'm afraid. Did ye know Daniel O'Connell once had half of Ireland on its way to the sacred grounds of Clontarf to hear him speak out against English rule? Of course the English forbade it, as they would, and what did yer man O'Connell do? He called it off. Why? He feared blood might be shed. Now lads, can ye ever imagine that?"

"He was a great man," Rory said softly.

"Of course he was, lad." I said. "One of our very best. But, like Parnell, he was a politician, and the day a politician becomes a hero will be the very first. I don't mean to assail the men, they did important things, but not heroic deeds. It's simply a matter of mismatched skills, lad. Politicians compromise. Heroes do not. The great Fianna warriors had three mottoes to live by: Purity of our hearts, strength of our limbs, action to match our speech. A politician brings only one... perhaps, and that's if he's great. But they're hardly the stuff of heroes."

"Conor," Rory said. "Let's go."

Conor could hear Rory's dander was up with me. "I'll just finish this bottle."

"Do you know why those grounds of Clontarf are considered sacred?" I asked Rory.

"I don't care."

"Well, if you fancy yourself a blood and guts man, you might want to stick around for just this story. Any blood and guts man doesn't know the Battle of Clontarf, might be called into question."

It was, I believe, that word *battle* that made all the difference. Rory's feet settled down. "No doubt you've heard of Brian Boru?" I asked.

"Of course."

"Now, he's no fairytale," I said.

"A High King of Ireland," says Rory. "Everyone knows that."

"Ah, very good… the Greatest and Last True High King of Ireland. And do ye know what you two lads have in common with him? What no lads in Dublin or even Limerick could ever claim?"

Have I ever seen such eager eyes? "Help me with a few more bottles here and I'll tell ye now." Rory put his hand to a bottle, but he didn't get straight to washing it.

Wasn't I gobsmacked to learn that these two fine Clare lads were well unaware that auld Brian Boru was a good Clare man his ownself, born only a spit up the Shannon at Killaloe. That was where his legend began, navigating those same waters the lads had floated upon only an hour earlier. Where they were riding high bringing in the Guinness, young Brian and his brothers took to the river for raids against the hated Vikings who'd conquered Dublin and Waterford and Limerick. The same heathens he'd seen viciously murder his mother when he was a boy.

Young Rory sat down in his chair at that. I surely had him now. Hanging on the words, he was. Conor as well. "Where did the Vikings come from?" he asked.

"From the north and the east, across the Irish Sea."

"From England?"

"Through it more like. The English couldn't stop them. They had already run amok over England before they came here. What's important to know is - they weren't Irish. Trespassers they were."

Brian's own father ruled the area that made up most of today's County Clare, and if there was ever a lad raised for warring, Brian Boru was him. As a lad he became literate in both Latin and Greek just to study the great generals, the works of Caesar and Charlemagne, learning their strategies of warfare to someday become a supreme tactician himself. Sure, didn't he even master the game of chess for the lessons in it?

He was a born leader and a brilliant innovator, coming up with his very own weapons and tactics to fight off the droves of enemies forever coming at them, even when they were far outmanned. He and his brother Mohan, who had become the King of Munster after succeeding their father, waged guerrilla warfare against Ivar, the Viking king that controlled Limerick City in them days. When Ivar killed Mohan, Brian himself became the King of Munster, and didn't rest one feckin' moment until he avenged his brother's death. He killed Ivar and all his sons and destroyed their Limerick fortress, taking it back for Ireland.

The lads came at me with all manner of questions. "How did he kill Ivar? How many sons did he kill? How exactly did he kill them? What fortress? How did he destroy it? Where was it?" They wanted to know just where each and every thing happened. They were astonished to learn that so much had occurred so near. So much blood spilled upon the very laneways they walked, the fields they ran... ghosts everywhere.

Answers I didn't know, I invented. After all, it's truth we're all after and a good truth is something like a good lamb chop - sure, it's enough on its own to fill your belly but you'll need to add a dash of something if you aim to draw the full flavor from it... really smack your lips. There's a lot of glory in history and I've never been one to allow a lot of facts and figures and dates and details to muck it up. Too tight a hold on those and its guts fall right out through your hands.

As the new millennium was only dawning, Brian expanded his kingdom across Ireland, from the shores of the Shannon outward toward all seas. He ended the Viking onslaughts of destruction and drove the invaders from his lands, finally bringing the regional chieftains under his rule as the one High King of Ireland. He ordered the construction of new bridges and roads to spur commerce, and built great churches and libraries and schools. He even sponsored poets and artists to lift the Irish spirit from its depths of darkness and wreckage. His reign brought over a decade of peace and order and prosperity to Ireland. Now that's a hero.

But Rory couldn't be arsed with all the peace and unity. He wanted battles and bloodshed, warriors and warfare. Of course, the great Battle of Clontarf would do just fine.

Rebellion would come, as it always will. The former chieftains were no more content living in peace and prosperity than Rory was in hearing tales of it, at least if it required obedience to Brian at the price of their own power. They recruited Viking warriors and more foreigners into an alliance of rivals to Brian, and then led sixteen thousand men to Clontarf to battle Brian's army… on Good Friday no less.

At that moment, I thought it worthwhile to consult the great Annals of Loch Ce for words better than I could offer, if only to assure the lads got the fullest dramatic effect. I keep an edition handy at the bar for just such occasions.

For Brian Boru, then in his eighty-eighth year, and after years of calm and harmony,

"it was like putting a hand into a griffin's nest to assail it. It would not be evading conflict, but seeking great battles and contests, to advance against the multitude that had then arrived there; for the choicest brave men and heroes of the Island of Britain had arrived there."

I closed the book with a most profound thud, for the next words are always strong in my memory and hear far better when preceded with a good dose of lingering silence.

"Warlike and haughty was the uprising they made!"

"Brian slaughtered 'em, didn't he?" Rory says. "I know he did."

"Let him finish!" Conor shouted.

"He drove them right back to wherever the feckers came from!" Rory cried.

"Well now," I says, "auld Brian was a deeply devout Christian and so he refused to bloody his own hands on such a sacred day."

"He didn't fight?" Rory asks.

"Sure he fought," Conor insisted. "Didn't he?"

"He wanted to. He even tried to postpone the contest, but of course the pagan hordes had no regard for faith on any day. But before he ceded command to his son, he led his army of Irish warriors to the great battle. He held a crucifix high in one hand and his valiant sword in the other…" I held up my glass and shillelagh likewise, "and he delivered a speech every Irishman should know off by heart, especially in these days. He stood amid his brave men and he said, 'On your valor rests the hopes of your country today; and what surer grounds can they rest upon? Oppression now attempts to bend you down to servility; will you burst its chains and rise to the independence of Irish freemen? Your cause is one approved by Heaven!'"

I suspect many youngsters might've been bored stupid between the yarn I was spinning and the endless monotony of the bottling, but Rory hung raring on every word and still never spilled a drop. He couldn't get enough of Brian Boru, the greatest Clare man of all. He drank it up like liquid gold, filling himself with a pride that shone right back through his eyes like torches. Engrossed as he was, I was even able to reposition my chair. He was no longer a threat to dash for the door. Sure, he'd have gone for a lock-in if I didn't finally send them off in the end. Long forgot all about his jam tart with custard as I continued into the night.

At dawn, the armies clashed. Where the Irish had numbers, the Vikings wielded superior weaponry and wore protective chain-mail armour. The battle was long and fierce and the blood flowed freely. Brian's courageous son killed one hundred of the enemy by his own hands, fifty with the sword in his right and fifty with the sword in his left, before he himself was cut down. The fighting nearly outlasted the daylight, but by dusk Brian's forces had vanquished the Vikings, scattering them to the sea, away and gone, leaving Ireland once more to the Irish.

"I knew it!" Rory shouts. "Didn't I tell ya, Conor?"

"I knew as well."

"Now, now. Don't get ahead of yourselves," I warned. "It wasn't all banners and parades."

Alas, poor Brian didn't ever get to enjoy the spoils of his great triumph. As the enemy fled, one stray Viking survivor chanced upon the tent where Brian was praying thanks of their success. He charged with his battle-axe and overcame Brian's lone attendant with a vicious blow. Brian raised once more his mighty sword, and with his final stroke took his assailant's leg, but the rotten foreigner was already upon him and the virtuous King's head was severed.

"Fuck's sake," Rory mutters. Pure gutted he was.

"But auld Brian had his victory in hand. He had his Ireland, united again. He had enough." I gave Conor a sly wink. "But it is said that when Brian's blood spilled upon his attendant's ghastly and near fatal wound, it healed instantly. Right as rain."

"Ah, Mr. Clancy!" Rory grumbled. "Now why would ya go on and add that shite to it?"

"Well, that's how I understand it happened."

"Sure, but ya don't believe it now?" Rory asked, in all earnestness.

"No, not at all," I says. "Sure, I don't believe it actually happened. But I am quite certain it's the truth."

Rory threw up his hands and chuckled. "Now I don't know what yer feckin' going on about at all."

I looked to Conor. "Do you?"

After a moment, he nodded softly. "I think so."

I think he did know, but somehow I couldn't seem to read his face, though I'll never forget the look that was on it: a kindly smile and sad but knowing eyes. I've no doubt nearly all the stories I told them over the years were as new to him as to Rory. Still, he always looked like he'd already heard them too many times before but just hadn't the heart to let on. I remember thinking that a lad of only twelve years shouldn't be capable of looking like that. Where was his innocence?

There are still odd days I wonder if somehow he already knew what their own story would be as well… knew all along. But there's a keen difference between knowing your history and really understanding it. If you don't know its secrets, you're wasting your time. A history without secrets is like, well, maybe something like a jam tart without custard. Did young Conor already know their secrets even? Could he have known the price they'd pay for keeping them?

A noble *seanchaí* didn't only pass the history along. He took a responsibility for collecting it as well. For sniffing it out and tracking it down, even reaching in and yanking it out of a well-girded hole now and again, if only for the sake of the good generations to come. Yet, when he finally has hold of it, it can be a right tricky grip.

It so happens these lads, young Conor O'Neill and Rory McCabe of Cloonlara, made my acquaintance and I fast grew a keen affection for them. I know now their secrets. Am I to keep them as well? What will be that price?

T'was a look I saw lately has me putting them down to paper this day. Kindly and sad, yet knowing.

Chapter Three

A Cloak of Blackness

The bottling work got done quite well and with nary a complaint, on that day and for many more that came after it. The lads delighted in our deal. They came in to me whenever they got free, at least two times a month, sometimes more, usually the two upon their trusty nag Oscar, but occasionally the long walk. I believe they even caught a lift with Captain Dinny a few times more. He never did stop blowing that tune for them. Still does today, I'm told… *Dublin Daisies* passing Cloonlara lock.

If there wasn't bottling to be done, there was always something else to keep them busy and me not. In exchange I'd feed them what I had going on the day and pay them a few pence for the sweet shop. I probably came out with the worst of it, what with all the free feckin' lemonade. They downed enough for half of Limerick. But sure it wasn't empty bellies or pockets that kept them coming back to Clancy's. They returned for the stories, I'm convinced. Everyone wants to know where they come from. Only natural. But with not a speck of Irish history being taught in their schools, and Liam McCabe as likely to speak of the past as his own horse, they were famished for it.

I told them of the darkness that befell Ireland after the death of Brian Boru. Even though he'd banished the Viking hordes, when no man came forward to tend the blessed flower of unity he'd cultivated, it withered into a tangled morass of confusion and turmoil. Alas, the vision was lost with the visionary. Weak regional leaders squabbled for power, forming and betraying alliances. It was all sheep and no shepherd, and sure didn't that eventually bring the Normans to our fine shores. A massive army led by old Henry II, who promptly declared himself Lord of Ireland, the poncey fuckin' prick.

And then he became it.

The boys would listen, and sometimes a slow dawning would come to their eyes; on other occasions they would just nod their heads and carry on with the bottling. Either way, vessels got filled... but this last bit caught their full attention.

"The Norman invasion, lads. The fuckers haven't left since."

The doors of Clancy's Public House welcome any and all. Always have. Position or persuasion have no bearing on it. If a man has a quid for me, I have a jar for himself. A smile doesn't greet everyone, but none first see a frown. Limerick's finest and feckless take a drink here, oftentimes shoulder to shoulder, and the lads came to meet many of them.

They were never very keen on the Church with all its commandments and chapter and verse, but with Father Stephen O'Dea more regular on my stool than at his pulpit only minutes away at St. Michael's, they eventually took a shine to him. To my knowledge, that's as close as either got to a genuine relationship with God - the friend of a friend.

They got early lessons in the perils of overindulgence courtesy of many, but most reliably demonstrated by my dear friend and preeminent patron, Old Man O'Mahony, a lifelong drunkard and ne'er-do-well who by any reckoning should no longer be with us, though he just might outlast us all. O'Mahony always listened as I told the stories, faintly swaying on his stool as he sipped endless whiskies from the short glass constantly clutched in his craggy, shaking hand.

He was a mute, rendered tongueless by a surprise uppercut, but sure he wouldn't let that stop him frequently offering his comment. An odd emphasis might be given by the sudden slam of his glass down upon the bar or by the silent trickle of an occasional tear, but more often than not a dry and croupy hum would rise from deep down in his tired lungs. It would frequently outlast his legs. Many a night its melodies kept me company while I've helped him home.

Of course, I usually know the words to go with it… always songs for Ireland. Over the years, the lads would have heard every one.

> *Proudly the note of the trumpet is sounding*
> *Loudly the war-cries arise on the gale*
> *Fleetly the steed by Lough Sweighly is bounding*
> *To join the six squadrons on Saimier's green vale!*
> *On every mountaineer! Strangers to flight or fear!*
> *Rush to the standard of dauntless Red Hugh!*
> *Bonnaught and gallowglass, throng from each mountain pass!*
> *Onward for Erin! O'Donnell Abu!*

In the late 1500s, Irish hopes were raised on the broad back of another great Irish hero, Red Hugh O'Donnell, from the far wilds of Donegal. Burying historical feuds with another powerful Irish chieftain of the day, the wily Hugh O'Neill, the two warriors joined forces and led their armies against the English occupation.

Perhaps I shouldn't have told the lads how Red Hugh came to his famous hatred of England. How, simply because he was the heir to the north chieftainship and might one day threaten their English power, he was kidnapped and imprisoned in Dublin Castle itself at only the young age of fifteen. How he spent three years and three months chained in a cold dungeon, longing for his rocky hills of Donegal. Perhaps that's too mighty a precedent to impart to a youthful imagination.

But omitting the jailing omits the escape, and nothing excites like escape. On a bitter sleeting Christmas Day young Red Hugh descended into the feculent castle sewer running deep under its walls and fled his pursuers into the Wicklow Mountains. With the dead of a harsh winter at his bare feet, he lost both big toes to frostbite for his trouble, but still made it home to take up his rule and lead his clan in a long rebellion against his English captors. "The Nine Years War."

"Nine years?" Rory asked, "Come on now, Mr. Clancy."

"We're only twelve," Conor says. "We'd only have gone three years without fighting."

Rory knelt down on the floor and took up his best boxing stance. "Ye'd wanna be Conor - the Wee Fighting Baba. Hurling dirty nappies from outta yer pram. Driving them Crown forces back across the sea with the smell of yer baby shite."

Conor knelt in front him. "If they fought like you, I'd have 'em well done in already."

They jabbed at each other, each landing a few good digs, quickly wearing the fun out of it.

"It was at the great Battle of Curlew Pass," I said, mostly to interrupt the shenanigans, "where Red Hugh almost did them in." That word again… always 'almost'.

They left their fussing alone, eager to hear of the action. They always reveled in the battle stories. I told them how O'Donnell and his Irish rebels stormed down from the rocky hills and barren bogs brandishing pikes and axes in close combat with the Crown forces trying to advance on his territory. It was bloody and brutal, but decisive, and they drove the hated English back. I told them as well of the famous Battle of the Yellow Ford, where O'Donnell marched south with five thousand rebels to meet O'Neill and his men at the Blackwater River. Concealed by barricades and trenches, they again lay in ambush, killing two thousand English and seizing their weapons and ammunition, even the pipe and drums that announced their fateful march.

The Irish had the English in shambles and on the run for the first time in four hundred years. But for every battle won, that putrid whore Queen Elizabeth sent more troops to our "rude and barbarous nation". Relentless reinforcements, endless across the sea like waves. Nine bloody years proved not time enough for even the likes of Red Hugh O'Donnell. Outmanned and underequipped, he made his last stand at the Battle of Kinsale. When the English prevailed, he finally fled to Spain in hopes of securing reinforcements for our own side. They never came. Red Hugh was poisoned while plotting his return to Ireland. Dead at thirty. Another hero gone.

Conor broke a lingering silence. "How can anyone fight for nine years?"

"We've been fighting for a lot longer than nine years," I said. "Sometimes there's no choice in it. Sometimes it's the only way to survive. When they take everything from ye, sometimes the fight is all ya have left."

I told them then how the English had commenced their persecution of Catholics in earnest over the years that followed, barring Catholics from public office and seizing our lands, even imposing fines on any who wouldn't attend Protestant church services. T'was like fining a fish for not walking... The goal was clear: cleanse Ireland of the Catholic stain.

Of course that policy provoked the Irish Rebellion of 1641, a bold plan to overtake Dublin Castle in yet another attempt to break the English rule. Another failed attempt, betrayed by an informer, the constant bane of rebel endeavors. Our feckin' gift of the gab, me arse.

Yet, the rebels persisted and the effort spread throughout the country, mostly in small but bloody clashes. Catholics who had lost position and lands chased their revenge, liberating the English Protestant colonisers of their homes and possessions, frequently by fire and often before the victims had even found an exit. The struggle lasted years, with merciless massacres on both sides, spiraling into an unquenchable hunger for vengeance, forever feeding off unspeakable brutalities. You can't get a grasp on that history without the blood dripping out through your fingers.

"Why didn't the people just leave?" Conor asked.

"Most couldn't. But many did. Many still do. I'd say many more will."

"They're just afraid to fight," says Rory.

"Perhaps, Rory." I said. "But if fighting means only sure death, is it not better to stay alive? Endure, to maybe fight another day?"

"I'd fight," he insisted.

"Then you're an eejit," Conor says.

"Better than a coward!"

"Yer mixin' bravery with stupidity," Conor answered.

"I'll mix with you," Rory said, shoving Conor and then getting shoved right back. For two lads who'd never spent a day apart, they were right quick to have a go at each other. I promptly interrupted the debate. "Well, those that stayed and fought had not yet seen the most vicious cruelties."

I told them how more English forces came forth again, over one hundred ships, this time trailing the most sadistic of all the scourges ever to cross the Irish Sea, Oliver-fucking-Cromwell. There were no

Irish victories to hope on here. Fueled by his zealous hatred of Catholics, Catholicism and anything keen on it, Cromwell laid waste the whole country.

He first slaked his thirst for Irish blood at the Siege of Drogheda. Heavy cannons and twelve thousand men breached the walls of the garrison and overcame the Irish forces. The beaten soldiers were pursued throughout the town. They sought refuge in homes and churches... but all in vain. They were killed in every spot they were found.

Larger contingents of Irish troops sought shelter elsewhere. A group near ninety-strong retreated into St. Peter's Church, which Cromwell's forces promptly set aflame. Fifty men were slaughtered as they escaped the inferno, thirty more burned to death high in the fiery steeple.

When another two hundred men found fortification in a gate tower, the surrounding army promised to trade their lives for their surrender. As soon as their arms were turned over, the men watched as their company leader was beaten to death with his own wooden leg. Then they were straightaway killed, the full lot of them. Forever gone were the gallant battles of proper armies. Honorable warfare was besieged by religious intolerance and finally replaced with savage sectarianism.

I'd watch the boys' faces to see how each story affected them. Rory's eyes would slowly narrow, his jaw tightening down ever harder with each tragedy revealed. Conor seemed to always lean closer but at the same time his eyes just drew further away, like he had to strain to listen because he was hearing every tale from an ever-increasing distance.

These stories I told over the course of many visits and many lemonades, spanning what must have been near a full year. At some point, Rory lost hope for a joyful episode. Of course he knew enough from present circumstances that there was no happy resolution of all the madness. Yet he never lost his interest, he only shifted it, becoming almost obsessed with the negative accounts. He'd press me for harsh details, mostly on the severity of the defeats and their brutalities. He wanted to know how many Irish died in every battle, how they were killed. He wanted to hear the particulars of the atrocities, the means of the tortures. It was as if he was filling an inner reservoir with rage and hatred to use on some future occasion should he ever discover he'd somehow run out.

With Cromwell the subject, it wasn't difficult to oblige. From Drogheda, his evil forces plunged into Ireland, giving no quarter. Surrender remained meaningless. Those who laid down arms were thrashed all the same, their women and children butchered and burned. Alas, the infamous Sack of Wexford. While the entire town negotiated a surrender, Cromwell's forces descended, slaughtering thirty-five hundred of its vanquished populace and burning every tatter of its capitulation to the ground.

His armies pushed onward, south and north and west, subduing all resistance and slaughtering any defiance. Until Limerick. Auld Limerick would not be taken, at least not by force. But though she couldn't be bested in battle, she was no match for time. The English surrounded Limerick and they simply waited. Finally, hunger and disease triumphed. Limerick fell in 1651. Survivors were killed or shipped off as slaves, scattered all to Hell. In the end, after only four years, Cromwell had rid Ireland of well over half its Catholics.

He imposed more Penal Laws across the country, ever more severe. Catholicism was barred outright, illegal. Bounty prices were offered for priests, hunted and killed as animals. Over one hundred thousand Irish children were shipped off to the Americas and sold into slavery. Catholic lands were seized indiscriminately and burned extensively. Crops were destroyed and famine soon followed, quickly trailed by the bubonic plague, as if it could smell the evil afoot and knew it would find helpless hosts adrift in Cromwell's cruel wake. The rampage left Ireland crushed and wretched for nearly two centuries.

T'was an evening of pissin' rain when Liam McCabe filled my door, probably the first time he'd set a foot in Clancy's since he'd become a father. He'd been a well determined drinker beforehand, and not unknown to kick up a shindy now and again, but he was rarely known to venture past his local in Cloonlara anymore. The lads had been in and gone that afternoon, so I presumed he wasn't after drink but, after a good long look about, he came on to a stool and ordered a pint.

"How ya keepin' there, Mr. Clancy?" Like he'd seen me only yesterday.

"Grand. How's Liam?"

"Just fine."

He lifted his glass to Old Man O'Mahony, down the bar with his swaying, then took a long swig.

"My lads giving you any bother here, Mr. Clancy?"

"Not at all. Quite the contrary," I says. "They're welcome anytime."

He finished his pint in the next swallow and stood up. "Slán."

"All the best," I said.

He dropped double the price on the bar and nodded toward O'Mahony, who raised his glass in thanks for his next drink. As Liam headed for the door, the old man just then commenced to hum. I knew the melody straightaway. It took Liam maybe to the door to recognise it - *The Old Fenian Gun.* Though I didn't dare sing them, I knew well the words. No doubt Liam heard them in his head as well.

> *It hung above the kitchen fire, its barrel long and brown*
> *And one day with a boy's desire, I climbed and took it down*
> *My father's eyes in anger flashed, he cried, "What have you done?!*
> *I wish you'd left it where it was, that's my old Fenian gun."*

He pushed open the door and looked out at the misty rain, pausing for a long moment to listen to O'Mahony's gravelly rumbling. Then he walked out.

There was a new breeze in the Irish air in those years after I first met the lads in 1912. Not yet a spirit wind of any mention, but a stir of sorts. Those old songs for Ireland were being sung a bit louder, for a bit longer. The Gaelic League had been well effective in bringing the Irish language back to its people, the lads even took some at school, and through the work of the Gaelic Athletic Association our sports and arts were becoming ours again. Those organisations endeavored to spread our history as well, often awarding nationalist books as prizes at their events.

One such book that had been passed around for years was Sullivan's *The Story of Ireland*. Remarkably, when the text was first published, the author himself was languishing in jail as a guest of the Crown for his previous publications of various essays of a nationalist disposition. Though "Written for the Youth of Ireland," I found his work quite engaging myself as it was chock full of lovely sketches and delightfully free of the usual English shite. Somewhere along the line, perhaps I was short of lemonade, I passed my copy on to the lads.

A few of those looking to add a hotter flame to the warming stir I mention were familiar faces at Clancy's. The Republican Brotherhood was still shrouded deep in the shadows then, but they were slowly becoming a bit less inclined to dodge the sunlight.

With his fine banker's suits usually picked to match his sharp blue eyes, Martin Sheehan was quite a dapper man of commerce by day, though his shine for style never stopped him from rolling up his tailored sleeves to get a job done. He worked tirelessly through the Land Commission to secure transfers to the benefit of the tenant farmers. His aggressive utilisation of compulsory purchases made him many an enemy of the rich land barons, but he helped far more poor families in Limerick put a permanent stake in their grounds for the first time in hundreds of years.

He kept his own home out the Ennis Road by Cratloe Woods, where he operated a small but fruitful horse farm. He was known to be a fine judge of the equine flesh and ventured often to America, having sold one or two prized Irish hunters to top breeders there. After America's anti-gambling rules shut down the Yanks' flat tracks for a good spell, he reversed the routing and brought home many a bargain thoroughbred looking for a place to race.

On one trip he even returned with a wife as well, a true Italian beauty whose parents had prospered in New York City after emigrating from Sicily. Martin and his bright Irish blues swept her right off her feet and, much to the chagrin of her family, he removed her all the way back across the Atlantic to his beloved County Clare. On the occasions the handsome couple stepped out in Limerick, all the heads would be turning.

But the fields of Clare don't compare with the lights of New York and poor Mrs. Lucia Sheehan, from Bay Ridge, Brooklyn, never became much more than a visitor to Ireland. They lived more apart than together. I suppose when they say the best marriages involve certain compromises on both sides, they're not referring to the shores of an ocean, but plenty of sea miles have been put into that love affair over the years.

When she was off in America, Martin could be found most nights huddled in a snug at Clancy's with his very few cohorts and confidants. I wouldn't dare presume to monitor their conversations, but even then it didn't take a keen ear to discern that they didn't all concern land purchase valuations or equine breeding cycles. It was a sorry secret around town that Martin Sheehan was the lead organiser for the Brotherhood in Limerick. Besides a wife and the odd horse, he was also known to come home from America with more than a few quid collected for the cause as well.

Nor was the other side of things a total stranger to Clancy's Public House. Limerick's been a garrison town for the British Army since they arrived and there are four barracks within spittin' distance of my fine establishment. It's no surprise then that the Crown soldiers, as well as the constables of the Royal Irish Constabulary, venture in for a drink now and again, much to my botheration. But their money spends as well as any and, at least in those days before the Great War, they sometimes even comported themselves as nearly civilised neighbors. Sometimes, that is. Mostly they were right pricks and general gobshites.

I won't bother here denying my nationalist leanings. Anymore a lean to me and I'd be on the floor. But, I'll dare say I didn't purposely foster these sentiments in the lads either. It just so happens that the fucking English government brutally oppressed our country for many long centuries. Facts are facts and truths are truths. I affix no slant. That said, I made note to them that not every Englishman was a bastard and not all Protestants were ruthless murderers.

Indeed, I told the lads how the great revolutions in France and America during the late 1700s, with their proclamations of rights of self-determination and liberty, inspired even some Protestants to advocate in opposition to English rule on general principles. The

United Irishmen, an organisation started by Protestants, grew to number over two hundred thousand members by then. They eventually rose up in the Irish Rebellion of 1798, but after some grand words and worthy battles, it was put down hard, ending in disaster for the Irish when the bulk of the opposing armies met out in Wexford, at the Battle of Vinegar Hill.

The rebels had at least equal numbers but they were woefully outgunned. Pikes can't match rifles, lads. It was a massacre Cromwell would have been proud of. Rebels who weren't lucky enough to be killed in the fighting were burned as they lay wounded or tortured for sport and hung as traitors to the Crown. The English rampaged nearby Enniscorthy, raping its women and burning their homes and churches. I told them how they dealt with Father John Murphy, the parish priest who fought with a rebel spirit unmatched. Not satisfied with his hanging alone, they stuck his head on a spike across from his church and burned his headless body in a drum of tar.

Old Man O'Mahony hummed the melody of *Boolavogue*. I sang the words.

> *At Vinegar Hill, o'er the pleasant Slaney*
> *Our heroes vainly stood back to back,*
> *and the Yeos at Tullow took Father Murphy*
> *and burned his body upon a rack.*
> *God grant you glory, brave Father Murphy*
> *And open Heaven to all your men,*
> *The cause that called you may call tomorrow*
> *In another fight for the Green again.*

Rory always inquired into the causes of our defeats. He was almost pleased to hear of a bastard informer or some other acts of deceit and trickery that turned the tides against us. He knew the Irish would prevail in a fair fight. Ten times out of ten. And he knew with certainty that Clare men were the fiercest fighters in all Ireland. Sure, Brian Boru had proven that. If there were enough Clare men at hand, the rebels couldn't lose.

I was thus stirred to tell them of Fireball McNamara, a legendary Clare man if there's ever been one, who himself survived the Battle of Vinegar Hill, though he took a bullet for his troubles. As a lad of just fifteen with a true adventurer's spirit, Fireball left Ireland to join the French Army, quickly becoming a master of pistol and sword. Those skills served him well in at least two duels with officers whom he had challenged after they'd insulted his Irish heritage. Fleeing a certain court-martial, he lit out to explore Europe but eventually returned to Clare. However, the dueling didn't end at home. He's said to have survived over fifty duels in his lifetime. His pistols even came to acquire their own moniker - Death Without A Priest.

Of course, it was only right of me to inform the lads that Fireball was indeed a Protestant himself.

"Then fuck him," Rory says.

"Why did he end up on Vinegar Hill?" Conor asked.

"He was fighting for Catholic Emancipation."

"A Protestant?" Rory asks.

"There's an old and well-proven approach to fruitful colonialism," I explained. "Divide and conquer. The English have carefully cultivated the animosity between Catholics and Protestants in Ireland for a long time now. They've always known their support and control depend entirely on that split. Most all have bought into it, but not everyone is so easily swayed."

"Fireball fought for Catholics?" Conor asked.

"Indeed." I told them how one of the more pitiless Penal Laws prohibited the ringing of bells for Mass at the Catholic churches. Well, Fireball McNamara wouldn't abide that. At Chapel Lane in Ennis, he once directed the bells be tolled for the day's Mass and, with his trusty pistols looming at his side, stood at the church doors to ensure they rang out entirely.

"What happened to him?"

"After Vinegar Hill, he went off to England."

"Why for?"

"Well lads, failing to defeat the English tyranny, Fireball took it upon himself to instead, shall we say, conquer as many young English ladies as he could, particularly those of high means. He greatly enjoyed relieving them of their fortunes, and their virtues, at every opportunity."

"He shagged 'em!" Rory exclaimed.

"What came of him?" Conor asked.

"He shagged himself silly!" Rory said, jumping up on Conor and miming a good riding for us.

"Feck off!" Conor cried.

"He was convicted of robbery, it's said twenty young ladies pleaded for his pardon, including the victim of his guilty offense."

"Did they let him off?"

"He was hanged."

"Feckin' Hell!" Rory shouted.

"By order of the Queen herself," I said.

"The fucking whore," Rory said.

Eventually our breezy discussions of days of yore reached the Fenian Rising of 1867, the most disappointing of all the Irish efforts at fecking the English out, or perhaps the least, depending on how one views such affairs. Perhaps both even.

The Fenians, as they called themselves, took their name from the Fianna. You'll remember those ancient warriors, led by the legendary Fionn Mac Cumhaill, your favorite giant of Irish history, who stood forever at the ready to defend Ireland. Supposedly, the Fenian Brotherhood had some fifty thousand members standing ready across Ireland, but when that call finally came, only a few hundred rose, and rather feebly at that.

They were disorganised, scattered and, as usual, betrayed from within. The most they could muster were a few skirmishes, some minor insolence and a general unpleasantness. Short of some strong words and great intentions, the best that could be said of the Fenian Rising itself is that very few men died in it, at least as compared with the usual massacres our rebellions have brought us. We were spared the bloody sacrifice to naught. It was over before it started and petered out into nothing. What they needed was their very own Fionn Mac Cumhaill.

"Would have been a grand day to wake him, lads," I said, with a hard pound of me shillelagh on the floor, trying my best to disturb our hero's ceaseless slumber deep underground. "A great giant to lead us. Maybe someday… seems there's always another rising coming."

"What happened to all the Fenians?" Rory asked.

"Well that's the question now, lads. Sure, fifty thousand angry men didn't vanish in the night. I don't know. Maybe their minds were changed. That can happen. Some men reconsider their principles, even change their beliefs. It's rare, but it happens. You'd be surprised."

"Maybe they just gave up," Conor said.

"That can happen as well. There's only so much any man can take, maybe some prices just aren't worth paying."

"I'd never give up," Rory said, softly though.

"We've been rising for four hundred years now lads, and we're still stuck, right deep thick in their English muck. But there've always been men prepared to fight for Ireland, and there always will be, God willing."

"I'll fight for Ireland," says Rory now, firm and sure.

"Three cheers for Rory Boru, the next High King of Ireland!" Conor shouts.

"Feck off!" Rory shouts. "I will."

I raised up my glass. "Then I like to think there are more just like you, Rory. More good men out there, waiting for yet another call; wishing for those three horn blows and never giving up... still believing. I know there are some. I've not a doubt of that, now."

"Who?" they both asked.

"That's not for me to tell but, rest assured, they're around. It's just like history. Simply because you can't see it, doesn't mean it's not all around you. Never forget lads, you live upon the very running grounds of Brian Boru himself. You swim in the Shannon, waters forever sacred with the suffusion of rebel blood, valiantly spilled defending Limerick on one bank, your beloved Clare on its other. Plenty of heavy history right close to home."

"There's no history in Cloonlara," Conor sighed. "Nothing ever happens in Cloonlara."

Of course, I wouldn't dare tell them of the genuine article of history living right smack under their very own roof. Not my place. Sure, they'd hardly believe me anyway. Indeed, they hardly believed the story I told them instead that day, a bit of proper Fenian action that occurred not all too far from Cloonlara.

"Ah, come on, Mr. Clancy," Rory said when I finished the tale. "Now you're just taking the piss. That never happened."

"I believe it," Conor declared.

"Of course you do," Rory laughed. "Just like you believe in dragons and fairies and feckin' giants."

But there was actual physical evidence of this incident, a ruined remain off in the woodlands along the Shannon, just below the treacherous Falls of Doonass.

"Why not see for your ownselves," I suggested. "Set your boots on the very spot and see if you don't feel its history reach right up through your bones."

And right off they went, armed with not just my vaguely recollected directions, but with my very own shillelagh for the march that was in it.

"I'd dare say I'll not be getting out that way again." I said when I handed it to them. "Give the old stones a wee tap with that. Just for luck…"

I suppose they never did tap it though. It's luck they were forever short on.

Chapter Four

Fenian's Trace

The lads rode auld Oscar out of Limerick City along their usual route home, Corbally Road over the five arches of Athlunkard Bridge to cross the Shannon back into Clare, then the lone road toward Killaloe. Once they crossed the River Blackwater at Annegrove, Oscar hastened his pace, just as he always did, whether they asked him for it or not.

It's a lonesome stretch of road there at Ballyglass, a mile or so before Cloonlara, where a long hedgerow of giant and gnarled old beech trees lean in to shroud the road and close out the sky. Even the brightest sun is humbled to a dull haze after fighting through that great canopy of twisted branches, all blanketed with moss and lichens and festooned with green ferns and ivy. At night, it's a desperate black tunnel. You'd want to keep your horse pointed dead straight or you'll find yourself in a ditch.

It's there that generations now have known the legendary *púca* to lurk and ramble. Most reported sightings are of a ghostly black horse, or at least its floating head, occasionally accompanying late riders for a short spell of their journey. Debates still rage over whether it's a good sign or a bad one for the soul that sees it.

Once Oscar sped his worried gait, Conor cast his eyes out over the misty fields, scanning the murk for the vaporous shape-shifting apparition. He'd been aching to catch even just a glimpse since he'd first learned as a lad that the name of their parish means 'meadow of the mare.' Not just any mortal mare, but a spectral spirit of haunted gallops. He didn't know if he really believed in it, so a wee sighting would go a long way, but he knew for sure he didn't not believe it. Where would be the adventure in that? Of course, Rory would have none of it, and would rail against any such talk as a lot of foolish *pishogue*.

Conor just loved to get a rise out of him. "Eyes peeled here now, Rory." he warned. "He could leap out from anywhere. Fair play, Oscar. Don't let him get onto us. Jaysus Rory, what was that? Is it ghost hooves I'm hearing?"

"You'll be hearing your feet walking if you don't quit your messin'."

Conor reversed his seat on Oscar and desperately slashed my shillelagh at the night.

"He's gaining on us, Rory!" he shouted. "I can't hold him off. We're in for it now."

"Feckin' right, you're in for it." Rory said, never so much as stealing a curious sidelong glance, adamant to never lend even a hint of credence to the superstitious nonsense of all that Irish folklore, no matter what Conor and Oscar might believe.

Still, and as Conor surely took notice, he never did endeavor to tighten the reins to slow Oscar's pace any.

That particular evening they took Oscar right past their regular turn to home and instead crossed over the Cloonlara canal bridge, even with the rain down on them. Where the good road turns north on to Killaloe they held east toward the Shannon for more than another mile. Where that road ends they found St. Senan's Well and past it the old ruin of Kiltenanlea Church, both landmarks they knew of, as did the many dutiful and devout from around the country who would seek out the holy well for a sacred spell of prayerful circumambulation.

A small *boreen* ran along past the crumbling church to reach its forsaken old graveyard, lying in neglect amid high grass and thistle, its range of scattered headstones extending all the way to the forest's shadowy edge. Of course, there's something in a cemetery that's irresistible to your more adventurous children - spirits summon youthful ears, desperate for hints of yesteryears - and the lads had explored the churchyard plot many times before. They would respectfully note the more familiar names they discovered tromping from marker to marker, but they much preferred to investigate the macabre stonework and grim epitaphs. An angel trumpeting, 'Arise ye dead & come to judgment.' The inquisitive skeleton, 'Be ye prepared for Death?'

That had been the extent of their expeditions to date, but it was still beyond there that I'd sent them. There were graves ahead they'd not seen. Not far into the thick woods a small circular arrangement of stones marked the burial places of the unbaptised or unknown, or maybe just the unlucky, alongside the abortions and the suicides not deemed fit to rest in the Christian cemetery. They were the forever ostracised, the innocence of their lives contaminated by the uncertainties and guilts of their deaths. Their stones held no inscriptions to read… they were blank slates. What became of their poor souls was anyone's guess. The lads gave those a wide and silent berth.

Another ways past that infinite purgatory the woodlands began to thin in spots nearer the river's edge, their cover interrupted by small clearings along the water. The tree-framed windows showed perfect views of the last run along the stretch of spectacular rapids spilling from the Falls of Doonass. In the autumn, one could watch the salmons' first leapings of the cascade on their annual travels upriver, but the mad din of rushing torrents eased as the fierce flow finally settled back into the lazier drift more common to the Shannon.

One small and otherwise inconspicuous opening was marked by a quite distinctive formation of great slabs of rock that curved well out into the dark water, creating a small sheltered cove on the shore side. The jutting stones served as an occasional safe-haven of sorts, the first available spot for a daring boatman to still his cot and catch his breath after navigating the cataract. There were few men who would chance it, mostly local *ghillies* guiding sportsmen to the salmon, and even fewer who managed to stay dry.

It was to that rocky port that I'd directed the lads. As the river is quite wide there, it's the furthest one can get into the Shannon without a boat or a swim. One can almost feel all alone at sea out on that rock. Still the ancient trees looming around its edges afford it an odd privacy, shielding it from view of anywhere far afield. They stood upon it and watched for a long spell as the surge of whitewater pounded the various masses of opposing rocks. It just kept on. One would think that the amount of power and violence behind the rushing water would eventually produce a change. Surely such a violent force demanded a result.

No. It just kept on.

When the rain started to fall heavier they finally turned away from the river to look back over the cove and across the clearing. In the shady thick of forest they saw just what I told them they'd see. Not a thing. High trees topping a sweep of dense underbrush, the same as anyone could see from the river.

"There's feck all out here," Rory said, squinting with the rain, his doubts as full as his shoes. "I tell ya, he's having a laugh. Sent us off on a wild goose chase."

Conor looked all around, and finally chuckled. "He did. And we're just two eejits standing out here in the rain."

They left the rock and joined Oscar below the shelter of the tree line. They looked deeper in but saw nary much more than darkness under the waning day.

"Feck all," says Rory.

Still as they waited for the rain to ease they waded a ways into the high ferns, just far enough to detect a hint of a design in the way that they grew, something of a rough pathway even. That led them further in until they discerned a rather strange shape darkening the shadows even more. Blanketed with mosses and snarled heavy with ivy, the remaining shambles of a seventeenth century tower house suddenly loomed over them.

"Fenian's Trace," Conor whispered. He was excitedly twisting the pendant under his shirt again.

"Fuck's sake, he wasn't joking," Rory says.

Hardly a castle, but with clear aspirations beyond anyone's simple domicile, the boldly Gothic structure was dominated by a circular stone turret of sorts, rising above its ornately arched entryway. The crumbled walls running off it still held second level height in places but were mostly collapsed to as low as your waist. They displayed a more basic rectangular plan, at least where they weren't completely concealed by the thick swathing of greenery.

A short rusted gate still manned its entrance. Though it was locked with a heavy timeworn chain, the wild tangle of briers seizing it provided even better protection. It was a delicate climb over to gain their admission.

"After you," says Conor.

Just inside, at the wide base of the tower, a broad stone bench sat opposite the lowest steps of a spiral stairway clinging to the wall. Where its narrow steps were still intact, they were crumbling and rickety… a perilous ascent.

"Let's go up," they said to each other.

The ivy helped as much as the stairs and by hook and crook they made it to the bastion at the top. They looked out over the parapet but the treetops were still above them, their broad leaves blocking any view of the river.

"Can't see a thing," says Rory.

"Not now. But listen…" Conor pointed out toward the river's roar. "He would've had a perfect sight of the falls."

They looked back and down into the house itself. The roof was gone entirely, but the huge beams that once supported it were scattered within, burnt-out and collapsed. A set of stone steps led up to a vanished second story, its remains charred on the ground below. Several craggy chambers were still identifiable but except for a large fireplace at the far wall their purposes were lost under a thick blanket of ivy and ferns and a determined attack of alder and sally trees.

Conor extended his arms and faced his palms downward.

Rory looked at him, puzzled. "Yer feckin daft."

"Mr. Clancy said you can still feel the heat of the flames."

"He's daft as well."

Conor kept his arms out a while. "I think I can feel it."

Rory spit down to the ground. "Madmen, the two of ye."

"You don't believe the story?"

"Who knows?" says Rory.

Conor finally pulled his arms in. "Well, you can see it was burned."

"What you can see is it's a feckin' kip," Rory said.

"No. It only looks like one." Conor said. "Think of what it was. Maybe could be again. That's what's so grand."

Rory pried a jagged stone loose from the wall, then used it to wrest free a second. He handed one to Conor. "Then this'll be our secret place. Where no one will ever know where we are… or what we do."

He cleared the moss off the flat stone top of the parapet facing the river and started to carve his name into it. And right next to his did

Conor take to carving his own. I'm told their names are still there today, just the same.

They were back with the next light of day and again at any free chance they had thereafter. They brought along axes, spades, and scythes and went at clearing the overgrowth like it was a mortal enemy, sprucing the site up right fit for regular dossing. They rigged a makeshift roof around the old fireplace and patched up its chimney, then nicked sods of turf off the clamps of neighbors to stoke blazing fires. They set rabbit snares and tried their hand at fishing but couldn't manage the patience, so they'd just pilfer the odd rhubarb patch or raid an apple tree and then feast by the fire heat until their bellies ached. When the sun was out, they'd loll on the warmed rocks and watch the rapids run. They even lopped some of the treetops to clear free a new view of the falls.

With their secret fort secure and operational, their visits to Clancy's abated in frequency for a good long spell. Save a convenient sweet shop, they had everything two young boys could want. Conor would sit atop the tower and read of our battles and struggles from *The Story of Ireland*. Rory would listen to every word, usually while surveying their demesne, ever-vigilant for the inevitable approach of enemy invaders. Sure, he knew his day would come.

When they did next visit, it was eventful. They should have stayed scarce.

The lads had soaked in many of the old rebel songs during their days at Clancy's, what with the occasional impromptu daytime sing-song or just from Old Man O'Mahony's habitual humming with meself joining in for a verse now and again. They knew many off by heart, but who's to say just what prompted Rory to choose *The Bold Fenian Men* to sound on that fateful day. Maybe their new sanctuary had them too long in the company of just such a ghost.

> *Side by side for the cause when our forefathers battled,*
> *When our hills never echoed the thread of the slave,*
> *On many a green field where the leaden hail rattled,*
> *Through the red map of glory, they marched to the grave,*

But we who inherit their name and their spirit,
March 'neath the banner of liberty then,
Give them back blow for blow, Pay them back woe for woe,
Out and make way for the Bold Fenian Men!

He sang it loudly along their whole route in, while swinging my long borrowed shillelagh about in tune, but the streets were noisy and full and no one took heed of two boisterous boys bulling their way through. Conor marched just behind him. He could never quite match Rory's brash exuberance, but always seemed to manage to keep right in faithful step nonetheless.

Just before the lads turned onto the long laneway for Clancy's, Old Man O'Mahony took my leave after a strong afternoon session. With a full room, I couldn't help him home, but he was in no worse shape than usual. He pushed open the door and shuffled out, frail and unsteady. The sunlight hit him like a weight and he slouched back against the door.

Then Rory's singing sailed to his tired ears.

Give them back blow for blow, Pay them back woe for woe,
Out and make way for the Bold Fenian Men!

The old man started humming along and hobbled out into the lane toward the tune. Conor pointed to him. "Old Man O'Mahony!"

Rory laughed. "Feckin' legless!"

The break in song left him confused and staggering, a bad state to be in, particularly in the face of a rushing carriage pulled by galloping horses, which is just what roared around the corner behind him. There was indeed a shout and maybe an effort to stop, but it was unsuccessful and the lead horse knocked him hard to the ground.

Its driver shouted once more. "Move off the bloody road!"

Then he stopped the covered carriage just ahead. It belonged to the Royal Irish Constabulary. Its driver wore their distinctive rifle-green uniform and spiked-top helmet. He got off and walked right past the old man, still down in the lane, bruised and bewildered, and went in to Clancy's to fetch the men from his local barracks. They'd been in for a good session and sure wasn't it the quality of their company inside that finally had O'Mahony exiting early.

Of course, the constables of the RIC were more often than not sound lads in them days... mostly local and mostly Catholic and mostly sound. The officers were largely a different story, but they weren't about much. Still, even the constables were shunned by some, and by me as well, if only to avoid the lingering stench off them for their actions during the land war, enforcing the evictions of poor tenant farmers to the benefit of Protestant landowners. Their badges featured the Irish harp, and that probably meant something to some of them, but still the English Crown sat right above it and at the end of the day that's what they answered to. As far as I was concerned the lot of them could all go to Hell.

Clearly, young Rory was no admirer either. "Fuck sake! Did ya see that?"

"Help him up." Conor said, moving to the old man, but Rory started the other way. "No. This way."

Conor hesitated. "Where?"

Rory yanked him by his coat. "Come on, for the *craic!*"

Rory sang aloud as they darted down the alleyway alongside Clancy's and hopped the fence to get around the back.

> *Give them back woe for woe,*
> *Pay them back blow for blow,*
> *Out and make way for the Bold Fenian Men!*
> *Glory O! Glory O! To the Bold Fenian Men!*

They hoisted a ladder to my back wall and climbed up its two stories to the roof. They crept to the front edge to get a good view of the lane below.

In short order, the RIC men filed outside and boarded the waiting carriage. Rory scurried back to my chimney and pulled off a loose brick. He slammed it down upon the roof, breaking it in halves, and darted back to the edge. He dropped a piece for Conor, still peering down as the driver slid behind his horses. Conor looked at the brick, then back to the broad metal roof of the carriage, but Rory was already in motion. He hurled it straight down.

The crash was so loud I heard it inside, clear as a gun shot, which it may as well have been. The horses startled and bucked, spilling a few of the constables to the ground. They scrambled for cover, then looked about in shock, eventually spying the brick and realising what happened. A man looked up. And there was Rory, looking right back down at him, skitting. Conor near yanked him right off his feet. "Run! We're trapped up here!"

The men tore off after them. The lads could run like rabbits but they couldn't fly like birds. When they ran out of rooftop they were well snared.

The knock on the door to his forge came hard and impatient. Liam knew it wouldn't be good, but he was punching holes in a red-hot wagon tongue and if it cooled too much before he flipped it for the final punch, its strength would be well diminished. He ignored the rude pounding. Anyone that bothered to knock was hardly worth the bother. When he was finished he quenched the metal, set his tools down and wiped the sweat and ash from his brow. The banging persisted.

He pulled open the door to find a uniformed officer of the Royal Irish Constabulary brandishing the fiendish half piece of brick in mid-knock. He was a man of about fifty years, rail thin with a fine mustache and clever, darting eyes. His second hand gripped his well-shined oak baton. Behind him two of the men from the carriage held Rory and Conor firm, their batons tightening against their poor necks with every squirm. Several others leaned against the carriage, cradling their carbines.

"Liam McCabe?" His accent was English. His breath was liquored.

Liam's huge frame came out through the doorway. He looked down at the smaller man's cold, narrow face. "I am."

"I am District Inspector Tyler Bowen of the RIC." He pointed to the lads. "Are those yours?"

Neither could manage to meet Liam's eyes. "They are."

Bowen pointed at Conor with his baton. "Your one says his name's O'Neill."

"T'is. He's mine by attrition. Not birth."

Bowen held up the jagged chunk of brick. "The little bastards thought they'd have some fun from the rooftops. A man could have been killed with this."

"If I'd wanted to hit ye, I would've," Rory hollered.

The man holding him threw him hard to the ground. As he yanked him back up, Liam stepped forward to take them. "If there was no damage then, I'll take it up with them here."

Bowen stepped into his path. "Right then, of course you will. Indeed I thought it best to bring them home. Far be it for me to impose any punishment, especially on such fine children. We all know boys will be boys?"

He theatrically tapped each of the lads' heads with his baton. Harmless, but that was enough for Liam. As he moved again to take them, Bowen raised up a hand and his men at the carriage leveled their guns at Liam. That stopped him.

"Tut-tut," Bowen warned. He slid his baton back into his belt and began tossing the brick from hand to hand, pacing the narrow ground between Liam and the lads. He was clearly enjoying himself. Rory's glare followed his every move. Conor kept his eyes on Liam. Maybe he noticed the almost imperceptible movement as Liam shifted his weight off his toes and back onto his heels, bracing himself as if he knew what was coming his way and knew just as well he had to accept it.

"I trust you do appreciate the gravity of their offense, Mr. McCabe. Am I not correct?"

"You are."

"Wouldn't you agree that it requires a lesson of some sort? Perhaps a reparation is in order, just to insure against any recurrence. After all, this sort of weaponry could render a quite dramatic injury." He crouched down to the lads, waving the brick in their faces. "Yes, a lesson there must be. And who better to give such a lesson than dear father?"

Suddenly, Bowen spun around, swinging the brick wide and catching Liam nearly full force in the jaw. He crumbled to the ground, his mouth exploding in blood. Bowen turned back to the lads and stuck the bloody brick under their noses. "A grave weapon indeed, wouldn't you say so boys?"

Rory struggled to get at him but his captor had him well restrained. Conor stood stock still but met Bowen's beady eyes directly. Bowen didn't hold them. He just dropped the brick at their feet and walked to the carriage. The constables there kept their carbines on Liam. "Let them go," Bowen commanded.

The men holding Rory and Conor released their batons. Conor ran to Liam, just raising himself from the blow. Rory picked up the brick and looked to the men climbing into the carriage. Bowen's back was to him, his head an overwhelmingly tempting target. Rory reared back to throw, but Liam just caught his arm.

He dragged him away by it. Conor dutifully followed.

A blazing turf fire kept the chill on the right side of the McCabe family's humble whitewashed walls that evening. Its blustery spring rains were no match for the constant shower of warmth Fiona lavished on her household, especially in times of strain. The outside world was of little concern to her in the best of times, but when it was assailing them she knew well to close ranks until the storms abated. It wasn't the first time.

She kept a hot towel on Liam's face and hot tea in his belly, his jaw far too bruised and sore to get any porridge into him. To ensure the talk would be especially scarce, she'd sent the lads, Katy, and little Brigid to their beds early. Conor and Rory both lay there sleepless, the day's events repeating through their heads. It was only a shock to all when a soft knock came to their door. Fiona quickly held Liam's shoulders to keep him firm in his chair. "I'll see to it, love. You rest."

Fiona made no effort to conceal her disdain when she saw it was none other than Martin Sheehan at their door. She didn't spare him any greeting at all.

He took it on, and gave her a long moment with it, for it was not unexpected. "Evening, Mrs. McCabe," he finally said.

She surrendered a nod, but only for the sake of decorum, not welcome. A stand-off it was. For a man known well for his head, Martin seemed full unaware of the rain falling upon it. He would have stood in it all night, and Fiona would have let him.

"Let the man in from the rain, Fiona." Liam called from his chair.

She turned her back and headed for the tea kettle and Martin stepped inside. He gave Liam's face a long look as they shook hands. Liam pulled a chair free from the table.

"Sit down, Martin." Liam was never too fond of chat anyway but with his injured jaw it genuinely pained him to speak. Not that he let on. "She'll have some tea for ya in a minute."

"That's fine now, don't bother," Martin said.

"No bother."

Martin noticed Rory peeking in from their room but so did Fiona and she quickly ushered him back in.

"What brings ya out on such a night?" Liam asked.

Martin pulled a bottle from his coat and set it on the table. He spoke quietly, near a whisper. "A bit of something to keep the heat in you."

Liam acknowledged the gift with a nod. "That's grand, Martin. But you're not one for the housewarming calls. What's on yer mind?"

"I was hearing you and your lads saw a spot of trouble today."

Fiona set a cuppa down for Martin and refilled Liam's. They waited for her to walk away before continuing their conversation. Rory peeked in again, straining to hear.

"And where'd ya be hearing that?" Liam asked.

"Come now, Liam. You didn't find that face in the forge."

"It's nothing a few days won't cure."

"There may be some other cures available as well."

Liam opened the bottle and poured a bit into each cup. "A few days should be enough."

Martin raised his cup in thanks and took a sip. "I'd like to hear what happened."

"I'm sure you know as much already."

"Just the same, I'd like to hear it from you."

"I'm not one for harping on the past, you know yourself."

"For God's sake man, we're talking about the afternoon."

"No, Martin, we're not. You are."

The look from Martin could well have lasted ages, for the long years of words unsaid in it. Liam returned it. For as much as he pretended otherwise, and as much as he smothered it all, those same years were mere days to him.

Martin stood. Then Liam as well. "I'll be on my way so." He looked to Fiona. "Mrs. McCabe. All the best." She opened the door for him.

Walking to it, again he noticed Rory peeking in. "Evening young Rory."

Rory straightened up like an eager soldier coming to attention. "Evening Mr. Sheehan, sir."

Martin just couldn't resist. "I hear you had quite a day for your-self."

Liam stepped between them, spinning Rory's shoulders back toward his room. "Back in with you now."

Rory sulked away, Fiona at his heels. Liam waited until Martin stepped outside his door, then put his large hand upon his shoulder. "Leave it alone with my boys, Martin. From where we've been, I trust you'll respect that now."

Martin shook his head. "As long as I can. My word on that. But it won't always be my choice - or yours. That lad just might have your spirit in him Liam, at least what you once had. And we both know what'll come of that Conor once he realises the O'Neill blood in him. When Ireland's time comes, so will theirs."

Of course, that's what worried Liam. Martin searched his old friend's battered face for any hint of something more. A thanks for the bottle and a shut door was all he got.

Fiona was turned in before Liam had it closed. She left him alone with his thoughts and his pain and the bottle. Wasn't it the best medicine for the day that was in it? She didn't have to ask why Martin had called. She knew who he was from long ago and most men can't change, even if they aim to, sure every woman in Clare knew as much. Her fella was the lone exception she'd ever seen or heard of. But then her fella was extraordinary. A rock he was, strong, steady and firm against anything at all that came their way. From childhood, Fiona herself was well familiar with those massive rocks out in the Shannon that stood their ground against the endless torrent. They'd been there always, and so would hers be.

As Liam sipped off the bottle, he couldn't hear the boys' whispers in the next room. If he had, the words wouldn't have surprised him. He knew he wasn't the only casualty of the day.

"Conor." Rory nudged him. He didn't get an answer but Rory knew there was no way Conor was asleep. "I'll bet your da wouldn't have let them hit him like that."

Conor closed his eyes as tightly as he could stand. After a good spell, Rory nudged him again. "We won't let them," he whispered. "We won't, Conor. Not ever."

Though Martin was on his best hunter, and the rain was still falling hard and cold, he maintained a slow trot over the near five miles to get home. He hadn't expected any more from the evening than he'd received. Hell, he was surprised he even got past the door. Still, he was frustrated. He just couldn't settle why he'd even ventured out in the weather in the first place. What was he after with Liam? Of course, Liam had been quite right, there was nothing in the line of information he could have provided that Martin didn't already know well before he arrived at his door.

Martin Sheehan had plenty of good men in the ranks of the RIC. Indeed, it was no great stroke of luck that he'd even had a man in the carriage Rory had bricked... one of the same men that pointed his Enfield at Liam earlier. Sure, only doing his job. He'd briefed Martin firsthand with a full account of the day.

When Conor and Rory had realised they were woefully short of rooftop, they'd kicked the ladder they'd climbed up on away from the wall. The constables set it up again but as soon as a man ascended Rory just slid it sideways until it fell away. The men couldn't climb it, but that didn't stop them from trying again and again. Of course, neither could the lads get down, but still, they weren't yet properly captured.

With Rory thwarting their pursuit at the back, Conor hung down from the roof's side edge and managed to swing himself into a window on the second story that also serves as my humble flat. From there he quickly found his way down to the pub. He tapped my shoulder at the back door as I was watching his pursuers flounder with the ladder. I told him to just leg it and head for the hills but he wouldn't desert Rory. I had him hide in the bar while I tried to negotiate a reprieve with the constables but my efforts proved futile. Even the offer of free rounds was snubbed.

When the men finally located a second ladder, poor Rory was outflanked and when they put hands to him there was no clemency. He took a bad hiding before they finally hurled him into that same carriage he'd only recently victimised with his brick. He hung his head and tried to take a study of the pains on him but his blood was still moving far too fast. He couldn't feel a thing. Just as he noticed the wheels starting to turn under him, he was hit with yet another hardy thump - as Conor jumped in and nearly on top of him - quite a cheeky surrenderer. It took the constables a moment to realise who their bold new passenger was. Once they did, Conor caught more than a few good wallops his own self, but his appearance sure bolstered Rory's spirits.

By the carriage they were taken to the barracks on William Street, which doubly serves as the county headquarters for the RIC. It was there Bowen got wind of the terrible incident.

What Martin didn't understand was why Bowen would have bothered with any of it. Two lads messin' about would hardly warrant the attention of a District Inspector, let alone his personal involvement. Men at that rank were mostly responsible for the administration of the various barracks in the district. They didn't have a regular role in the ordinary operational policing. They certainly didn't have a role venturing outside County Limerick to report the shenanigans of two Clare boys to their parents. It was all well beyond the bailiwick.

But Martin was beginning to learn that Tyler Bowen was no ordinary District Inspector. A Hertfordshire man, he had spent his first years in the RIC at Dublin Castle itself. Martin's contacts had information that he'd been involved there in intelligence gathering, investigating political agitators, mostly proponents of the Home Rule movement. He came to Limerick as a Head Constable and spent brief stints in charge of several of the main barracks before being elevated to his current post. Suspicions were strong that his intelligence duties were not quite finished, and that he was now charged with assessing the loyalties of the mostly Catholic constables and rooting out any rebellious souls. No doubt he was a man to be watched carefully.

Martin knew Liam wouldn't know anything at all of Bowen, but could Bowen have known something of Liam? His name would be well stale at this stage but would probably never be crossed off entirely. But sure Liam would be the last to know if Bowen had taken an interest in him, and Martin knew just as much before he'd gotten himself and his best horse soaked to the skin. Still he'd gone. For the life of him, he couldn't figure why.

Next day, Conor helped Liam affix the replacement wagon tongue to its shaft. Rory watched, mostly fidgeting. Purposefully perched nearby, Fiona hung the washing that Katy handed her while little Brigid tried to tug it back off the line. For a long spell, Rory didn't broach it. Then he did.

"Da?" he said, knowing maybe he shouldn't but helpless to stop himself. "Why did Mr. Sheehan call by last night?"

"Just to visit," Liam replied, hoping to snuff it out with that.

"Was it over the Brits that caught us?"

"He was after my account of it."

"Did ya tell him, Da?"

"There's no reason to be getting into it. What's done is done." He hammered the tongue into place.

"Would he be after seein' to the Brits then?" Rory asked.

Though it was well in place, Liam hammered the piece harder.

Rory pressed him. "Will he, Da?"

"There's nothing to be seein' to them about." Liam dropped his hammer and walked into the forge. "And I'll be hearing no more talk of that."

Fiona was forever on watch. She went to the boys. "Your father has enough to do with putting food on the table for the lot of us. He doesn't need to be answering for you lads out playing rebel. He's no use of it anymore and he needs no reminding!" She shooed the girls into the house. "Leave it be."

Liam's displeasure with the lads' devilment lasted well into that summer, affording them even more time off by themselves once their chores were finished. When he didn't need their hands in the forge, he didn't want to know them, so they made do at their ruin by the river. Rory had grand plans for it. They'd fix it up and live there as soon as they could get out from under Liam's roof. Sure, they'd both be hurling for Clare by then and busy winning All-Irelands, but when they weren't playing Conor could read and write all day, while Rory would catch salmon off the rocks.

Conor had different plans. On that same rock one fine and lazy sunny day, he wistfully watched the waters. Rory lay outstretched on the warm slab.

"I wish this was the ocean," Conor said.

"Go away," Rory answered.

"And all the land around it was the whole world." He pointed out at all the exotic locales of his imagination. "That was America… and South America down below it. Africa there, and the Orient there. Australia afar."

"What are ye goin' on about now?" Rory asked.

"I'd jump in and swim to everywhere."

"You're a feckin' eejit," says Rory.

Conor jumped upon Rory's back like he was mounting auld Oscar and gave him a good belt on the head. "I'd be a cowboy in America. Breaking wild broncos."

Rory bucked him right off and jumped up at him. Conor dodged him, dancing crazy and making faces. "And dance with gorillas in Africa."

Rory danced around him. Conor popped him with two quick jabs. "And box kangaroos in Australia."

Rory shoved him into the river. "Go on then, swim off, ya bollocks." He sat down on the rock. "I'll be right here when you come crawling back, stinkin' of your animals."

Conor climbed back up and sat down next to him. "Sure, you can have the lot of them," Rory said. "I'm never leaving here."

Conor held his silence for a long moment, then spit his secret mouthful of water at Rory, soaking his ginger head.

"Just for that, ya won't be welcome at my mansion." He pointed back at Fenian's Trace. "The fine seat of Mister Rory McCabe, Clare captain and Croke Cup winner ten years running."

"It'll take ya that long to fix it up."

"Sure, there's no rush in it," Rory said.

The poor lads thought they had all the time in the world.

I soon saw Liam once again, even before the bruising on his jaw had mended. The man fills a door frame, ye wouldn't even know it was open. He came in and I served him a pint. He took a long swallow, then pulled Sullivan's *The Story of Ireland* from his coat and set it on my bar. It was the copy I'd given to Conor and Rory, but with a new wear and tear quite noticeable. They'd been well at it.

"I believe that belongs to you, Mr. Clancy."

"Ah, yes. I believe it did," I answered. "Before I passed it on to some friends."

"Your friends won't be needing it anymore."

"Well, that's grand," I said. "I trust they enjoyed it." I pulled William O'Brien's *Irish Ideas* (a feckin' gem of a read!) off the bookshelf behind the bar and set it down. "Our friends might enjoy that as well."

Liam just pushed it back at me. "Your lessons are over, Mr. Clancy. Leave 'em be."

I replaced it with *A Book of Irish Verse*, Yeats' own collection. "That's poetry, Liam. Pure and innocent, on the Bible, but stunning just the same. Could stir a lad's heart."

He downed his pint, then pushed that book back as well. "You've stirred enough." He walked out and that was that. The lads were the youngest to ever be barred from Clancy's. I managed to keep Conor in the right books on the sly but the lads were scarce as hen's teeth for a few years.

And the whole world changed in those years - at least everywhere but Cloonlara. Rory and Conor went about the business of lads, enduring their schooling, working in the forge, training on the pitch and otherwise getting up to whatever devilment they could muster. The rest of the world erupted in blood and death.

Just as it did, Ireland finally won its right to self-government from England under the Third Home Rule Act, only the bastards strategically suspended its implementation for the extent of the war. That left a good upstanding Irishman facing a difficult dilemma in late 1914. The rest of us knew right certain that it was no affair of ours.

Citing the greater good, Redmond, our man in Parliament, called for the Irish to enlist in the British Army and fight the Germans side-by-side with Englishmen. Of course, the very thought of defending our great oppressor was too much for many to swallow. Rory would have rather taken his chances with the Kaiser than take orders from an Englishman. I suppose Conor thought about joining up, if only for the adventure in it, but having been born with the new century, they were both spared any difficult weigh up over it. They were too young for the gun.

Still, two hundred thousand Irish did enlist and a quarter of them died for it. The English had no qualms sending our men into their battles first. T'was no bother to sacrifice Irish blood at Somme Valley and Gallipoli while they finished their feckin' tea - the better to weed out any well-trained and willing soldiers that may go home and challenge their rule after the war. A crafty policy in case Ireland wasn't so overcome with gratitude to the English for saving us from the Germans that we'd forget all about the Home Rule. An empire could hope.

Lucky for us, the Brotherhood was too short of patience to wait and find out.

Chapter Five

A Rising Indeed

In my fanciful reminiscence, I find it easy to diagnose a certain ambition in the airs of those days, one that hadn't been known for ages. A vaguely resurgent pride, or at least something that felt akin to it, was after sprouting upon our fertile Irish soils. I know I saw it in the two lads. They seemed to carry notions of themselves beyond anything their present place warranted. I wouldn't presume to brand them dreamers, for Ireland's always been well full there and hardly a one's come true, but I believe they walked without the weight of fears familiar to most folks, as if they knew a secret of themselves, or their destinies, that spared them our traditional torment. Maybe it was the brashness of youth, but they were right keen for their tomorrows, and historically that's been a dodgy outlook for any Irishman.

The rain, indeed, will fall.

T'was a brimming boil of ambition and pride, along with a holy dose of revolutionary fever, that surprised the world by seizing the General Post Office in Dublin that Easter Monday of 1916. The barrage of it is still rumbling today - sure you'll have your slant on it and I'll have mine - but it was the bewildering cheek of 'em that was all the news in our little corner of Ireland.

The odd rumour of it, of a big something in the offing, had been passed in certain circles since early April, but when Easter came and went in Limerick without a stir or a shout, no one spoke much more of it. Then the stories of Dublin started to drift west. Mad they were. Totally inconceivable, yet still they kept pouring in. The speculation was rampant and every chancer on the street had a new version of it with his own half-witted theorising to follow. There was a fierce hunger for hard details, one that could only be satisfied by the veritable authority of the black and white.

I've little doubt then that there was an extra pep in his step as Rory rushed down the lane with that morning's fresh *Irish Independent* clutched in his grip. He burst into the house to find Liam and Fiona there at the table. "Where's Conor?" he asked.

"Delivery," Liam answered. "That you were supposed to help with."

Rory spread the newspaper open across the table. "Did ye see the news?"

The headline screamed it loud for them - Drama, Terror and Death!

Liam and Fiona didn't flinch. Somehow they already knew as much. "They're really fighting in Dublin!" Rory trumpeted. "A band of lads took it over."

Liam pushed the paper aside and stood up. "They took over the post office."

Rory grabbed it back. "It says other buildings as well." He found the description and pointed it out to Liam. "Look, the Four Courts, Jacob's Biscuit Factory, St. Stephen's Green."

Liam took it but didn't bother reading. "They've probably got them all done in by now."

"But they're bringing it to 'em, Da. The lads are fightin' 'em right in the open."

"Jaysus Rory, they toppled a biscuit shop. It's all a lot of blather and nonsense." Liam tossed the paper into the fireplace. "And they'll end up dead for it, sure enough."

Rory scrambled to save the paper but was too late. "Then I'll go to Dublin and carry on the fight."

Liam opened the door. "Then you'll end up dead as well."

"Liam!" Fiona cried. "Don't say such a thing."

He walked out. Rory shouted to the door. "At least I'd be fighting!"

Rory found Conor on George's Street, not far from the clock tower, just starting on his way back out of Limerick. The streets were busy and all abuzz. Newsboys were hawking their headlines on nearly every corner - Dublin in Flames! Rebels at War!

He leaped up onto the empty cart and plopped down right next to him on the seat, then smacked him with his rolled paper. "Did ya hear the news, boyo?"

"How could ya not?"

"Ain't it grand?"

Conor checked Rory's face to make sure he was serious. "Sounds like they're in trouble."

"Let's go to Dublin," Rory says.

"Dublin? For what?"

"Fuck's sake, ya know what for. To help the lads fight."

"They need a lot more than the likes of us."

"Sure there'll be loads of lads heading in from all over."

"I'd say it'll all be over before they even get there. Those lads don't have a prayer."

"At least they're fightin'."

"They don't stand a chance."

"Well they're doing something. And that's far more than anyone around here can say."

"They are at that. They're making a point."

They were quiet the rest of the way out of Limerick, momentarily content watching the city bustle along under the misty rain. Crossing Mathew Bridge, Rory looked west and out across the Shannon. He could see the old Strand Barracks on its bank, where a group of British soldiers were assembled just below its great carriage arch. Didn't that sight put a thought in his head?

"We should chat to Mr. Sheehan," he said.

"What about?"

"You know yourself what about."

"I've nothing to chat to him about, and he'd come to you if he'd cause to."

"Then I'll just have to go to him, won't I?" Rory answered. And with that he vaulted off his seat to the ground. Conor halted Oscar. "Are ya coming?" Rory asked.

Conor took a moment to answer. "I amn't.

Rory just turned on his heels, back into Limerick. Conor watched him go, then steered Oscar toward Cloonlara.

Rory found Martin easily. With his wife and daughter living off in America for the past few years, he began most of his days in his office and finished most nights in Clancy's. He'd been here for both over the previous few days, utilising the back snug as a makeshift headquarters as he received the intelligence coming in from Dublin.

The reports were distressing. Ambitious plans of insurrection were after going completely arseways falling into a right mess of confusion and chaos. Most in Dublin were entirely dismayed by the whole affair and some were even hurling abuse, throwing rocks and such when they weren't busy dodging the crossfire. The Brits were putting it down hard and had already rounded up the guts of the leaders so - at least at that stage anyway - it only appeared they'd made an awful hames of it. Of course, Martin and his men couldn't offer any help from Limerick but they had to be concerned with the repercussions that would certainly follow.

Lads came in and out with messages for him, but most of the time Martin just sipped tea or huddled in hushed tones with the two men that never strayed far from his side, Mick O'Keefe and Colm Crotty. They shadowed the dapper Martin everywhere, like two dark clouds chasing the sun they were. If not for the nose on Crotty, O'Keefe could claim the ugliest mug in Limerick - a sneezer like a frightened pig's mickey. And didn't the good Lord bless the two of them with the humour to match? I could hardly wait to see the back of 'em.

Rory got the full dose of their charms when he asked for a word with Martin. "Fuck off with ye," Crotty growled. But Rory just sat and waited.

After a while Martin noticed him there. "Rory McCabe? What brings you here, lad? Are ya alright?"

"Can I speak with you, Mr. Sheehan, sir?" Rory asked. He looked at Crotty and O'Keefe. "In private?"

"Of course," Martin said. He waved his men off to the bar. "Have a seat, Rory. What's on your mind?"

Rory held up his newspaper, damp and tattered. "Have you heard the news from Dublin?"

"What of it?"

"I want to fight."

Martin looked about, trying to make sense of the odd visit. "Are ya takin' the piss?"

"No, sir," Rory says.

"Ya want to fight?"

"Yes, sir."

"So why are ya comin' to me?" Martin asks him.

Rory leaned in to whisper. "With all due respect, sir... I've known you were in the Brotherhood since I was a little boy."

"Is that a fact?"

"Yes, sir."

"Does your father know that you're here?" Martin asked him.

"No, sir."

"C'mere to me, Rory," Martin says. "How old are ya now?"

"I'm fifteen."

"Fifteen? You've some size on ya for fifteen. Yer your father's son alright."

Rory straightened up even more. "And I can handle meself."

"I'm sure you can," Martin said. He stood and grabbed the newspaper, rolling it up. "But you're fifteen, lad. This fight..." he said, tapping Rory's shoulder with it, "isn't for boys."

Rory stood as well. He was already taller than Martin. "Red Hugh O'Donnell was in an English dungeon at fifteen."

"Is that so?" Martin replied with a tired chuckle. "Red Hugh, eh? There are some Dublin lads in one now. Limerick lads as well. Are you looking to join them?"

"I'm looking to help them," Rory answered.

"I'm afraid you're too late. That fight'll be over soon enough."

"Then what of here?" Rory asked.

"There'll be no fighting here," Martin sighed. "Not now at least... maybe someday. Soon, I hope." He gave Rory a pat on the back, ending their discussion. "Now, you'll excuse me, lad. I've business to attend to."

Crotty and O'Keefe somehow knew to return just then. Rory nodded to them, receiving only a pair of scowls in return, and then walked out.

"The McCabe boy?" O'Keefe asked Martin.

"Rory."

"What's he at?"

"Says he wants to join the Brotherhood," Martin said, sitting back down with a heavy sigh. "Fight for Ireland."

"I'd say right now Ireland'll need all the help she can get," Crotty mused.

"I've seen that lad on the pitch," O'Keefe said. "He's a tough fucker. Be a fine addition… if he could be trusted."

"Why wouldn't he be?" Crotty asked.

"Let's just say his bloodlines are suspect," O'Keefe answered.

Martin cut it right off. "He's too young."

"Too young?" Crotty asked. "Fer fuck's sake, Martin, since when does that matter?"

"Since I say it does."

Crotty held his tongue. He was surprised by Martin's stance, but he knew him well enough to be sure there was a sound reason for it, and that it certainly wasn't the one he was just given.

O'Keefe would likely have known the real reason, though he didn't care for the explanation either. He looked at Martin. "As the cock crows, the young bird chirps."

Martin didn't bother looking back. "And pity him who makes an opinion a certainty."

It wasn't the galling failure of our Easter Rising that set Ireland off on this rocky road where we find ourselves today. If doomed rebellions were the solution for English occupation, we'd have seen the back of them centuries ago. The grim brutality they responded with is what brought us here. With every man they put up against the wall, Irish hearts broke a little more. The fields of revolt were well barren when they set out, but didn't their blood steadily nourish those same grounds until they were fertile enough to feed our blessed uproar?

Now let it never be forgotten that there were fine Limerick men among those that faced the execution guns. Con Colbert, Edward Daly, and Sean Heuston, it was their sacrifice too that eventually transformed a perplexed and unsympathetic public into a defiant and determined citizenry.

But sure, we were none too soon in getting there. Martin's hopes were a long time coming. Ages it took us.

God moves slowly, yet his grace ever comes.

While Ireland waited, the adventuresome business of lads was quite quickly forsaken for the more visceral pursuits of young men. Of course, the hurling started at the top. Like nearly every other young fella in Ireland, the lads were rarely seen without their hurleys in hand. With each other always at the ready to test one's mettle, their individual skills swiftly sprouted to noteworthy levels, but it was in tandem where they were truly remarkable. They spent endless hours racing the fields together, passing the ball back and forth between them for miles. They'd dodge trees and leap stiles, risking life and limb to be sure each wasn't the one to let it hit the ground. They came to know nearly every move the other could make, every lift and strike, every check or chop, even before it occurred.

Word spread wide of the Cloonlara lads' hurlin' feats. Rory was a terror, with physical gifts not to be matched by boys even two and three years older. He could speed by you, knock you off, or just plow you over. Pick your poison. Conor wielded the handiest hurley around, quick and nimble with an exceptional dexterity, but it was his innate feel for Rory's fierce movements that elevated them to the full potential of their togetherness. He always knew where'd he'd be. And if he didn't find him in just the right place, he'd maneuver to get him there, most every time.

Of course, a bit of sporting notoriety for a teenage boy is worth its weight in gold, so when the lads weren't chasing the *sliotar* around the pitch, they were chasing the girls down the path. Every scant hour they could squeeze free of Liam and school was spent chatting someone up. They may not have been as adept in the romance department as on the pitch, but no doubt they were just as keen to score - the only acceptable excuse to drop a hurley. When they found their pickings were a trifle limited out in Cloonlara, didn't Limerick City offer a great treasure trove of quarry to quest?

Now, it should be known that the River Shannon is named for the young goddess Sionann, grand-daughter of the great Sea God Manann Mac Lir. As the story goes, she lived temptingly close to the legendary Well of Knowledge, only all but the king were forbidden from visiting it, quite a problematic prohibition, especially for a young lass with an irrepressible longing for wisdom beyond her years. Alas, didn't the poor girl's curiosity eventually get the best of her? When she opened the well a great wave of endless water rose up and drowned her, carrying her across the heart of Ireland and out to sea, its wake furrowing the great river that bears her name forever.

It seems some knowledge just isn't worth the knowing.

After its long run through Ireland, the snaking Shannon splits Clare from Limerick, where it finally begins to open up and stretch full for the Atlantic. There's something special there, a wellspring of Sionann's feminine enchantments must still swirl in those waters, for as all the world surely knows, the fairest colleens in Ireland, and thus the world again, hail from that blessed region. I suppose a man can argue over which side of the river can boast the best bounty - sure I'll take My Beauty of Limerick over your Darling Girl From Clare - but no doubt you'll agree we'd both be doing grand by herself. Who could blame a lad for casting a rake of lines? A rag on every bush, as they say...

By the time they were seventeen the lads were already capable of hurling against full grown men and generally holding their own. Though they mostly played with their junior club in Cloonlara, many of their matches were played right here in Limerick. Of course, Clancy's has long been known city-wide as the best spot to quench a sporting thirst, and players and spectators alike gather here to recount the day's contests and enjoy a jar or two.

When Rory and Conor eventually came to appreciate yet one more seductive treat for an idle hand, my lemonade went the way of their custard concerns and I found myself drawing them pints of

Guinness from those same barrels that once only appealed as river riding seats. Oh, how the days can pass.

After every local match, or at least the victories, I'd hear them coming even before the door swung, marching down the lane in a boisterous sing-song. T'was music to my ears. A winning squad always delivers their supporters, and Clancy's hosted many a celebration over the years that Rory and Conor were playing. Great *craic* it was. Even Liam would occasionally find his way in for a pint or two after taking in a match. Even he couldn't hide his pride.

Inevitably, it was Rory who led the team in, the cock of the walk, usually in mid-song:

> *Up to mighty London came an Irishman one day.*
> *As the streets are paved with gold, sure, everyone was gay,*
> *Singing songs of Piccadilly, Strand and Leicester Square,*
> *Till Paddy got excited, And he shouted to them there -*

Conor and their teammates all joined in:

> *It's a long way to Tipperary, It's a long way to go,*
> *It's a long way to Tipperary, To the sweetest girl I know,*
> *Goodbye Piccadilly, farewell Leicester Square,*
> *It's a long, long way to Tipperary, But my heart's right there!*

A raucous applause would always follow. The day's crowd didn't need to be won over, it was already theirs. Not so for the noble publican, not being one easily swayed generous by the trappings of success, nor compassionate to the pities of the odd failure.

Rory was a true showman. Why walk to a bar when it can be reached just as well with a strut? "Ah, the very handsome Mr. Clancy," he says. "We're after winning another one for auld Munster today… hard fought and well-earned to be sure. But man, it's thirsty work, don't ya know?"

He'd beckon the whole team up close in a circle, like there was a sacred secret to be whispered. "Any chance ya might stand a round fer the lads now? In recognition, like?"

Now meself, I'm not a complete stranger to the working of the boards. "Well done there lads. 'T'is grand," says I. "And now ya want I should stand ye a round? For the accomplishment in it, is it?"

The place echoed in shouts. "Go on now!" "A round for the lads!"

Conor joined in as well. "It'd only be a grand gesture of support for the team and for your dear beloved Munster as well, Mr. Clancy. One only a fine and very handsome man such as yourself could give."

Rory hoisted him right up onto a stool. "A man, I might add, who's looking as handsome today as I've ever seen."

"A cheer for the handsome Mr. Clancy, boys!" Rory yells. The room roared gracious for my abundant beauty. That sort of appeal, submitted so passionately, warranted great consideration, week in and week out. I took a long moment, and then a longer one.

"What say ya, Mr. Clancy?" Rory asked.

"Man or mouse?" Conor asked me, with a sly wink.

I held up my arms for silence. Yes, the verdict at hand required it. There could be no misunderstanding.

"C'mere 'til I tell ye lads. If it's free pints you're after, well I've said it before but sure I'll say it again... I will in me feckin' hat!"

Conor fell back off that stool, right into Rory's arms as the crowd erupted in boos and cheers and every manner of bold celebration. And with that, the drink would flow and yes sir, I'd be well up to me bollocks in it. Times to hold dear...

The lads were on the pig's back and full of vim and vigour, snug in that brilliant span of life between adolescent innocence and adult burdens, and loving every moment of it. I'd say even auld Liam was well chuffed watching their antics. Even in on the rounds he was.

Oh, if I could only button up those days and tuck 'em away.

Martin Sheehan himself chanced the fray for a congratulatory word. "Alright there, lads. A fine match today."

Rory straightened right up on his voice. "Thank you, Mr. Sheehan."

"Some thundering runs, Rory."

"Thank you, sir."

As always, O'Keefe and Crotty were with him and quick hullos and nods were passed. Rory called for a round for Mr. Sheehan and the lads.

"No thanks, Rory. We're on our way."

"Ah, of course you can stay for the one now, Mr. Sheehan," Rory implored.

Liam put a quick end to it. "He said they're on their way, Rory."

Crotty and O'Keefe shot Liam some surly looks to mark the terse snub, but Martin diffused it with his usual charm. "Sure, we are on our way. There's yet work to be done. Another time maybe." He shook hands with the lads, "A fine match today though," and he gave Liam a warm nod. "All the best."

And they were off, to talk of more than the hurling maybe. Liam wasn't long after them, but the lads hung on a good while after, enough to leave them well scuttered and talking shite.

Rory was up and down, zealously re-enacting the day's plays, though with far less balance and agility than his more sober legs had mustered only hours before.

"I knew, Conor," he insisted, though Conor wasn't offering any objection. "I knew right where you were going to put that ball. I knew it. Even before you struck it… before you did now. I knew it then. That's the guts of it. What do ye think of that?"

"I think you're fuckin' locked," Conor said.

And he was right. A fine time to clear the room and send them off home, but ah sure, one more round. What harm in it?

Then the door opened and three teammates from the other side of the hurling match staggered in.

"Sorry lads," I says right quick. "All finished now."

"Well then that makes you a right bollocks!" says the biggest one. Bigger even than Rory by a few stone, and probably more pissed, though that was a closer call.

Rory hopped up quickly. "Alright there lads. No need for the carryin' on. Allow me a word with good Mr. Clancy here and we'll see if we can't scare up a few pints for ye." He patted the giant a good rankling thump on his massive chest, then turned to me, quickly mustering up the most of his charm, near begging me to keep them around. "Please Mr. Clancy, just one round for the lads?" Friends or foes, he was looking for the fun to be had in it, though there was little hope for affections to bloom. Still, credit due to Rory for first extending the olive branch. "I'm buying," he says.

The monster raised up his meat hook of a hand. "We'll buy our own drink."

"No, no, no. The least we can do. Right, Conor?"

"The least we can do," agreed Conor, though he couldn't resist stirrin' the pot a bit. "Especially after the long, hard, disappointing day the poor lads have had."

"I said we'll buy our own fuckin' drink ye culchie bogtrotters." He led his teammates toward the bar, but Rory intercepted them. "Fine then. Ye buy it. Just be careful not to drop it. As we seen today, ya got hands like me granny's feet."

The big man shoved Rory into the bar. "Maybe I'll drop you as well."

Conor jumped between Rory and the giant, "Come now lads, for Mr. Clancy's sake." He got an even fiercer shove for his trouble but moved right back between them. "Alright lads, there'll be no fightin' now."

Now Rory pushed him. "Piss off, Conor. I'll box his ears."

Conor quickly grabbed the two pints I'd put up and flashed a wink at me. "Jaysus lads, hold your hour. If fightin' it will be, why not a bit of sport with it?" He got back between them, holding each pint out. "Since Mr. Clancy's been kind enough to pull these two beautiful pints here, let's try not to wreck his fine establishment while we're at it."

The big lad and Rory didn't break their hard stares, but they held onto their fists a moment. Conor seized it. "Take a hold of these, each of ye, but don't sup it." They each took a pint in their left hands, leaving their right hands ready to fly, but Conor continued before either twitched a nerve. He had their curiosity.

"Here are the rules," he said, nudging them in opposite directions. "Give us about twenty paces here." They each backed up, still keeping at their staredown, just across the span of the bar now. Conor pulled two stools for the others. "Top seats, lads. A bit of *craic*, now, is all. Ye can be the judges."

He stood in the middle, refereeing the contest. "Each of you gets one charge on the other. A full-on wallop now, but the one taking it has to hold on to his pint glass. Now, whoever spills the least amount of drink is the great, grand champion for all time and eternity. Our loser... buys the round."

"Who goes first?" Rory asked.

"You go first, boyo," says the big lad. "You won't be gettin' up when I'm done." Conor got out of the way. "When you're ready, gentlemen."

Rory set his full pint on the floorboards next to him and crouched into an attacking stance. The big lad lowered himself into a human wall. Both hands gripped his pint firm against his chest, his burly arms in a blocking position.

"Alright there, big fella?" Conor asks.

He grunted his assent, and Rory sprung at him instantly, with all the speed and strength he could muster, a coiled spring battering ram. He crashed into him with his full force. The big lad was sent sprawling backward. He slammed into the wall and slumped to the floor, the best of his breath knocked clear from his lungs. He looked down at himself, newly splattered with Guinness, but then held up his pint glass - still about half full - for the optimists wondering on it.

"Judges," Conor called out, taking the glass off the big lad and handing it to his teammates. "For your consideration." He dabbed a tea towel on his damp chest. "Looks like the spilt half is safe and sound right here on his *geansaí*."

Then he helped him up, finally appreciating the full size of him. His eyes barely met the big lad's shoulders. "Jaysus, you're some mountain, aren't ya?" He walked back toward Rory, who was crouching himself into a similar defensive posture. "Mind yourself, Rory. He's feckin' massive."

Rory girded up for the bash in it, fortifying his pint glass high against his chest. "Don't be mollycoddlin' me now, ya lumbering tank. Bring yer best or don't bother." The big lad's blood was boiling. He bent into a sprinter's stance, steaming for it.

"Buck up now, Rory," Conor warned, his voice betraying a bit of genuine concern. "Alright?"

"Grand," says Rory, and the big lad broke for him - but didn't Rory tilt the pint to his mouth and gulp the whole of it in one swallow? Drained it empty, just as the charging bull himself blasted him clear off his feet. He tumbled into the far wall, even lost a boot in it, but he held safe the glass.

Conor quick took it off him and passed it over to his judges.

"It's empty!" they declared.

"And not a drop spilt!" added Conor. He grabbed Rory's arm and held it up, the only part of him able to move yet. "The champion!" As he pulled him up Rory posed a quiet question. "Fancy one day you might take the hit?"

"Never work," Conor said. "You've a far faster swallow."

The big lad made good and bought the round. I'll admit to one last on the house as well. And wouldn't you know, the lot of them fell outta the place, arm in arm and singing *Tipperary*.

Still, after the hurling and the drink and the songs and the *craic*, it was a weighty world the lads were facing in 1918. As the war dragged on, England looked to the Irish to supply fresh soldiers to throw at the German army piercing their Western Front. They enacted a bill to bring conscription to Ireland. Both Conor and Rory were then seventeen. At eighteen they could be called up. Even as the death tolls rose with every read of a newspaper, it wasn't so much the prospect of braving the trenches that burdened their young minds, it was the notion of doing so at England's behest. Same with the rest of Ireland… conscription hadn't a hope.

The executions and internments of the rebel leadership carried out by England after the Rising had soured a taste already too bitter in the Irish yap. We'd had two years to dwell on that treatment. When even the bishops threw their support behind the resistance movement, compulsory conscription was laughed right out of Ireland. They drafted not a single Paddy.

Our nationalist sentiment was growing strong across the land. The secret aims of the Brotherhood, once whispered only in back rooms and far fields, were after being voiced aloud across the laneways and at the fairs. Though few were rarin' for another rising, there were far more who wouldn't have been caught surprised by it and even more again who might lend a bit of support this time. Not to say there was a sudden surplus of rebels. We're a country of farmers and fishermen, along with the odd smithy, and most were just trying to get by and couldn't be arsed with the politics. Especially that odd smithy...

Still, there was something strong blowing in the air alright.

And there was something in the alley outside the McCabe forge when Rory stepped out of their house late one misty morning that spring. There hadn't been a constables' visit since Rory'd bricked the RIC carriage over five years prior and he hadn't grown any fonder of them in the interim. Now there were three sitting in a lorry outside their forge.

A fourth was inside speaking to Liam as he looked over some papers. "I trust you'll find the pay more than fair for the work required," the constable said.

"There'll be measurements needed," replied Liam.

"At your convenience. Arrangements will be made for you."

Liam signed one of the papers and handed it to him. "It won't be me."

Just then Rory stuck his head inside. "What's going on?"

"Wait outside," Liam answered.

"Are ya alright, Da?"

"Wait outside!"

When Liam came inside, Rory and Conor were waiting at the table. Fiona had the girls outside and was giving the men a distance, but just a small one. Rory stood up just as Liam sat down. "What's going on, Da?"

Liam passed the papers to Conor. "Measurements," was all he said.

"For fuck's sake," Rory says. "I knew it."

"Rory!" Fiona scolded. "Your language."

"You're after taking a job on for 'em, aren't ya?" Rory asked.

"There's not the work to keep the three of us busy as is," Liam said, without looking up to Rory. "A job like this won't come along again. We can't turn down that money."

"I wouldn't work for the bastards for any amount of money," Rory avowed. "I can't believe yer even thinkin' of it."

"I'm not thinkin' of it," Liam says. "It's done."

"Well it'll be done by yourself then," Rory said, moving to stand behind Conor. "We won't be helpin' any."

Liam looked to Conor. "Is that true?"

Conor toyed with the pendant under his shirt for a long moment, twisting it nervously. He finally spoke, though in barely a whisper. "I'll help ya, Da."

Rory spun Conor's chair right around and shouted at him. "Ya must be fuckin' joking!"

"Rory!" Fiona barked.

"Jaysus! Do ye not see what's goin' on around ya?" Rory asked.

Liam remained steady. And deliberate. He finally looked at Rory. "We have to take what work there is."

Rory swept the papers off the table. "I'd rather no work at all!"

"And no money as well?" Liam asked.

"I'd rather none than your English fuckin' blood money," Rory answered.

"Rory!" Fiona cried again.

With that Liam put his giant hands upon the table and stood, eye to eye with Rory now. "Yet you'll sit to eat at my table?" The two huge men together were simply too much for the room to hold.

Conor scooped up the papers and stuffed them into his waistcoat. "Da and I will take care of this job." He stood up and faced Rory. "You can handle the rest."

Rory broke his glare from Liam to look at Conor. "How can ya be a part of that?"

Conor didn't answer. Rory opened the front door but stopped and looked back at the two of them. "You'd think I was the fuckin' orphan."

Chapter Six

Jodhpurs and High Boots

Martin Sheehan's farmstead was set back against a rugged wooded hill and only approachable by a long *boreen* that cut through acres of low potato fields. They were awash in their purple and white spring blossoms, and with the showers down the earthy odour off them filled the afternoon's air. Rory inhaled the scent deep into his lungs after the long run he'd put in from Cloonlara to far out the Ennis Road, but when the Sheehan place came into view, he finally slowed his feet to give his mind a chance to catch up with his plan, whatever that might be. He really hadn't a clue why he was there.

The very thought of Liam taking on a job at the New Barracks was wrecking his head. That barracks was the seat of English power in Limerick City, housing both British Army troops and a good number of RIC men. Hundreds of 'em. You could hear the bastards drilling on their acres of parade grounds inside its walls. You could see them as well, with a peek through the massive stretch of iron gate that led inside, at least until you were ushered along by the soldiers stationed at the two guard posts on either side. How could he agree to work for the fuckers?

For Rory's whole life, Liam was as far from political as a man could get. He did his work and that was that. Rory had never seen him take any interest in Republicanism, never heard him speak a word on the movement. Still, the Sinn Feinery was the talk all over Ireland in them days. Hell, Rory himself rarely stopped yammering about it. There was no way Liam wasn't aware of the message he was sending by taking on that job. People would wonder what side he was on, and maybe not for the first time. But he never cared what people wondered. Liam did his work and that was that.

The whole way over he'd tried to suss out a reason that might make sense in explaining it to Martin. Could it really be the money? Was it enough that the Brit's job would be after paying three or four times what they'd get anywhere else? Sure, money was tight. With the war on everyone was skint. But that was always the case and they'd always gotten by. No way Martin would accept that as a justification.

But fuck's sake, what did he really think Martin could do about it anyhow? Could he talk Liam out of it? Rory'd never known Liam to be talked out of anything. Could he maybe bring other pressures to bear to make Liam reconsider? Rory knew well enough who Martin was. Is that why he was nearly to the man's door?

He stood out in front of the house for a long moment. It was hardly surroundings that would suggest a regular meeting place of the upper command of the Brotherhood for Limerick. Horses could be heard from inside a large barn, set a ways off to the side just next to a small riding ring. The house itself was a fine two-storey, stone Georgian with a large brass claddagh knocker hanging in the center of its bright green door.

Martin's wife answered it. The beautiful Mrs. Sheehan spoke to Rory with an accent he'd never before heard the likes of. A beguiling mix of New York and Sicily was a voice entirely alien to Clare. "Ciao," she smiled. "What is it I can do for you, my dear?"

She sounded to him like an angel singing poetry. "Mr. Sheehan?" is all he could muster in reply.

"Just a minute," she said, disappearing back inside to find him.

As he waited, Rory heard a horse neigh off by the riding ring. For a small stud farm, Martin had earned a reputation for breeding some of the soundest horses in Munster, and Rory was always keen to get a good look at one of them. Indeed, it was an impressive stallion being led into the ring, but Rory couldn't even take notice of it, for his eyes were captured by the even finer beauty pulling the reins. He was gobsmacked.

"Rory McCabe?" Martin said when he opened the door.

Rory near had to pull his own head back around to face Martin. "'T'is, sir," he answered. "Hello, Mr. Sheehan."

"Are ya alright, lad?"

"I am," Rory said, taking a quick glance back to the ring to make sure he wasn't having visions.

"What can I do for ya?" Martin asked him.

"It's my father, sir. He's after taking on work for the Brits. At the New Barracks."

Martin didn't answer, but clearly this wasn't news to his ears. Rory looked back to the ring again but the only half that was visible to him was empty now. "Well, I thought you should know of it," he said.

"And I do," Martin answered.

Rory's thoughts were barely hanging together when he'd arrived. Now, he'd nearly lost the plot altogether. "Well, it's bollocks isn't it?" Rory asked.

"Ah," Martin sighed. "I can respect the decision. A man has to earn his bread."

"Well I'm not having any part in it," Rory says, stealing another glance to the ring. There she was again. Feckin' amazing.

Martin finally noticed the cause of Rory's distraction.

"I just thought… I wanted you to know that," Rory stammered on.

"And I can respect that decision as well. Even more so." Martin says, offering a handshake. "Fair play to ya, lad." It was a clear send-off.

Rory shook his hand, but held onto it. He finally collected himself and refocused. "I want to join the Brotherhood, Mr. Sheehan. I can help."

Martin looked at him for a long moment. "Does Liam know you're here, lad?" he asked.

"Does it matter?" Rory asked him back.

"Maybe," Martin says.

"I'm not fifteen anymore," Rory answered. "I can help."

"Not now you can't," Martin says, finally pulling his hand away. "But leave it with me." He gave him a good clap on the back. "All the best now, Rory." Then he turned to go back inside. That was it.

Rory didn't know what to make of it, but then he heard the horse again. "Wait, Mr. Sheehan!" he shouted, nearly yanking him back out the door. He pointed to the ring. There she was, riding along its rail, deftly guiding the stallion. A vision she was. "Who is that?"

"That, is the prettiest girl in all of Ireland," Martin says. "My daughter, Maria."

"Jaysus, I'd forgotten you had a daughter."

"She's been off in America living with her mother's family for the past years. Only back a week."

Now, like any good Irishman, Rory was a great admirer of our fair-haired colleens but, having inherited her mother's Italian features - long, silky, raven black hair and soft, tawny skin that made him think of a warm, milky tea - Maria was a beauty unlike anything he'd ever seen.

"She'd be almost… near my age then, wouldn't she?" Rory asked, his curiosity bursting.

"She would, almost," Martin said. "I tried everything I could but, much to my consternation, *she's* not fifteen anymore either."

But Martin liked the match. He headed over to the ring, calling out to her. "Maria! Come here. There's someone I want you to meet."

Rory trailed, trying to collect himself as she rode over to the rail.

"Maria, this gentleman is Rory McCabe, the finest young hurler in County Clare." Rory reached up and shook her hand. Her splendid, velvety hand.

"Rory, my daughter, Maria Sheehan."

"Pleased to meet you," Maria said, with an American accent.

He could hardly contain himself. "Not half as much as me."

Martin knew enough to take his leave. "Well Rory, I've work to attend to."

The horse nudged Rory and he gave him a pat. "He's some horse, Mr. Sheehan," he said, though he never took his eyes off Maria. "Would you mind… if I watched him for a spell?"

"Not at all," Martin says. "I'll leave you to it then."

"All the best, Mr. Sheehan," Rory says, never even looking back to him.

Rory watched Maria ride a smooth canter, though she could have been on a drunken, three-legged mule for as much as he watched the animal. She was perfectly prim in a red riding coat, jodhpurs and high boots. She was also the first girl he'd ever seen ride astride on a horse and not sidesaddle. "You've some way with that horse."

"Thank you," she said. "I rode every day in America."

"A bit fancy maybe," he added quickly.

"To each his own."

"I could show ya a bit if ya like," he offered, never a lad to shrink when he could stretch.

"I think I'll get by," says Maria. "Would you mind pulling the gate open?"

Rory hopped down and put his hands to the gate - but held it fast. "Only if you'll be my dancing partner at the *céilí* on Saturday. It's out at the crossroads by Ballyglass."

"I'm busy Saturday," she answered.

Rory lifted his hands. "Shame in that. I guess you'll just have to open it yourself, so."

As he made himself a great show of walking away, Maria spun the horse and ran it hard at the gate, leaping him over it and right at Rory, who just managed to dive himself out of the way. She slowed the horse and circled back around him, laying there on the ground. "I'll expect you Saturday then," she said.

And with that she gave the stallion a kick and tore off into the meadow. Rory stayed on the ground and gazed up at the sky for a spell. He watched the sun slowly break through the clouds thinning above him and just waited until its rays eventually came shining down, landing warm on his face... a kiss off heaven.

Wasn't it nearly that same time that Conor lay back upon one of the makeshift hammocks they'd hung within the walls of Fenian's Trace and felt the heat off the same glorious rays of sunshine? When Rory'd taken off after the dust-up with Liam, Conor figured for certain he'd be at their hideout in the ruin. This wasn't the first cross words the McCabe walls had heard, and Rory always headed there to settle his blood. It was a sanctuary of sorts. Conor gave him some time of his own before wandering down.

It was strange he didn't find him there, but he knew he'd turn up like always, so he chose a book from the stash he kept in one of their secret chambers. He had every intention of getting stuck deep into its pages, the quickest route to forgetting the day that was in it, but with the sudden early summer heat hitting him, and the rare quiet without Rory there rabbitin' on, he instead closed his eyes and dozed off into a brilliant slumber.

He would've slept for ages had the hoof beats of an approaching horse not stirred him. Their secret spot was that way for good reason. Few still knew of it and callers were scarce. Conor quietly moved out to the arched entryway, shrouded in the shadows. Then he stopped dead.

After growing up together the lads had plenty in common but their near identical reactions were nothing strange. Maria was just that enchanting. Still is. There's not a healthy eighteen-year-old boy in the world who wouldn't have been similarly spellbound.

She dismounted her horse and walked out onto the rocks. Kneeling down, she swept a hand through the water, feeling the cool current on her fingertips. She splashed some onto her face, rinsing off the glow of sweat from her brisk gallop through the meadows. Then she sat and pulled off her riding boots and stockings. She stuck her feet in and laid back upon the warm stone.

Conor could only stare. He was helpless to look away, wondering if maybe he was still lost in a dream. After a while, Maria stood up. She took her boots and walked back to her horse who was having a drink at the edge of the small cove formed by the outcropping. When she had a good hard look around, Conor ducked back into the entryway, yet he still had a fine sight of her when suddenly she took off her riding coat. It nearly stopped his heart.

She draped it up onto the horse's saddle, but wouldn't you know it, as she did so the big beast took a few steps to his side and put himself directly in Conor's view. All he could see was her lower legs. Not entirely unsatisfactory mind you, but a bit disappointing all the same, especially when it was her blouse that followed the coat onto the saddle. When next she slipped her jodhpurs off, he almost fainted. Her stallion was as handsome a horse as he'd ever seen but had Conor a rifle that day the animal would have been stone dead.

Maria waded in up to her waist, then turned and fell back into the frigid water, unwittingly emitting a soft cry as it grabbed her breath.

Conor strained for a better view but the feckin' horse thwarted him every angle and Maria was soon out. It was only a few stirring glimpses he caught as she quickly dressed and mounted up, but then she suddenly steered her horse in a straight dash to the stone archway. Conor ducked deep into it and pressed his back hard against the cold stone.

"If I'd wanted to put on a show, I'd have charged an admission," Maria called out to the shadows. She peered in but it was too dark to see much of anything. Conor closed his eyes and held his breath and hoped to God he'd disappear... gave it a good effort, too. When he didn't, he knew he was caught rotten.

"If I'd known there was to be a show, I'd have bought the horse's ticket," says he. Finally, he leaned out into the light. "I didn't mean any harm. Ya kinda took me by surprise."

"I took *you* by surprise?" she cried. "You nearly put the heart crossways in me."

Getting his first good look at her face, he was immediately taken by her eyes. They were incredibly blue, much like her father's, but where his held a tight and steely gaze, hers seemed to overflow with a softness that illuminated her entire face. They were the color of the warm, faraway seas of his imagination. And from that moment, he longed to swim away in them.

"I was just trying to read my book," Conor says, holding it up. "If I'd known it was your bathtime, I'd have found a quieter place."

"Well I guess I owe you an apology then?" Maria replied. "You see, I've been away for a while and somehow I didn't realise this was now a library. Somehow I mistook it for a tinker camp. And I suppose you're the good librarian then aren't you, and not the head tinker himself?"

Conor laughed. "You talk like a Yank."

"Well, maybe this is better," she said, before putting on her thickest Irish brogue. "Sure boyo, aren't you only a right eejit?"

Conor was completely taken aback. For such a sight to look at, she had some cheek on her. "I guess it's well true what they say of a swim in the Shannon then."

She reverted to her own voice. "And what is it they say? Mind the peeping tinkers?"

Conor smiled. "They say it confers the gift of impudence."

"Is that so?"

"T'is indeed. But only if it's a swim such as yours," he said. "That is, one wearing nothing but a smile, ya might say." And with that he gave her a sly wink.

Her eyes narrowed and a stroppy look came over her face. "You really are a nitwit, aren't you?"

"Jaysus! I'd say the river's rewarded you with abundance."

"Well, I say take your book…" she said, pointing into the entryway, "and creep back into your God forsaken hole."

With that she set herself to ride off but Conor grabbed the horse's reins. "Have a go at me if ya like, but you'd want to mind yerself. This God forsaken hole happens to be a historic landmark."

Being her father's daughter, this settled her for a moment. "You don't say. And what bit of Irish folklore supposedly happened here?"

"Don't tell me you've never heard the story of Fenian's Trace?"

"Why do I suspect I'm about to?" she asked, chancing a slight smile.

That was all Conor needed. He gently moved to take the reins from her. "May I?"

She eyed him for a long moment. "You may."

Conor pulled the horse under the entryway. "Mind your head now." Maria ducked under and they came through to the inside of the ruin.

"Back in the 1860s, Fenian times, this place belonged to an old English lord. But he was a good man, a Fenian himself," he said, as he slowly walked her around the house. "For a long time it was a meeting place for the rebels because the Brits never bothered with the old man. They all thought he'd gone a bit daft, living out here alone for so long."

Maria had a good look around the place and by that time the lads had it well outfitted. There was peat for the fire, a roof for the rain and their hammocks for rest. It wasn't difficult to picture a rugged band of rebels assembled there, plotting their insurrections.

"I presume you've heard of the Rebellion of 1867?" Conor asked her.

"Of course."

"Well, not long before it, a load of guns and ammunition, and a good bit of dynamite even, were stashed here in anticipation of the big day." Conor pulled away a loose board leaning against the wall to show her the small chamber hidden there, which was now stuffed with his books. "Of course, wouldn't you know, some scoundrel of an informer told the Brits what they'd find here. So, they set out to collect the weapons, arrest the old man and burn the house to the ground, as they were in the habit of doing back then."

Conor had a way with his words and was pouring it on thick. Maria couldn't help herself being drawn into the story.

"The old man got wind of this, but the rebels were well scattered about at the time, so it was just him here alone when the Brits came on to him."

Conor climbed up the steps that led to the old second storey and sat on its edge, about even with Maria on her horse. "Well, as the story goes, he piled up near all the dynamite in the middle of the second floor, which was right here. Then, he took the guns and ammo up there," he said, pointing up to the tower. "And just when they got through his doors, he blew the house into bits, along with more than a few of the Crown soldiers, and then proceeded to hold off the rest of 'em for the guts of the night."

"Then what happened?" she asked.

"When the house finally burned itself out by morning, this was all that was left of it."

"Did he live?"

"This was it. There was no sign of the old man."

Maria took a long look around the place as Conor came back down the steps. "But why do they call it Fenian's Trace?" she asked.

"Because it's got a better ring to it than 'God forsaken hole.'" he teased.

"Tell me," she said.

"Mind your head," he said again as he led her horse back out under the archway. "As the story goes, when the old man was told they were coming to burn his house down, he spoke his very last words, 'The only one's gonna burn this place is me, and I won't leave the bastards a trace'." He turned the horse around to give Maria another look. "Fenian's Trace."

"Sounds like a story from the Irish fairies," she said.

"It's all true. Ask your da. He knows."

"How do you know who my father is?" she asked.

"'Cause you're Maria Sheehan. I remember you as a young lass."

She was taken aback slightly, but mostly flattered. "But I've been away a long time. How did you know it was me?"

Conor looked straight into her eyes. "I'd remember those eyes forever," he said. Of course Maria loved hearing this, as any girl would, and could hardly hide her blushing smile.

But she quickly stifled it when she saw the sheepish grin spread across Conor's face as he looked down at the horse's legs. "'Course I shoed Blackie here for your da last month as well." He winked at her. "Two and two together, is all."

Maria yanked the reins from his hands and pulled her horse away, embarrassed for letting her guard down. "Well, I'll have you know that his name is now Brooklyn, not Blackie," she said. "That's after a burrough of New York City where I lived, though I'm sure you know nothing of it."

Conor just smiled, a bit amused by her petulance.

"Well don't worry, you can name a horse after your own home," she said, turning Brooklyn away to head off. "Just call him God Forsaken Hole."

And with that, she tore off. Conor quickly climbed up into the turret and watched her ride away, catching only glimpses while she passed through the woods and over the hills, but he didn't turn away once until she finally disappeared completely.

It wasn't long after that both lads found themselves at Clancy's. Rory was in first, with their mates Michael and Eamonn. He was in quite a celebratory mood, his frustration with Martin's rebuff well forgotten amidst the wonder he'd discovered at the riding ring. The three were already well-oiled when Conor arrived, feeling nothing short of brilliant his own self.

"Hey, ya bollocks!" Rory roared at him "I've been waiting on you."

Conor got a look at the state of them. "I see you lads put another day to good use."

"A pint for Conor, Mr. Clancy." Rory says, raising up his own. "I've an announcement to make. Was holding onto this for you, Conor. It's a toast is in order, lads… a toast to the future. To the future of Ireland…"

The others gave up their obligatory encouragement, these proclamations being typical of Rory when he was in his cups. Conor especially had heard it all many times over, but still he always enjoyed Rory's antics.

I handed Conor his pint when Rory continued on, at least that's how I remember it. Maybe I only imagine it now, knowing the future in it, but I swear I saw his face fall on the very next words from Rory. "… and to the future Mrs. Rory McCabe."

"Fer fuck's sake, what are ya goin' on about?" Michael says.

"Feck off with ya,'" Eamonn added, a lad not known for his eloquence.

"Whose acquaintance I just happened to make today," Rory continued. "And who will be swinging on my arm at the crossroads on Saturday. And who just happens to be the daughter of one Mr. Martin Sheehan."

"The Sheehans don't have a daughter," says Michael.

"Oh, they've a daughter alright," Rory says. "And a finer looking lass you won't ever see."

"Where've they been hiding her all these years?" asked Eamonn.

"She's after spending the past five or so in America," Rory answered, hardly able to contain himself. "Some very, very formative years, lads."

He threw an arm around Conor and pulled him aside. "Jaysus Conor, I wouldn't mind only I hardly know meself. Wait'll you see her. She's a vision. Ya won't believe it."

Conor took a long drink of his pint, then wiped his lips with his sleeve. "No, Rory," he said, somehow mustering up a smile. "Sure, aren't you gushing with it?" He finished his pint right quick and called to me for two more. "I believe it alright."

It was only later that week that Martin and Lucia Sheehan and young Maria took a walk through the town. And didn't they stand well out amongst the more regulars and common folks? Martin always commanded a certain respect and the unique features and indisputable beauty of his wife and daughter drew them loads of attention. They hardly noticed it.

"Is it as you remember?" Martin asked them.

"It looks mostly the same," Maria answered. "But I think it feels different."

Martin was curious. Maria's time in America had transformed her. Of course, she'd done all the normal growing up and was no longer his little girl, as was to be expected. But it was clear to him that she was also developing a personality not common to most Irish women, especially around Limerick City.

He knew a large part of this was due to the lifestyle she enjoyed in America. Her mother's family had seen some success in various New York City enterprises and, with Martin's financial contributions added in, she wouldn't yet have made an acquaintance with misfortune. Is there an Irish lass can say the same?

In Ireland, every Catholic girl already knew the path of her life before she turned sixteen. There was no way of escaping it. The Church knocked them down young and the social order kept them there. If they dared fight it, they'd get kicked from both sides. If they still somehow managed to stand up, to somehow come even to a man, the English were always there to remind them we were all still second-class citizens.

Irish women hadn't a hope.

But his Maria did, and Martin could see it in her. Sure, didn't she nearly glow with it? She was far from resigned to her place. She'd even fought their return to Ireland initially, but relented when Martin insisted on it, even if she didn't like his reason. Part of her was still her daddy's little girl and she missed him. She knew her mother did as well.

Martin just hadn't expected her to return so different, but he was enjoying every second. No man ever wore a scarf as warm as his daughter's arm around his neck.

"How is it different?" Martin asked her.

"I can't say exactly," she replied. "I don't remember everyone seeming so restless and agitated. Everyone's in a tizzy. Maybe it's just the war, but it's not like this in America."

"I'll take that as a compliment," Martin says.

"Well, it isn't one," she said, rolling her eyes to high heaven.

Just then Rory snuck up and tapped Maria's shoulder, then hopped in front of her as she turned. She fell for it.

"Good day Mr. and Mrs. Sheehan," he said. He smiled wide at Maria when she turned back. "Looking for someone?"

She smiled. "Hello, Rory."

"Good day, Rory," Martin said. "You remember Mrs. Sheehan?"

"Ciao," she said.

He nodded and took off his cap, then chanced it. "Ciao," he said.

Maria laughed at him.

"I understand you're to be taking Maria out Saturday," Martin says.

"I am. To the *céilí* - if she'll still allow."

"Of course," said Maria.

"I hope you remember your steps, Maria," Martin said. "Or Rory here may be tough to keep up with."

"Is that so?" Maria asked.

"I'll take it easy on ya," Rory promised with a wink.

Martin pointed down the road a ways. "Isn't that Conor there?" he asked. Indeed, Conor was guiding Oscar and their cart along. He was heading in their general direction but hadn't taken any notice of them.

"It is," Rory answered. "Head in the clouds, like always." He suddenly held his hands up to the Sheehans. "C'mere lads," he said. "Would ye wait here for just a moment now? Would ye mind?"

"Of course."

Rory dashed over to Conor and grabbed his arm. "C'mere!" he said, almost pulling it from his shoulder. "There's someone for ya to meet."

Conor steered over and hopped off the cart. "Mr. Sheehan," he nodded. "Hello, Mrs. Sheehan," he said, pulling off his cap. His eyes checked Maria's quickly but he didn't speak. He wasn't sure if he could and he hadn't a feckin' notion what to say to her anyhow.

Martin saved him. "Conor, this is my daughter, Maria."

"Pleased to meet you," Maria said, offering her hand.

"Maria's the girl I told you about," Rory says. "Remember?"

"Of course I remember," Conor answered. "You could hardly contain yourself."

Rory smiled at Maria. "I told him a lot about you," he explained.

When Conor shook her hand he finally mustered a look in her eyes. "Indeed he did," he said. Their sparkle gave him a bit of a boost. "But I must say, it's far better seein' you in the flesh."

Maria was sure the whole street would notice her blushing, but it was only Conor who did. It took her a long moment to reply, "Well, I do hope you're not disappointed."

Conor stammered for a response but Rory interrupted. "Where ya off to?" he asked.

"Only a few chores."

"Grand, I'll give ya a hand."

Conor climbed back up onto the cart, waving him off. "I'll be alright."

But Rory jumped in next to him. "Ah sure, we'll finish up and go for a pint." He nodded to the Sheehans and waved to Maria. "Saturday, Maria. I can hardly wait."

"All the best," Conor said, waving to the Sheehans. "Maria," he said, tipping his cap to her. "Nice to finally have met you."

Rory could hardly wait 'til they were out of earshot. "Have ya ever seen anything like her? I was tryin' me best to talk to Mr. Sheehan but I couldn't keep my feckin' eyes off her."

They rode along a while, both thinking of her. "Didn't I tell ya, Conor?" Rory said.

"That you did," Conor confirmed as he steered Oscar alongside the high, cut stone walls of Lord Edward Street.

"Those blue eyes of hers are amazing," Rory went on. "Jaysus, look at me. I'm blabbering like a schoolboy."

When Oscar turned the corner, Rory's demeanour changed entirely. He suddenly realised where they were - approaching the wide gates of the New Barracks. A few soldiers looked at them from their guard posts.

"Yer goin' to the barracks," Rory says.

"I told ya I didn't need your help."

"For fuck's sake now," Rory exclaims. "Will ya just cop on already? Yer probably making the same bars they'll be puttin' us behind some day."

"Fencing for a storage yard is all," Conor replied.

"That's not the point, Conor."

Conor couldn't look at him. "There's more to consider."

"We'll get by without the work," Rory said. "We always do."

"That's not my decision to make," Conor answered.

"Well ya can't leave it up to auld Liam," Rory said, as he got out of the cart. "He'd let 'em burn the whole country to the ground so long as they left him his fuckin' forge and food on his fuckin' table!"

"Some people might be grateful for that," Conor said quietly.

Rory just walked off. Conor snapped the reins and Oscar made for the guard post.

Come that Saturday Rory could hardly contain himself, so he set off to O'Connor's Cross to help set up for the *céilí*. It was bucketin' though when he arrived and there was strong talk being given that a cancellation might be in order. Rory wouldn't hear of it, and it was his insistence that carried the day. Of course, the lad wouldn't have given up on that dance if a wintry blizzard had landed in Clare that afternoon. He would have put up the tent and lay down the dance platform by himself if he'd had to.

Indeed, the turnout was strong that night. Young and old alike would attend in them days and you could see a face from every family for six miles. The best musicians around gathered up just behind the platform and the worst nudged in at their elbows. The men would drift to their side and the women to theirs, but the bit of *poitín* that usually made the rounds would eventually bring them together again and ensure that anyone with half a note in their head would be up for the sing-song.

Martin decided to use the occasion to celebrate the homecoming of his wife and daughter and all eyes fell on them when he arrived with the two ladies on his arms. They were as fine-looking as any family Clare had ever seen and Martin was proud as a peacock. If it weren't for the grisly scowls on Crotty and O'Keefe trailing them all night, no one would have peeled their eyes away.

As soon as the music kicked up, Rory promptly asked Maria for her hand and led her out onto the platform to join in line with several others. The *bodhran* player put them right into the beat of *The Haymaker's Jig* and the fiddle and flute carried it away. Everyone was watching the couple, with more than a few envious eyes staring daggers at the newest arrival in Clare. Rory was known as a class dancer and there was never a shortage of girls hopeful to be his partner. He'd generally spin every one of them, but his attentions never left Maria that night. Nor did many others. Both Michael and Eamonn quickly joined in to get a swing with her, but Conor just lurked at the edges. Of course, he watched every step.

Rory loved his dancin'. There was many a night he'd swung Conor around their floor, half just for the *craic* but half for his practice. He had all the jig steps - rise and grind, quick-sevens, promenade - but didn't Maria keep up with each of them? After *The Siege of Ennis* and *The Walls of Limerick*, the crowd cleared a bit. Ever the showman, Rory took the opportunity to break off into a *Sean-nós* dance, battering up a storm and putting your man on the *bodhran* through his paces. The crowd clapped and stomped along to the tune. Even Martin's ill-tempered companions joined in.

Then, Rory all of a sudden darted off the platform, swept the unsuspecting Conor up into his arms, and carried him right back. Poor Conor was raging, but he was helpless in Rory's mighty grasp. Everyone loved it and Rory swung him about until he finally pulled a smile out of him. And when he put him back to his feet, didn't Conor even give the crowd a few smart steps of his own?

Chapter Seven

Mr. Yankee Doodle

Just one night swinging Maria around the floor had Rory chasing her every day. Fierce smitten he was. When she wasn't asleep or off to the shops in Limerick with her mother, he was at her side. When she had a horse in the ring, he'd be at the rail, chatting her up and watching her every move. When she finished, he'd help her with the tack and the grooming just to stay near. On her free time, when the weather was fair, he'd ask her to the city for walks on George's Street or down along the quays. When the rain was down, they'd loll it away here in Clancy's, playing draughts or dominoes.

He called in to me on his own more often as well. He'd trade hours at the old chores to ensure a few bob in hand for his outings with Maria, but mostly he was avoiding the forge after all the shoutin' and roarin' about the English job at hand. At first he tried to take some responsibility for the other work they had in, but there was still a fierce frost between him and Liam that showed no signs of thawing out, so he'd call in on his mam and sisters and maybe make the odd delivery if it didn't require time in the forge, but for a good spell of that summer's nights he took to sleeping on the spare scratcher in Clancy's storage room or on his hammock at Fenian's Trace.

He'd cross paths with Conor out at the ruin on occasion, but all the staying away from home had Rory missing his faithful companion. They'd been nearly attached at the hip their whole lives and Rory hadn't ever for a moment considered that might someday change. But since he'd gone missing at the forge, Conor had all he could do to keep up with the work. He found precious little time for dossing.

Of course, when he did, Rory was right there to greet him, often with Maria already in tow. Even with all his courting of her, he still wanted Conor beside him. He was at his happiest in their little triumvirate and he wouldn't have any of Conor's begging off to give the two of them some time alone. And, if Conor's truth be told, he didn't need much convincing to tag along. At least at the start, he couldn't stop himself.

It was one fine late summer Sunday afternoon when Rory and Maria caught up with Conor in the city. He was just after making another delivery and had taken his regular stop at Daly's Bakery on William Street before heading home. The smiling young lass at the till was no stranger to him. Mary'd had her eyes on Conor for years and was only thrilled to see him alone for the odd chance to flirt a bit, at least before Rory knocked on the window and squished his face up against it.

"Hello, Mary!" he shouted, with a good gander to her ample bosom. "How're yer floury baps?"

"Rory!" Maria cried, pulling him away.

"Ah, I'm just having a laugh."

Inside, Mary gestured toward Rory. "Feckin' eejit he is."

"A gobshite," Conor added.

"And the rest," she agreed.

"See the two of them together all the time now," she said, handing him a bag of brown bread. "Like the two of ye used to be."

"I guess they are at that," Conor says.

Her hand lingered on his when she gave him his change. "Well, I hope it's not leaving you lonely."

He gave her a warm wink and walked outside.

Rory and Maria were already sitting up on his cart. "And where are ye headed?" Conor asked them.

"Yer taking us on a leisurely ride out to Fenian's Trace," Rory answered. "I believe there are some stones in desperate need of a good skipping."

Maria smiled at him. "But only if you're already going that way."

"I am," Conor replied as he got in. "But I've still a few things to…"

"Whatever about a few things," Rory interrupted. "Da'll be down the pub now. Your work is done for the day."

"Then you can join us?" Maria asked.

"Of course he will," Rory answered.

Conor snapped the reins on Oscar and off they went, Maria snug between the two lads.

"Now," Rory asked him. "Did ya get it?"

"I didn't look yet."

"Get what?" Maria asked.

Rory grabbed the bread bag and checked inside. Sure enough. "Your one always slips him a free scone on the sly." Rory said, taking a bite and then passing a piece to each of them. "Mmmm, blackberry," he mumbled.

Maria nudged Conor. "She must fancy you."

"She always has," Rory said.

"She's a very pretty girl," Maria added.

"She's a slapper," says Rory.

"Rory!" Maria scolds. "How rude."

"I'm only coddin' ya," he says. "She's a lovely girl, right Conor?"

Conor didn't answer.

"Not perfect though," Rory said.

"What's wrong with her?" Maria asked.

"Doesn't matter," Rory answered. "He always finds something. He's waiting for the perfect girl." He put his arm around Maria and pulled her close to him. "But I've already got her."

At Fenian's Trace the sun was brilliant, glistening off the waters and heating up the great rocks. Conor and Maria laid back on them, eyes closed and taking in the warmth. Meanwhile, Rory was taking off his trousers. Stripped to his jocks, he ran out with a shout and suddenly leaped over them on a bold flip into the river.

He swam back over. "Come on lads, jump in."

They only ignored him, but he wasn't having it. He splashed Maria.

"Rory!" she scolded.

He splashed her again. "Come on for a swim."

"No," she said. "Stop it!"

So he splashed Conor. "Hey, sleepy head."

Conor's silence only got him wetter.

"Come on, Conor. In for a swim. Don't make me come up for ya."

Conor lay still, but gave Maria a sly wink.

"Alright, work away," Rory said, as he quietly started climbing up toward him for a sneak attack. "A bit of kip'll do you good after all your hard workin'. Just doze away…"

As he was almost onto the rock, Conor sprung up and tackled him back into the water. They wrestled there like two little boys, dunking and splashing each other, Conor in his full clothes and Rory in his jocks. Maria watched and laughed and cheered them on until they tired each other out and climbed back up to catch their breath.

When Conor pulled his shirt off to wring out the water, Maria noticed the pendant hanging from his neck. It was cut of rough metal, in a design of three almost leaf-like shapes interlocking in a criss-cross of sorts. Rory noticed her staring at it and so did Conor. He began to twist it.

"It's his Trinity Knot," Rory said.

"I've been wondering," Maria replied. "It's lovely, what does it mean?"

"Means he's all tied up in knots," Rory joked.

"No, really," she pressed. "You're always playing with it aren't ya?"

Rory laughed out loud at the double meaning. "He sure is!" He hopped up and gave them his crudest portrayal of an ample-bosomed creature. "Everytime he thinks of his sweet Mary and her big floury baps!"

"Rory!" Maria shouted, as Conor leapt up and shoved him back into the water.

"He is though." Rory said when he popped back up. "Whenever he's nervous."

"I am not," Conor insisted. "Feck off!"

"You are," Rory said. "Just watch him, Maria."

"I'd still like to know what it means," she said.

"It can mean many things," Conor explained. "It represents any three things that are connected, like."

"The Father, the Son and Holy Spirit?" she asked.

"Sure," he answered.

Rory climbed back onto the rock. "But it was around well before all that," he added, "so it can mean other things as well."

"But what does it mean to you?" she asked Conor.

He took it in hand, and started at it again. "Me mam and Da..." he said before letting it fall, "... and me."

Maria wasn't sure how to respond. She'd learned the odd bits on his family from Rory, but had never heard Conor mention his parents before.

"Did you make it in the forge?" she asked gently.

"No," he answered.

She waited for more, but it didn't come.

"It was his da's," Rory said.

The silence lingered lightly at first, but gradually grew heavier.

Rory pointed out over the river toward the rapids. "So, where will we swim?" he asked. "America or Australia?"

Conor had a few loose stones next to him. He threw one out toward the west. "I thought I'd try America first."

Maria put a hand on each lad's shoulder and sat down between them. "What are you two talking about?" she asked.

"Conor used to imagine he could swim to anywhere in the world from here," Rory said.

"Wouldn't it be wonderful," she said. "Where would America be?"

Conor pointed at the rippling water where his stone landed. "Out about there, to the west."

"And not so bad a swim at that," Rory says.

"I'd love to visit Australia," Maria said. She pointed off in the other direction. "It would be over there, right?"

"No. That's only Africa," Conor replied, pointing even further out. "Australia's way over there."

"Feck's sake, Maria," Rory teased. "Did they not teach ya yer geography in America?"

"Not starting out from the River Shannon," she answered.

"Well I think you best stay right here from now on then," Rory said. "Ya clearly don't even know yer east from yer west and it's a mighty big world out there. I wouldn't want ya getting lost."

"Don't you want to see the world?" she asked him.

"My world is right here," he replied, spreading his big arms wide. "Look at all this. There's everything ya could ever want or need, right there in front of us." When he brought his arms down he draped one over Maria's shoulder and pulled her closer to him. "There's no reason to leave it. None at all."

Conor was down to his last stone. He hefted it in one hand while he began twisting his Trinity Knot again with the other. He stopped when he realised, annoyed with himself. After a moment, he tossed in the stone. "I am leaving."

"Leaving for where?" Rory asked him.

"America."

"When?" Maria asked.

"He's not going anywhere," Rory says.

Conor stood up and headed off the rocks. "I am. Soon as this job is finished."

Conor'd spent hours on that rock skipping stones off to the foreign destinations of his imagination. Still, it wasn't until he heard the very words come out of his mouth that day that he realised he was actually going to leave. It took him by surprise, but what had always been only a dream to him was suddenly an absolute certainty. He'd have packed his bag that night if not for Liam.

He returned to the McCabe house just as Fiona was fixing dinner: a lamb stew, and with spuds just as he loved them, a hunk of butter with a dash of salt and a big schawll of milk. The young girls were setting the table while Liam sat waiting for the meal.

"I swear I could smell supper before I was over the bridge," Conor said when he walked in. He handed Fiona the loaf of soda bread but not without first pulling off two chunks and dipping them into the pot over the fire. He handed one to Liam for a taste.

"Delicious. If there's a better cook in Clare, she's off hiding with the fairies," Liam declared. Conor needed only to hear that from him to know he'd had his pints that day.

"Did you see Rory?" Fiona asked him.

"I did," Conor answered. "He's grand, Mam."

"Will he be in?" she asked hopefully.

"He won't."

The daughter Katy sat up on Conor's lap. "I bet he's with Maria Sheehan."

"You'd be right," Conor said, giving her a teasing tickle.

Young Brigid, climbed aboard as well. "When I grow up I'm going to look just like Maria Sheehan."

"But even prettier," Conor promised.

"He's spending some fair time with her of late," Fiona said.

"She's a fine girl," Liam responded. "I'd say he sure fancies her."

"They make a dashing couple," Fiona added.

Conor said nothing.

I'd say it was about that same time of the evening that the dashing couple themselves were strolling George's Street, on their way to Clancy's. Rory had Maria on his arm but Conor on his mind. He'd been hearing forever about Conor's plans to go roving and never gave them a second thought, but there was something in his voice earlier that had him fretting.

Maria sensed it. "Do you think he's serious?"

"Nah," Rory bluffed. "He's always goin' on about leaving but never does. Even if he is serious this time, I'll talk him right out of it."

"Why would you want to do that?" she asked.

Rory wasn't even sure how to take the question. "So he won't go," he said, as if it was only so obvious. "I just can't get my head around why he'd even want to leave."

"Does he have relatives anywhere?"

"No. We're the only family he's ever had. We're his whole life. All he knows."

"Couldn't that be the reason right there," she said, though not quite as a question, which suited Rory just fine, for him not having an answer handy anyhow.

Clancy's was right buzzing after the long, lovely day that was in it, but with a lot of drink taken on all counts. Always grand for the till, but a bit chancy for the finishing up... I especially had my eye on the five members of his majesty's Crown forces who'd stumbled in at midday and only proceeded to get rat-arsed drunk and generally unruly. Their antics had already inspired Father O'Dea and even O'Mahony to make an early exit, but it wasn't me first time pulling pints for eejits and I had a long experience with keepin' men peaceable.

Perhaps it was due to the few jars I'd had on me ownself, but no alarm bells went off in me head when Rory and Maria came in. Rory had been with me on this side of the bar enough nights by then to know well not to lose the head on account of any harmless messin' about, even off some drunken soldiers. Of course, he'd never had anyone looked like Maria by his side on those occasions.

"How's the form, Mr. Clancy?" Rory asked. "Are ya well?"

"Grand, I am. And how's Maria?"

"Hello, Mr. Clancy," she said.

"What will ye have?" I asked, though with all the effin' and blindin' off the soldiers, I was hoping they wouldn't have anything at all.

"Ta, but we're right off again," Rory answered. "C'mere to me though, if Conor sticks his head in, will ya tell him to wait for me to get back?"

"I will, of course."

Rory noticed the clamor coming from the soldiers and nodded toward them. "Are ya alright there?"

"Grand. No bother," I says, hoping to see the back of him right quickly.

"They wreckin' yer head?"

"T'is grand," I assured him. "On yer way. I'll hold Conor for ye."

And didn't I have them walking for the door? Nearly gone... and then yer man rushes over and makes a grand show of opening it for them. "Never saw a Paddy pass up a drink for the sake of a shagging," slurs out the ignorant Brit.

Rory stopped dead, feeling Maria's hand tighten hard on his. He heard the rest of the soldiers standing up behind him but he just stared at the one bastard, making sure he wasn't taking him up wrong, though he knew without a doubt he wasn't. Yer man's sneer said as much.

I darted out around the bar and put myself between Rory and the others, just as they were grabbing hold of the rifles they'd left leaning against the back wall.

"Yer alright there, Rory!" I shouted. "No harm done now. On your way, lad!"

"Rory, please!" Maria urged, pulling him forward. "Let's go."

But your man was still there in front of them, swaying in the doorway as he ogled Maria. "She must be a hell of a fuck."

Rory tore his hand from Maria's and landed a fist square on the fucker's nose, shattering it to pieces and knocking him out into the street. Then he took Maria's hand again and walked outside. They passed right by the downed soldier, there on the seat of his cacks cupping his hands over his nose as the blood flowed out like a river.

I tried to block the door from the others rushing after him but they pushed me right out through it. They raised their guns and called to Rory. "Hold it there, Paddy!"

Rory stopped and turned around. He held Maria behind him, shielding her.

The soldier he'd walloped was just after standing up. "Wait chaps!" he shouted. Still staggering, the feckin' gobshite managed to hold his arms up and get in the way of the other's rifles. "Don't shoot him!" He spit out a few thick gobs of blood while making a strange and vile snorting sort of sound. Wouldn't you know yer man was fucking laughing?

He took a few steps toward Rory, but this time kept himself well out of punching range. "Don't worry, Paddy. I won't let them shoot you," he said, smiling at him. "Just give that little tart a right rodgerin' for me and all is forgiven."

Rory took a step toward him but Maria quickly got back in front. She tried pushing him away but he wouldn't budge. "It's them or me," she says.

The others raised up their guns again as yer man gave Maria a long lascivious look up and down. "Go on for the shag, Paddy," he said, still snickering. "I would."

Rory just looked at the daft bastard... deciding, but then Maria grabbed his head and pulled it to hers. She kissed him hard. When she let go, he looked down at her, then back to the soldiers. "Come with me now, Rory," she said. And then she quickly strided away.

Rory looked at the guns aimed at him. "Go on, Rory!" I shouted at him. "Don't be a fool!"

After an interminable moment, he finally turned and followed after Maria. He could probably hear the soldier's drunken cackling until well after he caught up with her. I've a notion he never stopped hearing it.

"If you didn't come with me I would never have spoken to you again," was Maria's greeting to Rory when he did catch up. "Not that it would have mattered, as you'd now be dead."

"Well you've a strong power of persuasion." He wrapped his arms around her and picked her up off the ground. "Would ya mind showin' me that again?" he said, leaning in to kiss her.

She pulled out of his arms and shoved him hard. "Are you a fool?" she yelled. "Did you really expect me to just stand there while you get yourself into a stupid fight?"

"It's not stupid," he said. "You should know that, of all people."

"Is that so?" she said, angry. "And why should I know? Because of who my father is?"

"That's right," Rory answered. "I'd say he'd understand."

"Oh, come on, Rory. Do you see my father taking on drunken soldiers in the pub? He fights in the courts."

Rory realised he knew far more about Martin's activities outside of the courts than Maria did, but that wasn't for him to spoil. "We should be fightin' them everywhere," he said calmly. "Every chance."

"Oh, really?" she continued. "Even when you're outnumbered five to one? With only your fists to their guns? That is stupid, Rory. And it's senseless, not to mention it's futile, too!"

Rory was taken aback. He'd never been challenged by a girl in his life, especially with this kind of passion behind it. He'd never been as attracted to one either. Not as just then. Her fire nearly took his breath away.

Of course, there was still only so much giving out he could take. "Well, that's just it now, isn't it Maria?" he said. "There are always more of them. And they always have guns, where we've got nothing. But what are we to do? Sit and wait for them to leave? Ask nicely?"

"You could have died back there, Rory!" she cried, finally overcome with her anger and the fright of it all. She sat down, hugging her knees in a tight crouch as her voice dissolved into hushed sobs. "And me, too," she wept. "You didn't have a chance."

"The lads in Dublin didn't have a chance," Rory said. "But they fought all the same."

"And they died for it, too," she whispered.

He tenderly tilted her chin and looked down into her eyes. "Some things are worth dying for."

She stood up and put her face right close to his. "And some things are worth living for."

Their kiss stretched nearly as long as the light in the late Irish summer sky, all the way out the Ennis Road and past the potato haggarts on the run down to the Sheehan's house. Maria found it was nearly as hard to hold herself back as it was to hold Rory off, but the affections had to stop somewhere and her father's door was as good a place as any. "Safe home now," she said.

"I'm hoping to see Conor at Clancy's."

"You're going to try to get him to stay," she said.

"He'll stay," Rory declared.

"You'd miss him if he left."

"Ah, shite," Rory sighed. "It's just better he stay."

"For you or for him?" she asked.

"Jaysus, Maria," he says. "You do get to yer point."

She kissed him again. "Goodnight, Rory."

As she headed inside, he stopped her. "Maria?" he asked. "Would ya mind askin' yer da if I might have a word with him?'

Sure, this would've caught her surprised, but there's probably no quicker flutter for a lass of seventeen, than when a lad asks for an audience with her father. "Of course," she said. "Let me get him for you."

Martin brought his smile to the door. "What can I do for you, Rory?"

Rory looked past him to the hallway to be sure they were alone. He was done with the whispering. "I want in to the Brotherhood, Mr. Sheehan."

Martin sighed, then pulled the door closed behind them. "We've been through this, Rory. I couldn't use you now, even if it was my choice."

"For fuck's sake, man," Rory says. "Do ya think I don't know yer in charge of the whole lot here? The training and all? I know half the lads in yer command."

Martin took a long hard thought on getting into it all, but decided against it. "They're boys in the fields with sticks. Nary a gun among the lot of them."

"Fine then," Rory scoffed. "Give me a fuckin' stick."

Martin was well twisted inside over it, but he'd chosen his course long ago and wasn't keen to change it now. "There's just nothing happening. Not yet."

"Maybe it's time something did happen," Rory says.

Martin glared at him. "Get one thing straight, lad," he said. "I'll decide when it's time." He opened his door to go back inside, but then softened a bit and looked back. "'Til then Rory, you best spend your time worrying about that daughter of mine. She's a handful."

Rory didn't bother to reply. He just walked away.

When Martin returned to his study, O'Keefe and Crotty were at the window, watching Rory go. They'd heard the whole conversation.

"Fer fuck's sake Martin," Crotty said. "Why are ya pushin' that lad away? He's just what we need. All the young lads idolise him and the older fellas respect him just as much. Sure, ya know yourself."

Martin looked at O'Keefe. "You of the same mind?"

"I wouldn't go anywhere near him," O'Keefe said. "Why take a chance on another McCabe?"

"I don't know what happened with his father and I don't much care," Crotty answered. "But we're gonna need every man we can get. Ya can't put him off forever."

Martin pushed some papers aside on his desk and took a bottle of Jameson's from a drawer. He poured three shorts for them. "I can put him off so long as he's asking."

"He's only asking out of respect for you," Crotty says.

"And I'm only refusing him out of respect for his auld man."

"That man doesn't deserve respect," O'Keefe said.

"You've no idea what he deserves," Martin scoffed. "You don't know any more what happened than anyone else."

"I know enough," O'Keefe muttered. "And I know he still has no problem helpin' the Brits. They're keepin' that fuckin' forge of his well busy."

Crotty raised up his glass. "To Hell with Liam McCabe," he declared. "We best give that lad a chance to get some proper training under his belt, so he can be ready when the time comes."

Martin downed his drink. "He'll be ready when the time comes. You can count on that." He poured himself another. "And as for Liam McCabe, don't be worryin' yerselves after him and his destinations. I'd say he's already been to Hell."

There was tea by the turf fire at the McCabe house after supper. With the young girls asleep and Fiona and Liam settled in, Conor figured his time was now. It was weighin' on his shoulders since he'd come in.

"Da, I've been thinking," he said. "Once we finish on this job, I'll be heading off to America."

"For God's sake, why?" Fiona cried out, in spite of herself, as that wasn't her way. She looked to Liam, but he'd barely flinched. He just watched the flames.

"Just to see it," Conor answered. "Something new."

"There'll be enough work for us all, even after this job," Liam said. "You wouldn't be going on account of that now?"

"No, but yourself and Rory can surely handle what there is, and there'll be more for ye."

"That's no reason to leave," Liam says.

Conor stood up. "That's not the reason." He waited a moment for further questions but was relieved when they didn't come. Fiona had quiet tears instead, next to more silence from Liam. Conor got his coat. "I'm off to meet Rory, so."

Fiona wiped her face and girded her voice. "Bring him home, Conor. Will you?"

"I'll try, Mam," he answered, though he knew he'd fail. "He's grand though. Don't be worryin' yourself." And he walked out into the night.

Fiona waited a good spell for first words from Liam, though she knew well it was in vain. Sure, that was only their way. "You knew he was leaving?" she said.

"I knew he'd leave someday."

"Do you think it's over the forge?"

"He knows it's Rory's by right," he answered. "And I'd say for the first time he can see Rory thinking of the future."

"But that's not the reason, is it?" she asked.

Liam stood up and put a new sod of turf into the fire, then sat back, closer to Fiona then where he had before. Somehow that still wasn't close enough, so he pulled her in snug. "There's a sorrow in Conor that runs deep," Liam said softly. "There from the day he was born. If he's ever to be rid of it, he'll have to get away from here. And he knows it."

"I'll worry after him," Fiona whispered.

"It's Rory that needs worryin' after," Liam said.

"Rory?" she asked. "Rory's big and strong like you. I don't think anything could hurt him. Conor's just a gentle soul."

"They're both strong lads," Liam said, staring into the fire as the low flames grabbed onto the new turf. "But Rory's only strong 'cause he doesn't know any better. Sometimes that comes with a price. I'd say Conor already knows that."

After all the clatter with Rory and the soldiers I cleared the place out and locked it up. Clancy's doors hadn't been closed that early in years but I was well knackered from it all and just couldn't be bothered. With achin' feet and a wrecked head, I was only desiring of a soft seat and a quiet pour by me lonesome. Well, I managed to get me arse up on the stool and the whiskey down in the glass, but it was still short of my lips when Rory knocked on the window.

Even on a look out through the manky glass I could see he was worse off than me. I let him in and produced a second glass.

"Sorry for losin' me head earlier," he said.

"No apology necessary," I says. "A rake of savages they were."

"I should have never let the fucker get up."

"Don't be foolish now. He wasn't worth a bullet in the head."

"If Maria hadn't been there, I'd have killed him."

"If she hadn't been there, they'd have killed you," I says. By the look on his face I don't think the prospect had ever crossed his mind. "There's an old saying Rory: T'is better to be a coward for a minute, than dead for the rest of your life."

"I wasn't scared, like," he insisted.

"I've no doubt of that, Rory," I said. "Me? I was feckin' shittin' meself."

He got a good laugh outta that but I could see in his eyes he was still nearly comin' apart at the seams. Conor was leaving, and he just was after falling for Maria and falling out with Liam, all in the same go. And now, with all his ragin' at the Brits, yet being spurned by Martin to do anything with it, the lad didn't know which way to turn.

The bottle was handy though.

I was grateful when Conor finally called in, but Rory'd already had a good sup by then and got thick with him right off. "Ah, look who it is now. Mr. Yankee Doodle himself."

I quickly produced a third glass and filled it for Conor. "You'll wanna get that into ya," I warned.

"Ta, Mr. Clancy." He knocked it back, then looked around at me empty pub. "I see Mr. Stroppy here has them all clamoring for his company."

Rory didn't even grunt for him.

"Don't worry Rory, there's still someone loves ya," Conor said, throwing an arm around him. "Mam's after askin' for ya. Ya might call in soon."

Rory shrugged his arm off his shoulder. "Feck off."

"Ya can see why she misses him, like," Conor says to me.

"Well, we're after havin' a bit of the excitement earlier today, Conor," I told him, with a nod to Rory.

"Yeah?" Conor asked. "What happened?"

"What do you care?" Rory growled. "Shouldn't you be swimming off to America?"

"Think I'll have to catch the boat for this trip," he replied, with a wink to me. "What happened, Mr. Clancy? Are ya alright?"

"Grand, I am," I says. "Just a bit of a scuffle Rory had with -"

Rory held his hands up to interrupt me. "Don't bother with it, Mr. Clancy," he said. "Conor here couldn't be arsed with our little scuffles. He's got his own big plans to worry about."

Conor poured himself another and raised it to Rory. "Here's to you, Rory." He drank it and set it down. "Ya feckin' eejit."

He turned for the door but Rory stood up and grabbed his arm. "If you're leaving over the forge," Rory said, "there's no need. You can fuckin' have it."

Conor yanked his arm away. "It's nothing to do with it."

Rory shoved him. "Then why ya goin'? What's so fuckin' grand about America?"

Conor shoved him back. "What's so fuckin' grand about Ireland?"

"Ireland's day is coming," Rory said.

Conor laughed out loud. "It's been coming for a few hundred years now, Rory. Where is it?"

"It'll be here when people are willing to fight for it," Rory shouted. "And not running off to fuckin' America!"

"You think I'm running off?"

"I think every Irishman should be willin' to fight for his family's homeland," Rory declared. "Amn't I right, Mr. Clancy?"

I poured one more for meself and took the bottle away.

"And what of my family and our wretched homeland?" Conor came back at him. "Near the lot of 'em dead in the famine, the few left scrapin' for life itself. Then soon as they do finally get something sound to grow outta that cursed soil they get fucked off their land!"

Rory was near exasperated. "That's why we have to fight!"

"Like me da, Rory?" Conor asked him. "Gettin' stuck in jail for doin' his bit for Ireland. Leavin' me mam alone and sick, pregnant with me. Dyin' with me! And what did he get for his troubles, Rory? Fightin' for the fuckin' glory of Ireland... what did he get for it?"

Rory finally backed off and Conor walked to the door, wiping the tears off his face. He turned back to Rory. "A bullet in his head he got. Didn't he, Rory?" He reached for the door. "I'm to fight for that?"

Then he opened it to go. Wasn't it pissing rain...

Conor just laughed. "You think I'm running off?" he says. "Well yer right, Rory. First fuckin' chance!"

And out into it he went.

I had a notion our night would end with me helpin' Rory find his bed in the storage room again, but then yet another knock landed on Clancy's tired door. I opened it to the fright of Crotty's twisted nose stickin' in at me. "Any chance of a last jar, Mr. Clancy?" he asks me. "I'd like a word with Rory."

Of course, I let him in. "Ah, fair play to ya, Mr. Clancy," he says. He took a stool next to Rory, dropped down his coins and asked for two pints. "Would ya have one yerself, Mr. Clancy?" He asked in just such a way as to let me know my answer. It was clear he was in on business.

"I won't," I says, setting down their pints and pushing his money back to him. "And those are on the house. Last of the evening though, lads." I caught Crotty's eye and nodded to Rory. "It's been a long day."

"Cheers, Mr. Clancy," he said. "I won't be long."

As I went about my tidying up, Crotty leaned closer to Rory. "I'm hearing you had a bit of a run-in earlier."

"Where'd ya hear that?" Rory asked him.

Crotty just shrugged, in a clear indication that he's the sort of man that hears of these things.

"I should have taken the whole lot off," Rory said.

"No point in fighting over nothing," says Crotty. "You'll get your chance."

"As I hear it there's nothing happening."

"Come on now, lad. Use your head."

"Then why won't he let me in?" Rory asked him. "I can help. He has to know that."

"I wish I knew," Crotty answered. "Sure, you've got my support."

"It has to be Maria," Rory figured. "He must be thinking he's protecting her somehow."

"Can't say he says anything about that," Crotty replied, trying to steer him back on track. "But I do know he fancies you courting her. He said himself she mightn't do better."

"Would it have anything to do with the work we've taken on at the New Barracks?" Rory asked.

"Can't say he's in favor of it now, but he knows where you stand," Crotty answered, though it was only afterward that he actually gave that situation any real thought.

"My da just won't see it," Rory went on. "Somehow he's no worries on taking the job, but then won't go anywhere near the feckin' place himself. Has Conor in and out like a fiddler's elbow. There's something quare there. I can't get my head around it."

Crotty considered it further. "You never know when that sort of access might prove useful."

"Sure, they're nearly finished now."

"Another missed opportunity," Crotty sighed.

"I'll just be glad when the fuckin' job is done."

"Sometimes good things happen from bad things," Crotty said. "If ya look at 'em hard enough."

Rory was still pondering Martin's reasons. "I don't know what else it could be."

"It's a deaf dog, as they say," Crotty offered, finishing his pint and standing up. "Very hard to call."

"Would ya put a word in for me?" Rory asked him.

"I have and I will," Crotty assured. "But he's always been a hard man to impress, like. Everyone has to prove himself."

With that parting hint, he gave Rory a pat on the back. "Cheers, Mr. Clancy!" he shouted over his shoulder as he went to the door.

Rory sat there in deep thought for a long while. Finally, he stood and finished his pint. "I'm off, Mr. Clancy," he said, catching me surprised. "Sorry for bending your ear."

"It's pissin' rain, Rory," I said, knowing he was in no shape to go anywhere. "Stay in the storage room tonight. I'll put on a breakfast for ya in the mornin'."

"Thanks, but I'll head off," he said, making haste for the door. "Sorry again for all the clatter before." And off he went, disappearing into the weather.

Conor and Rory had shared the same bed since the day they were moved into it from outta the same crib. After eighteen years, they were so used to the company in it that they could each roll in and out and over and arseways without stirring a single snore off the other.

Yet that night, when Rory quietly slipped in next to him under the blankets, Conor did wake for a moment. He didn't open his eyes or say a word, but when he nodded off again, he dozed deeper than he had in many weeks.

Chapter Eight

Bloody Gates

That next morning after breakfast Rory followed Liam and Conor into the forge and took up the work with them. They were already after fashioning over forty-odd sections of fencing in all manner of shapes and sizes and with all the necessary attachments and hinges in their appropriate locations. It was intended to replace the front sections of several storage and stable areas where a relentless corrosion had the old iron falling out of the walls. Conor'd been into the New Barracks on several occasions to take all the measurements and he'd come up with a design to facilitate an easy installation, though that wasn't part of the McCabe job.

There were plenty of idle soldiers available at the barracks to labour at that chore, but they'd got stuck for the complex metalwork behind it when their long-time smithy had passed away. They found they didn't have anyone with a notion of how to properly bend metal. There were other smithys in Limerick and even a few more well closer than Cloonlara, but those that were asked all passed up the work. To a man, the Catholic smithys all cited their disinclination to work for the Brits, and the two Protestant forges that were consulted simply weren't up to the task. In any case, they all said Liam McCabe was the right man for the job. A few added that he probably wouldn't give a shite either way if the King himself came asking.

Conor was well adept at determining all the angles and proportions to construct the sections, but there was no doubt that Liam's adamant refusal to enter the New Barracks had complicated the process. They'd fallen behind schedule and were getting stick from the Brit officer managing the work, so when Rory finally joined in with them, he quickly got them back on track. It was less quickly that he got back on track with Liam, but a smatter of communication was restored in time. What started as the odd grunt or nod, eventually progressed to a few words concerning the work at hand and, eventually, a bit of chat about the weather. Music to Conor's ears...

His own discussions with Rory covered everything under the sun, but mostly Rory just went on and on about Maria. At first Conor didn't want to know, but as Rory was learning more about her life, he couldn't stop himself relating it, and Conor couldn't help himself taking an interest. Liam's curiosity hooked him as well, and he found himself listening for details. He never said as much but he was quite pleased to see Rory so obviously smitten. He knew better than most that the grounding the right woman could provide might do his son a world of good... maybe make all the difference.

After much remembering, both lads decided they'd probably already crossed paths with Maria as a young lass many years earlier. As it turned out, both families, just like almost everyone else in southwest Ireland claimed, had attended the 1910 Munster Championship in Tralee when the great Tyler Mackey led Limerick to a stunner of a result against Cork. At least they determined they would've been in that same crowd, and that seemed to count for something of an early connection.

It wasn't long after that most glorious of hurling matches that Maria and her mam went off to live in America. Mrs. Sheehan had fallen terribly in love with Martin at first sight but, after giving Ireland nearly ten full years of her life, which she swore didn't include one sunny day, she still couldn't muster even the least of affections for it. The things we do for love, we only do for so long. With no other family here on either's side, and Martin regularly traveling back in any case, they decided Maria should take her schooling in New York.

Martin never gave a thought to his own leaving. He had his work in Ireland and it wasn't finished - far from it. When Maria graduated, or survived those American nuns thumping their lessons into her more like, he insisted they come back across for a good spell. She wasn't sure how long that would be, she only knew it wasn't really up to her anyway. She liked Ireland though, at least so far, but she'd barely even caught her breath. Rory was seeing to that.

When Liam stepped out of the forge on some matter, Rory told Conor about his run-in with the soldiers at Clancy's. Conor had already got the story from half of Limerick City, but he was well interested to hear it firsthand. Rory told him he knew there'd be trouble the moment they walked into Clancy's, though he insisted he wasn't looking for it. He just knew Maria would draw it.

He told Conor how he would have killed the filthy Brit bastard had Maria not been there. He was still thinking maybe he should've all the same. When Conor pointed out the guns they had pointed at him, Rory only shrugged it off.

"I wasn't even a bit nervous," he said. "I'm not boasting, like. And it's not bluster," he explained. "I mean, I know I should have been afraid. Probably should have legged it right away, but for some reason I was feckin' sure those rifles couldn't hurt me. You know that kind of way?"

Conor couldn't understand it at all, but still he couldn't help believing him. "You're a gas man, Rory."

"I'm not coddin' ya," Rory insisted. "It's right quare, I know, but I didn't feel a dash of danger in it. It was just some men pointing sticks at me."

Conor looked at him, just as worried as confused. "Fair play."

"You think I've gone daft, don't ya?" Rory asked him.

"Well, you're not the full shilling. That's for sure."

They also spoke of every single aspect of the barracks job, and of the barracks itself. Conor'd been inside it several times at that stage and Rory had a million questions. He wouldn't let Conor spare a detail.

When finally the fashioning was completed, the lads hitched up the long wagon and began loading the fence sections upon it for delivery to the barracks.

"I'll take these over," says Rory.

Conor caught his eye. "I'll manage."

"Give me a go," Rory pressed. "Just for the *craic*, like." He was smiling innocently, like butter wouldn't melt in his mouth, but Conor knew he was scheming something.

"Would ya ever give it over?" Conor said. "I know what yer after."

"I'm after nothing. Just curious is all."

"They won't admit you, Rory."

"Ah, I'll talk me way in," Rory says. "Sure, I'll tell 'em you're locked. Tell 'em ya had two full pints all by yerself and fell right over. So it's me in or they're out of luck."

"I was put through a full check and all manner of hassle. They know me now."

"Oh. So you're mates, like?"

"Feck off," Conor replied, continuing to load up the sections. With the various shapes and sizes of them there was a bit of a puzzle to it all. They had to take their time and arrange them just so in order to fit them all in the one load.

"Or maybe I just tell 'em ya already fucked off to America and couldn't give a shite anymore what happens here."

Conor softened a bit. "I'm not going anywhere 'til we get payment for all this. You make a hames of this now and that might never happen."

"We'd all be better off."

"Just help me get it loaded up. We can strap it down and I'll go."

"Fine," Rory says. "I'll just come along with ya."

"They won't allow any more than one man in," Conor explained. "That's been clear from the start."

"Tell them I'm yer helper, like."

"I wish," Conor replied. "They won't lift a finger to help. Shiftless bastards."

"Feck's sake," Rory says. "Ya mean they'll just stand and watch ya unload all this yerself?"

"They won't watch me either," Conor told him. "They don't pay me a lick of attention once I'm in."

Rory stopped working and thought for a long moment, staring at the few remaining sections of black iron fence yet to be loaded. Than he looked at the big black stack of pieces they'd already arranged into the wagon. He started pulling them back off. "They'll never know I was in."

Conor read his mind. "Not a chance," he said.

Rory went at it fiercely, yanking the sections off so fast Conor couldn't even get a hand in to stop him. "They're coming off. You can watch or ya can help."

Indeed he was right, so Conor joined him. Rory gave him a wink. "Come on. It'll be good *craic*… my chance to see how the other half lives."

When they had nearly all of them off, Rory started carefully repacking them. Where before they were using every inch of free space, now he was creating some. He laid them in crossways and arsewise until he formed a small covered compartment, with just barely room enough to maybe jam himself into. He smiled at Conor. "And Bob's your uncle."

"This is for delivery, smartarse," Conor says. "What's to cover you on our way out?"

"Whatever all this is replacing."

"What's on yer mind, Rory?" Conor asked him, deadly serious. "I need to know."

"Just a bit of reconnaissance," Rory answered. "Nothing to ever concern you. You'll be far off by then."

Conor just shook his head, bemused with himself for even considering it. "We won't even get past the gates."

But soon as Rory heard him say *we*, he knew Conor had given up on stopping it.

When Conor was ready to leave, Liam came out and gave it a quick lookover, making sure everything was all there and well strapped in. Rory had obscured his secret compartment with various covering pieces, and with several tons of steel packed onto the long wagon there was no prospect of Liam ever noticing it. He gave Conor the paperwork on the job along with their bill and they discussed the payment details for a moment. Then the two lads climbed up onto the wagon behind auld Oscar.

Liam looked at Rory. "It's a one-man job from here."

Rory smiled at him, for probably the first time in months. "Sure, I'm just taking the lift in to meet Maria."

Liam nodded. "Off ye go then," he says.

Conor was unable to even meet his eye. He snapped the reins and off they went.

They only took a brief detour for a stop at People's Park in Limerick City. Rory pulled off the sections concealing his hidden chamber and somehow managed to cram himself into it, leaving barely the room to breathe. The way he'd done it, he was belly down and arms tight to his sides, with his head up close to the front of the wagon, almost under the seat. He'd left a small gap in front where he could see a bit if he craned his neck up, but mostly all he could set eyes on was Conor's feet.

Conor quickly replaced the metal pieces and strapped it all back down, then leaned in close. "Can ya hear me now, Rory?" he whispered.

"Of course I can feckin' hear ya."

Conor couldn't resist a bit of messin'. "Well? Is it cozy, like?"

"Are ya taking the piss?" Rory asked.

"Sure, I'm just wondering. I'd say it's nice and snug, no?"

"Snug like a feckin' coffin."

Conor laughed. "That may be bang on."

"Very funny," Rory said. "Just get this yoke moving."

"Sure, we'll be off in a minute," Conor replied. "It's just me nerves are shattered, Rory. I don't suppose you'd mind if I went for a quick pint or two?"

"Feck off, ya eejit!" Rory yelled.

Conor got back up onto the seat. "Right. I'm the eejit?" he said, promptly steering Oscar straight toward a high curb. "Who's the gobshite kissing the steel?" The wagon bounced abruptly, hopping Rory's head hard off the metal, just as Conor'd hoped.

"Ah, me head!" Rory shouted.

"Sorry there, Rory," Conor teased. "Didn't see that one."

The slagging stopped when the walls got high at Lord Edward Street. Conor suddenly felt right queasy in his gut. "Last chance, Rory," he whispered. "You'd want to cop on now."

"We're grand," Rory assured him. "In we go."

Conor drew the wagon up to the guard post at the side wall. A soldier came out, casually pointing his rifle in Conor's general direction. "What's your business, Paddy?" he asked, looking over the wagon.

Conor handed him the job papers. "Delivery. From the McCabe forge."

The soldier didn't even glance at them. "Tad late for a delivery, isn't it?" he asked.

Conor didn't bother answering. He was half hoping the git would refuse them entering. The soldier took a stroll around the wagon, even shook the metal in spots, not out of any suspicion, but just general curiosity and a chance to ply his authority. "What's all this for?"

"Replacements for rotted sections of fencing," Conor answered.

"Sections where?" the soldier asked.

"Storage yards."

The soldier handed him back the papers and hit a quick, shrill blow on his whistle. "Delivery coming in!" he shouted.

After a long moment, the massive iron-barred gates fronting the New Barracks were slowly pulled apart, permitting their entrance to the huge parade grounds and the main quarters buildings that surrounded it, housing over a thousand men between the soldiers and the RIC troops. The entire complex encompassed over a full square mile inside its walls. Its ancillary buildings included a chapel, a hospital, and a jail, with endless stables and sheds and garages wedged in wherever space allowed. With even a balls court and a skittles alley to ensure the Crown forces their recreational comforts, it was an outright village onto itself.

The soldier walked through the gates and waved at Conor to steer the wagon along behind him. "Bring it in, Pad. I'll show you the way."

"I know where they're at, like," Conor said, looking off toward the route he'd taken before, past the large garage bays just inside the gates.

"Well, you'll bloody follow me regardless."

The soldier took a shorter path, cutting right across a corner section of the giant parade ground. Plenty of soldiers were about, but no one paid them any attention. A few groups were drilling in the open spaces and some others were bustling about near several large vehicles - open lorries and cargo trucks - randomly parked near various buildings.

It was a different route from the way Conor had previously gone, so just like Rory, he was seeing some areas for the first time. The soldier turned between the two main buildings where the officers billeted and led them along a narrow passageway. In front of them, down the end, was a smaller structure fronted by a broad verandah with long tables and benches.

"Jaysus," Rory whispered up to Conor, a tinge too loud. "Their own fuckin' pub."

"You'd 'ave a pub too if you were stuck in this bloody dungeon," the soldier replied. "Walls everywhere, bloody rain never stops."

When they turned again at the pub, and next passed by a long row of stables, Conor started to recognise where they were. Ahead he saw the old storage sheds he'd measured. Their fencing was bent and rusted and falling off the walls. Their gates barely hung on their hinges. The soldier pointed at a long, bare concrete wall opposite them, the back side of the jail building. "You can stack the lot of it against there."

Conor halted Oscar. "Any chance of a hand?" he asked.

"Not bloody likely," the soldier laughed. "That pub you saw? I'll have two pints down before you're halfway finished." He turned and headed off, skitting to himself. "Chance of a bloody hand? Good luck."

Conor watched him leave and looked around. They were fairly well tucked away and a long sight off from the pub, but still situated in a spot where someone could turn the corner in any moment.

"Get this shite off me," Rory said.

Conor quickly started unstrapping the bands. "Spot of luck getting set with that git."

"And you're after asking him for a feckin' hand, ya bollocks."

Conor pulled free the sections screening Rory's feet. "You're all clear here."

Rory tried to wriggle himself backward but he was wedged in too tightly and couldn't gather any impetus. "Give us a pull," he said.

Conor grabbed his boots and yanked him out. "Stay outta sight," he told him as he quickly started unloading their metal.

Rory moved into the shadows under the walls and looked all around. "I'd no idea it was so massive."

Conor pointed over to the battered shed. "Enough sightseeing. You best get to those old sections."

Rory trotted over and pried a bent gate open enough to see inside the storage area it sheltered. There was all manner of equipment scattered about haphazardly - barrels and boxes, lumber and sandbags, wire and rope and the odd wheel or old door. "They've an interesting collection."

"Just get it off, Rory," Conor urged. "Or there's nothing to cover you going out."

Rory pulled on a large piece of the old fencing. It was crumbling and decrepit but it was still iron set deep into concrete and took a mighty strength to disturb it. He wrenched it back and forth with all the force he could muster until its hinges and joints finally broke free from the concrete. It crashed to the ground with a huge racket but he went right at the rest, tearing each off and moving ahead until he had the face of the first shed completely gone.

Once he had the first piece off the second shed, he checked the contents inside. It was more of the same, old tools and materials, disorganised and forgotten, only this assortment included about ten long crates, stacked against the back wall. "Jaysus," he whispered.

He quickly ducked inside and pried one open. There sat six Lee-Enfield rifles.

Conor was just pulling the last of the sections off the wagon when he saw Rory come out carrying a crate in his arms and grinning ear to ear. He could hardly believe his eyes. "Have you gone stone fucking mad?"

"They won't miss a few crates," Rory said excitedly. "Sure, they hardly know they're there." Laughing he was.

"We'll never get out with 'em," Conor says.

Rory slid it onto the wagon and quickly covered it with a section of the old metal. "We're gonna try," he said, dashing back in for another.

Conor pulled off the last piece and placed it with the rest of their delivery, stacked up orderly against the wall. When he turned back, there was Rory with another crate. He stepped between him and the wagon. "Rory, this is too far," he insisted. "We get caught and they go straight to Da."

Rory pushed right past him. "Then we best not get caught."

Conor was raging, but he knew there was feck all he could do about it. There wasn't time to talk sense into him and he was already back in for another crate anyhow. "Hurry then ya fuckin' eejit," he said as he went at loading the old metal to hide the crates. "Or we'll both be shot."

Rory came out with a third and slid it underneath, leaving just the room for himself. "Slide under there and I'll cover you with the last of it," Conor said.

Rory inspected his getaway compartment. "We can fit another one."

"Not with you under, we can't," says Conor. "Get your arse in there."

"I'll find my way out," he said as he ducked back in to the shed.

Conor followed him this time. "Have you a fuckin' brain in yer head? We've three already."

Rory came out with the fourth. "Every one counts."

"We'll be lucky to get out as it stands," Conor argued.

Rory jammed a few pieces of metal in against it. "We'll never get out if you keep moaning." Then he checked the other sides to make sure they were all concealed.

"Where the hell are the bloody gates?" shouted the soldier.

The lads froze. Conor right there at the back of the wagon and Rory just around the other side of it. They never heard him coming. But yer man wasn't looking at them. He was staring at the sheds, utterly confused. Their entire front sections were suddenly gone. He walked straight to the first shed and raised his free hand up, the one not holding a rifle, and actually felt for the vanished metal. Like a fucking mime, he was. "Where the hell are the bloody gates?" he shouted again.

Rory silently grabbed a loose iron bar from a section inside the wagon, then crouched down behind its wheel. He was mostly screened from view by the load in it, the same load Conor then pointed out to the soldier. "We can put the scrap iron to use at our forge. No point in wastin' it."

Rory gripped the bar tight in his fist as the soldier moved closer, coming right over to the wagon and looking at the big pile of bent and rusted metal. "You can make use of that rubbish?" he asked. "You're just bloody tinkers."

"And I'd say we'll be affordin' ye a big discount for it," Conor promised. "Now that ya mention it."

The soldier was still confused. Half-drunk as well.

"Course I'll let 'em know it was you that thought it up," Conor said with a wink. "On the way out, like."

The soldier finally copped on. "Of course it was me thought it up," he affirmed as he checked out the pile. "Can't take the whole bloody gates without affordin' back a big discount." He walked around the other side toward Rory, but Rory quietly circled away from him, only feet apart.

Conor hopped up onto the wagon seat, right between them, but finally the soldier took his nose outta the wagon and walked back out in front of Oscar. "Follow me out, Paddy," he said, heading away in a direction opposite from that they'd come in.

Conor took a peek back as he snapped the reins. Rory gave him a cheery twirl of his iron bar and quickly ducked into the shed for cover.

From there, Rory crept out and back to the walls behind them, figuring the fastest way out was over one. He hadn't a hope. Even if he could get up one, they were all topped with wide stretches of barbed wire. If he got caught up in it, he'd be bollocksed.

Still, he knew he had to stick close to the walls, as anyone not in a uniform crossing the parade grounds would be noticed immediately.

He scrambled along them, stealthily maneuvering through the narrow spaces that ran behind most of the buildings. Where there was no structure to screen him, he chanced a run for it, boldly faithful that the falling darkness would provide cover enough.

He recalled all the descriptions Conor had given him, so when he saw the two huge garages that housed the barrack's large fleet of vehicles he knew he was getting close to the main gates. If he could get inside the first garage sight unseen, the rows of parked-up cars and lorries provided an easy enough route through to the other one. But with a big group of soldiers picking at the motor of a cargo truck parked right up front, it was getting back outside the second garage that posed his problem.

While he was considering his predicament, he caught a glimpse of Conor on their wagon, trailing behind the soldier, who was ever so slowly strolling across the parade ground. He suddenly felt a sharp twist in his gut when he thought of the crates in the wagon. Conor was about to reach the gates. If any other soldiers decided to check his cargo, he'd never get out of this place.

He felt the cold iron clenched in his hand, then made his dash into the garage. He scurried all the way along its back wall and, counting his stars lucky, found an interior door leading right into the next. Along the back wall again and then flat onto his belly to slide forward under several parked officer's cars lined up all the way from the back to the front.

Conor was at the gates now. Rory could see the soldier from the other gatepost was checking his papers with the first soldier, but he wasn't quite close enough to hear what was being said. If it all went arseways, he wasn't going to leave Conor alone for it. He needed to be near enough to pounce.

He ran clear out into the open for a stretch of near fifty feet, then slid right underneath the back end of that long cargo truck with its motor getting all the attention. But no one saw a step, and suddenly he got to thinking that maybe he was invisible. It was the same sort of feeling he'd got when he faced the rifles, like he was completely invulnerable, almost ghostly.

He could hear the mechanic's conversation like he was a part of it. Your one was going on about his wife's drinking, giving out that she was more able for it than himself. Fuckin' eejits, these Brits. Through their legs he watched Conor talking to the soldiers and could see that some negotiating was taking place. "Ah, fair play, Conor," he thought. He knew he was after providing them that lovely discount.

The sudden shrill whistle ran right through him, but then he remembered what it meant. The gates slowly opened and Conor steered Oscar out for home, their chancy freight safe and sound.

On the other hand, Rory was well fucked.

At least he thought so, until another banjaxed cargo lorry drove right in through the open gates Conor'd just gone out. This one carried its own shrill whistle and was throwing great blasts of steam from the motor. The driver steered it right next to the one parked above Rory, but further from the gate, and didn't the full crew of mechanics switch right onto it?

No more legs in front of him. The gates were still open, and Rory could see that both soldiers were over at the far post, probably arguing over how to divvy their discount. His coast was well cleared.

He dashed to the near gate without being spotted, then quickly slipped past the unmanned guard post. He was out. Invulnerable.

But when he looked back to be sure he wasn't seen, wasn't it what he did see that caught him? The guard post wasn't entirely empty. The soldier's rifle was leaning against its door, exposed and helpless.

Rory didn't hesitate. He ducked back in, grabbed it and turned - just as another lorry pulled up to the gates - open-sided and full of soldiers, each one holding a rifle.

And there he was, caught rotten - trapped between their guns and the bloody gates closing in behind him. Entirely vulnerable.

After clearing the gates and leaving the barracks behind, Conor returned to People's Park and waited for Rory to appear. Of course, there was no plan pre-arranged but he was hopeful Rory would have the same thought and be right along behind him. That hope quickly faded with the last of the daylight. Still, Rory could have needed to wait for darkness to find a safe way out, so Conor held on for him a bit longer. His minutes felt like hours. Finally, he headed home.

Liam was there waiting on him, pondering the delay. When Conor arrived, Liam held a lantern up near his face. He thought he looked a bit off, and then he noticed him fiddling with his Trinity Knot. "Are ya alright?" Liam asked him.

"I am," Conor lied.

And Liam knew it straightaway. He looked at the battered metal in the wagon. "Where's this from?"

"The barracks."

"The old fencing?"

Conor nodded, and just watched as Liam immediately put the lantern close and lifted up a few sections of it, revealing the crates underneath. "What's here?"

"Rifles, Da."

It didn't take much for Liam to piece it all together. "Rory?" he asked.

"Be here any time," Conor replied, only it came out a lot more like a question than an answer.

Liam looked him in the eye. "Are you sure?"

Conor could only shake his head. At that, Liam re-covered the crates and climbed up next to him on the wagon's seat, taking the reins out of his hands. "We best get these to a safe place."

Even the most astute ear wouldn't have detected the difference in sounds, but when Martin pulled his best draught horse out of his stable, the noise his hooves made upon the floor went from a clop to a clip. That's what happens when you move a horse off a secret trap door, even one covered with pissy hay and stale shite. That's the hay Martin was clearing while he asked his questions. "Did anyone check Clancy's?"

"He'd have come straight home," Conor replied as he dragged a crate into the stable.

"How do you know?" Martin asked.

Conor set it at Martin's feet. "That's where these were going."

Martin pulled up a section of the barn floor, revealing steps leading into a large hold underneath. He climbed down and Liam and Conor lowered the crates in to him. Conor could see enough to know they weren't the first guns going under Martin's ground.

"Well, if the bastards have him," Martin said. "I'll be hearing soon enough."

"If the bastards have who?"

Their heads all turned to the unexpected voice at the barn doors. Maria's silhouette was illuminated by the moonlight, but then she came in close enough to see it was just the three of them. "Where's Rory?" she asked. But of course, no one had the answer.

She turned and walked off. Conor went after her.

Liam passed the last crate down to Martin, who grabbed a pry and opened the top. They'd never even been touched. He now had two dozen brand new rifles he'd never figured on. He was well impressed.

He looked above to Liam, waiting there with the piece of floor in hand, ready to cover the hole and be done with it. "I'd nothing to do with this," Martin said to him as he climbed out. Liam just dropped the flooring and got into his wagon.

Conor had rushed to catch Maria before she got back to the Sheehans' house to get inside, but when he got to their door the house was still dark. He sat down on the porch step and dropped his head into his hands.

"How could you let him be so stupid?" came her voice from the darkness.

"His head was set," Conor answered, without even looking up. "I'd no idea what he was after 'til we were already inside. I'd say he didn't himself."

Maria sat next to him. "What will they do to him?"

Conor looked at the tears fresh on her face, glimmering wet in the rare moonlight. All he wanted in the world was to wipe them away, but his hands wouldn't move for him. "There's no sayin' they even have him," he said. "He could just be -"

"Conor," called out Liam softly.

He stood up. "It'll all be grand," he said.

As he turned to go, Maria grabbed his hand. "Conor," she cried. "Why is he in such a hurry to get himself killed?"

He could feel the soft warmth of her skin clenching his. Even the moisture from her tears on her fingertips.

"Conor!" Liam called again.

He slipped his hand free. "Not to worry," he promised, as he ran off into the darkness. "No one's getting killed."

Chapter Nine

Of Course

The district prison building in the New Barracks was in an even more dreadful condition than the shed fencing Rory had torn free from its walls only hours before. There were over fifty detention cells within its three storeys, but they held enough spare filth and foulness to stock many more. Should have been pulled down itself... the stables were far cleaner.

For a lad his size, the spot where Rory now found himself didn't leave much room to stretch his arms. The front wall was barred from floor to ceiling and faced with a stretched wire netting to keep its occupants from throwing anything out. The other walls were solid concrete, with only five- or six-odd feet side to side. They'd dumped him on the floor upon delivery, instead of on the three raised planks and block of wood meant to make a bed and pillow, though he'd hardly have known the difference in whatever kinda way they left him. Hard is hard. And cold is what he got under the tattered blanket they tossed in, thin as a weak wafer and it wouldn't even cover the space of his shoulders.

Of course, having been beaten senseless after he was nabbed robbing the rifle, Rory hadn't yet gained an appreciation of his new accommodation. The odd spot of tea that had been tossed on his face every few hours since he was brought in had thus far failed to revive him. When one piping splash finally elicited a few pained moans, the sipping soldier notified his commanding officer that the subject of his interest was stirring.

Highly polished boots marched your man in on a crisp step, as an accompanying soldier conveyed the details of Rory's capture. "The lorry came around just after he'd rushed in to nick the rifle, so the men were right in on him before he could scarper… gave him a good hiding for his trouble, too."

"Bring me that bloody rifle," the officer ordered. "And I want the man who left it unattended at the gate post replaced and docked a month's pay."

Somewhere deep in his stupefied suffering an inkling of recognition came to Rory… a remembrance disagreeable enough to pull his mind out of the puddle of agony soaking his body.

"Open this cell and get him on his feet," ordered the officer once the rifle was produced.

Rory hadn't tried to twitch before then, but hearing that, he struggled with all his might to stand on his own strength, rather than allow anyone to lift him. Well teetering he was, but still up before the key turned in the lock.

The soldiers took his arms and held him steady and the officer came in with the rifle in hand. "What's your name?" he asked.

It was then Rory was certain. He didn't even need to open his swollen eyes to confirm it, but still he forced them apart somehow or other. He tried to focus, but all was hazy.

"Your name!" demanded Mr. Tyler Bowen, now nothing less than the RIC's County Inspector for Limerick, but still the same bony-faced bastard Rory knew from years before.

"Brian Boru," Rory muttered. And he wasn't all too surprised when not one of the ignorant fuckers reacted. They wouldn't be giving a rat's arse about Irish history.

"Do you see me, Brian?" Bowen asked him. "I wouldn't want you to miss your reward. His Majesty's Government aims to please."

Even though he was being held by the soldiers, when Bowen raised the rifle up in front of him, Rory managed to shift his weight back off his toes. He knew a blow was coming.

"If it's a rifle you covet, it's a rifle you will get." Bowen said, and he smashed the butt into Rory's face, knocking him out of the soldier's grasp and onto the floor.

"Pick him up," Bowen ordered calmly.

The soldiers hoisted him to his feet, though not easily.

"What did you want with a rifle?" Bowen asked.

Rory's head just hung down. He was barely conscious, but his mind found him the memory of the day Bowen had struck his father with that brick. Rory'd picked it up to fire it at the back of Bowen's head. He never had a doubt he would have hit him flush.

"Fancy yourself a rebel do you?" Bowen continued. He positioned the barrel of the rifle under Rory's chin and slowly lifted it.

But Rory'd hesitated his throw for a split second on that day. He knew it ever since, and that momentary pause had allowed Liam to catch his arm and pull him away.

"You know how we deal with rebels?" Bowen said, looking to one of the soldiers. "Hold his head steady." Then he slid the barrel along Rory's chin and jabbed it hard into his mouth.

Rory'd always puzzled over his hesitation then. As a boy, he had attributed it to that strange sensation he'd heard people mention called *nerves,* but as he grew older he realised he'd never known that feeling. His other explanation was doubt. Had he maybe suffered a twinge of distress over an undertaking of such violence? Had he balked at the commitment in it?

In the moment Bowen cocked that rifle, Rory obliterated every uncertainty of his being. He opened his eyes and looked right at the fucker.

Bowen pulled the trigger.

A click.

Empty.

Bowen lowered the weapon. "You're no bloody rebel," he scoffed. "You're just a foolish boy." He handed the rifle to one of the soldiers. "Let the boy down."

They dropped him to the floor, walked out and locked the cell. As Rory slipped back into oblivion, he heard Bowen's voice trailing his footsteps down the corridor. "Ireland does not belong to the Irish," he pronounced, almost singing it out. "Ireland belongs to His Majesty the King. You are simply guests at his pleasure and should be grateful for the Crown's hospitality."

It was days before the barracks put out any official information on Rory, but Martin had his sources inside to suss out what they were doing with him. Despite Bowen's pronouncement that Rory didn't possess the makings of a rebel, his attempted theft was charged as a seditious offence and he was prosecuted by court martial. Rory was essentially defenceless without a witness to testify on his behalf, and with nationalist sentiments increasing across Ireland, the British government had started taking a hardline approach toward anything and everything that might possibly be considered Republican activity. They'd clearly decided harsh examples were in order.

And so it was, the stairs leading to the Sheehans' second storey suddenly got far steeper when Martin got word of the verdict. He knocked at Maria's door and opened it. She'd barely left her room since she heard Rory was arrested.

"He's been sentenced to six months hard labour," Martin said.

Maria didn't answer. She'd hardly spoken since that night.

"It could have been worse," Martin claimed. "Judging by that length, I don't think they even know anything's gone missing. Would've been harder on him."

She wouldn't even look at him. "I'm sure you're glad about that."

"I am," Martin admitted. "I won't lie. It was a brave thing he did. You should be proud."

"I should be proud?" she cried, finally turning and pointing at him. "You're the one that should be proud. He definitely didn't do it for me."

"Maria, I swear I had no idea what he was up to. It was entirely on his own."

"You may as well have ordered him to do it, he's so desperate to impress you. You're some kind of hero to him," she said, squeezing back the tears that spiked in her eyes. "Though I can't imagine why."

"I'm no hero," Martin said softly. "I am impressed though. He's become a fine man, just as I always thought he would. And I'm delighted to see you with him."

"Well now you won't be seeing me with him, will you?" Maria said, turning back to the window and her silence.

"You'll be standing by him now," Martin said, leaving no question on it.

Maria wouldn't turn back.

"Six months isn't so long as it seems now," he said. He lingered for a moment, searching his mind for the right words. Perhaps something he could say to provide her a bit of comfort. Finally, he just closed the door.

It was in late 1918 that the armistice finally ended the Great War and this tired world let go a heavy sigh of relief. On the continent, as the deathly dust of warfare gradually settled upon its ravaged lands, the Allies began all their swapping and shuffling of the broken puzzle pieces.

A no longer quite so great Britain limped home to lick its wounds and tally its costs. A high price it paid for that victory. Its far flung dominions had suffered too many dead under the British flag to remain in its shadow. By their own accounts, they'd bought their way out of the union with a payment of bodies, and then some. When Australia and New Zealand and South Africa attended the Paris Peace Conference, they represented themselves. The British Empire was finally starting to see its sun set.

The Yanks, they sailed back home to America to make their cowboy pictures.

But in Ireland, there was still that old itch to be scratched. The last round had hardly been fired in Europe when the Sinn Féiners swept our elections and sat the first Dáil. First days of 1919 we declared our independence from England. That should have been the end of it but, while the Brits gave the Aussies and the Kiwis seats at that fancy French table, our own demand for recognition was ignored by the Allied powers divvying up the new world. One might think independence could have been bestowed upon auld Ireland along with all the other sweeping allotments goin' around, but England held fast, breaking its promise of Home Rule without giving a second thought.

But no matter, Ireland had no peaceful notions on it any longer. Across our new nation, what few guns we held were already being loaded, and even emptied, as two unlucky constables were advised of at Soloheadbeg, over in Tipperary. And thanks to Rory's exploits at the barracks, there were two dozen more rifles at the ready under a trap door in Martin Sheehan's barn, which was up and down like a hoor's knickers in those months. Martin and his men were drilling the younger lads on the use of 'em, and training them on tactics in general at every opportunity. There was no specific plan in place, or any targets chosen, but they were being cooked up - and the underfire was scorching.

Of course, Rory still had no idea where the rifles he'd stolen had landed or that they were being put to any use, and he had no knowledge of any vague intentions toward bloodshed while sitting there in a cruel cell, cold on the hard floor, with only his own raging imaginings for company.

He was tinkering with tiny strands he'd twisted off the wire netting fronting his cell when a warder shattered his concentration with a skillful flick of his cigarette. "Up on your feet, Paddy," he said. "You've a visitor." With the help of another warder they led Rory's shackled steps to a slightly larger cell on the ground floor, though this one shared a barred wall with another adjoining cell.

Conor was standing in that one. The warders locked Rory's chains to an iron ring cemented into the concrete floor, then walked out and closed the cell door. "You'll have five minutes."

Conor didn't let on but Rory's bruises were savage, and it was clear his pained walk wasn't due to the chains on his ankles. Still, he smiled wide at the sight of Conor. "What's the *craic*?" he asked.

"Not so bad," Conor answered. "How ya keepin' now?"

"Not so bad," Rory claimed. "Just takes some getting used to. Did your delivery work out?"

"All's in good hands," Conor assured him.

"That's grand. I'd have been along as well if I'd been just a bit swifter."

"Or a bit smarter," Conor added.

"If I want a sermon, I'll get me a priest."

"Yer lucky a priest wasn't giving ya yer last rites."

Rory gave him a hard look. "Did ya really go to all the bother to call in, Conor, just to have a fuckin' go at me?"

Conor just left it at that and Rory eased off a bit. "I'd say Maria's not so impressed either."

"She's grand," Conor said. "Just worryin' about ya.'"

"More like givin' out about me, I'd say."

"She's grand," Conor repeated.

"I can't stop thinking about her," Rory said softly, suddenly struggling a bit to keep himself together. "I'd love to see her. If she'd come, like?"

Conor couldn't remember having ever before seen him even the least bit vulnerable. "She'll come then," he promised, though he had no idea if she ever would. The assurance seemed to bolster Rory though.

"I want you to look after her for me," Rory told him. "I know you would all the same, but just to mention it. She's already enough worries being her father's daughter. I wouldn't want her hearing grief over me as well."

Conor looked away, and up at the tiny barred window where the day's dull grey light peered in on them. "Rory, I'm off to America in less than -"

"Enough with that America shite!" Rory shouted.

"Keep a lid on it!" called in one of the warders.

Rory glared in their direction, coughed harshly and spit a blood-soaked gob on the floor. He turned back to Conor, gritting his teeth in anger. "What's a few more month's time gonna matter? You'll have to be covering for me at the forge now in any case."

Conor knew there was no point in arguing with him. "That's no bother," he smiled. "Sure, you're only feckin' useless in it anyway."

Rory softened. "I'm just asking you to make sure she's looked after 'til I get out. If you're set for America then, work away."

"I will then," Conor promised.

"Fair play to ya," Rory said, managing to smile again. "C'mere to me, how's Mam and himself?"

"Grand. They thought it best I come."

"Da have anything to say?" Rory asked.

"Not so much."

"Sure, he'll only be thinkin' after his forge."

"Time's up, Paddy!"

As the warders unlocked the cell, Conor could see Rory set his jaw and muster up a brave face. When they came in and took hold of his chains he scowled hard at both of them. "T'is yer time is up, lads. And ye don't even know it."

"You mind yerself, Rory," Conor urged. "Keep the head down and get yerself through it." He reached through the bars to try to put a hand on him, but the warder just pushed it away.

"Don't you go worryin' yer little old head over me, lad," Rory said with a wink for him as they lugged him out of the cell. "They had Red Hugh in their jails for over three years," he called back. "And you know how that story went." His voice faded into a trailing echo as he disappeared up the stairway. "Sure, six months is hardly pissin' time!" he shouted. "It'll take far more than the likes of these!" That was the last Conor heard from him before his shouting was finally drowned out by the clang of his leg shackles, dragging along on each stone step.

After leaving the barracks that afternoon, Conor crossed over Sarsfield Bridge for the long ride out the Ennis Road. He hadn't even told Maria he was going in to see Rory. He first wanted to see for himself what state he was in, preserving the choice of not telling her at all if it was as rough as he'd feared.

And rough enough it was. No doubt Rory'd taken a storm of a beating already but Conor couldn't help feeling he might be courting even more of it with all his bluster. Why couldn't he just cop on and shut his gob for once? He was only lucky they still thought he was just nicking the one rifle for a bit of *craic*. If they knew the rest of the story he'd be dead already.

Now he had to tell Maria at least something of it if he was to pass on Rory's plea for her to go in for a visit. A girl like her should have nothing to do with a place like that. And who could know how she'd find him?

"Hello, Conor," Mrs. Sheehan said when she opened the door to him. She had the most welcoming smile he'd ever seen, leaving him shy but sure of himself all at the same time. "What can we do for you?"

"I'm after seeing Rory," he blurted out, surprising himself even. "At the jail, like. I thought I should call in to Maria with the news."

"Oh, dear. How is he?"

"Not all the worse," Conor lied, though as he did didn't he even notice that saying it aloud somehow made it that small bit more true? "He'll be grand."

"Well, that's good to hear," she said. "He's such a strong boy, isn't he?"

"He is."

"And what about you?" she asked. "I understand you have a ticket booked for America soon."

"I do," he answered. "But I won't be off so soon as I thought. I'll be waiting for Rory to come home now."

"Of course," she said. "But you'll be going to New York City, right?"

"I will," he said.

"Oh, Conor, you're just going to love it," she said. "I miss it terribly. It's just wonderful… a different world."

"I hope so."

"I'll give you all my family's information and I'll write them that you'll be in touch. They can help you with everything and get you settled in."

Conor hardly knew what to say. "Ta. You're very good."

"Of course," Mrs. Sheehan said. "Now let me get Maria for you."

"Mrs. Sheehan?" Conor said, stopping her. "Is she alright?"

"Not too bad. She's quite strong herself."

"I'd say she takes after her mother," he said.

Mrs. Sheehan leaned in to him. "And I'd say you are right," she whispered. "But you men don't make it easy on us, do you?"

Maria suggested they walk her horse out through the meadow and so they did. Conor reported on Rory and, once again, as he voiced the words of how he was coping, they continued to become truer. He started to think Rory's suffering might be only in his own mind. After all, what he saw as Rory's reckless defiance sounded far less worrisome when he described it instead as spirited bravery. Sure, Rory was nothing if not bold and cheeky. That was no surprise. He'd be grand.

Of course, he made the barracks and the detention cells sound something less than daunting as well. "He asked for you. It would mean the world to him if you'd visit."

Maria was silent for a long while. "I think I'm supposed to say *of course.*"

"You can say whatever you please."

"I almost don't want to visit him, Conor," she confessed. "I do want to see him, but I have this feeling if I visit him now, I'll be going forever."

"It's only six months," Conor said. "It'll pass quickly."

Maria stopped, holding Brooklyn steady at her side. "Six months this time, but who's to say how long the next time? Or if he'll even end up alive the next time? My mother's had that worry forever. Every time my father leaves she wonders if it's for the last time. That's why we were in the States for so long. She loves him still, but she just couldn't be here and face that anguish every day."

"But she's here for him now?"

"Because he insisted we come back," she said, starting to cry. "And it's worse now than ever with him so busy with the Republican movement."

"Well, she doesn't let on, so."

"Because she's always been strong for him, Conor," she said, tears trickling from her dark eyes. "I don't think I have that in me."

This time he couldn't help himself brushing a tear from her cheek. "You're stronger than you know."

"But I don't know if I want to be," she whispered.

Conor pulled his hand away and stepped back from her. Once more he tried to bend his reality with his words. "It's only a visit, Maria," he affirmed. "And it'd mean the world to him."

She looked away, then pulled Brooklyn around and headed back toward home. "Of course," she said.

Conor arrived home to find Liam alone in the forge. There was nothing strange about that and Conor naturally looked in to join in on whatever work was going, but that was the difference in it. The fire was blazing ready but Liam was working on nothing at all. He was just sitting on a workbench, staring at the flames.

Conor had never before seen him idle in the forge. "Are ya alright, Da?"

Liam stood and grabbed the nearest spare rod. He thrust it into the fire. "Well, how is he?"

"Seemed sound enough," Conor answered, though his voice was shakier than he would have liked.

"Is that all then?" Liam asked.

"I'd say they had a bit of go at him."

Liam turned and studied Conor's face closely. The worry was all over him. "He'll be grand," Conor added weakly. "If he just keeps his head down."

And with that, Liam knew well what Rory was in for. He pulled the rod out and examined the redness of its heat, then stuck it back in.

"He asked after ya," Conor said. But Liam had no answer for him. "Had ya thought at all of goin' in to see him, Da?" he asked. "I'd say it'd do him some good."

"I'll not go in that building," Liam answered, pulling back out the rod, glowing pale yellow and ready.

"Ah, it's not so bad once you're in is all," Conor explained. He waited for Liam to put the rod to the anvil, but Liam just watched it slowly cool again. "I could put your name down on the visitor's list if you like. Shouldn't take long to set a time."

"I'll not go in that building," Liam repeated, and then he dropped the rod on the floor and abruptly walked out of the forge.

Conor took a seat on the workbench himself. For a long while, he just stared into the fire.

Later that same night Conor called in to me at Clancy's. He gave me the report on Rory and I gave him his pints. It was clear he was well rattled from the day.

"For fuck's sake, Mr. Clancy," he says to me. "He was goin' on about Red fuckin' Hugh O'Donnell! Winking at me, like. In shackles and chains and all beat to Hell and he's fuckin' winking at me?"

"Sure," I says. "He wouldn't want you worryin' after him."

"But it's me, Mr. Clancy. I know him better than anyone."

"All the more reason."

"Ah, I could see he was in bits, and he knew it. He's no reason to be grandstanding for my sake."

"Perhaps it's for his own sake," I suggested. "Maybe that's who he needs to be to get himself through it."

"If that's who he needs to be, he won't be him for long if he doesn't stop baiting the guards like he was. You'd wanna be a fuckin' eejit."

"Fair play to him," I says. "Putting on the brave face. Don't let the bastards know he's afraid."

"Well that's the trouble, isn't it?" Conor says. "He's not afraid. I've never seen Rory show the least bit of fear of anything."

"I'd say I seen that the night he faced down the soldiers here, with Maria," I remembered. "I've seen enough donnybrooks in here to know the difference. A man can't bluff that sort of pluck."

"He doesn't bluff it. Rory's fearless," Conor said. "But the guards don't care if he is or not. They'll beat the head off him either way."

A few stools down the bar Old Man O'Mahony began to hum an old song, which I recognised from the start, though I don't believe Conor was familiar with. I put up three shorts and took down a bottle of the John Jameson's. I meself was hard on the whiskey in them days. With Sinn Féin sweeping the elections and declaring our independence, the nerves were at me something fierce. Sure, it's one thing to go on about independence in the comforts of yer own pub and sing the rebel songs with a bit of the drink taken. It's quite another to see lads taking up arms and doing something about it - especially when they end up dead for it, or beaten rotten. Some steps forward offer no retreat.

Easy enough for me to say I was all for it coming, I wasn't going to be holdin' a gun. But I knew enough of them that would be. And I knew Rory was already well down the path. That wasn't something I was prepared to stand sober.

I raised a glass for Rory and sang out on O'Mahony's tune;

Fill up once more, we'll drink a toast to comrades far away,
No nation upon earth can boast of braver hearts than they,
And though they sleep in dungeons deep, or flee outlawed and banned
We love them yet, we can't forget, the Felons of our Land.

It was on a morning within a few weeks that Martin and Mrs. Sheehan, with Maria between them, rode their car straight up to the gates of the New Barracks. They could see the parade grounds through the iron bars, where several squads were drilling. Behind them were the massive buildings that housed hundreds of soldiers and RIC constables tasked with keeping Limerick under English control.

Martin offered Maria his hand to help her out. When she took it, he held it firm for a moment. "You don't have to, dear."

She drew deep a nervous breath, then stepped onto the ground, though she was unsure if her trembling legs would even keep her standing. They did, so.

"You be strong for him now, Maria," Mrs. Sheehan urged.

She walked hand in hand with Martin to the guard posts. "I always thought it would be you I'd be coming here to see," she told him.

When Martin gave her name, the guards informed them that he couldn't accompany her onto the grounds, which was disconcerting for Maria but not entirely unexpected for Martin. Though few folks had any true knowledge of Martin's sidelines, everyone knew of his successes in banking and horse trading. He was one of the most prominent Catholics in Limerick, and that only assured him a steady dearth of common courtesies off most Protestants he had dealings with, especially there at the very seat of English power in Limerick. The long look-over the guards gave Maria right there under his nose was proof in fact.

When the guard beckoned her through the gate, Martin took her hand once again. "You don't have to, dear," he repeated, hoping she'd relent. But Maria pulled her hand away, straightened up her shoulders and walked in. Even when she was led past the parade grounds and the drilling fell sloppy with leers and whistles, she carried herself with a certain grace and dignity that robbed most of their enjoyment from it.

She was brought into the dismal prison building and kept waiting in the visit cell for what seemed to her forever, though it was only long enough to allow the warders get a look in at her once the word spread. Maria managed to pay it no heed at all.

Rory was still looking rough, but the bulk of cuts and bruises on his face had healed some by then, swapped out for a cast of cold hatred. His hard look vanished when he was led in to see Maria. He hardly even noticed the warder taking a good gander at her when he locked his chains down to the floor ring. Rory couldn't take his eyes off her himself.

"You're a vision from Heaven, lass."

"And you're a damn fool!" Maria said.

"Jaysus, Maria," Rory laughed. "It's grand to see you as well."

"It's not grand to see you," she cried. "Not in here. How could you be so stupid?"

"I know it." He leaned in and whispered. "If only I'd come out when I'd had the chance, they'd never have caught me."

"You don't even see," she chided. "You didn't have to be there at all."

"It was a chance worth taking," Rory replied. "What'd yer da say?"

"Maybe you'd rather he came to visit?"

"No Maria, no. I miss you so much."

She pressed against the bars and he leaned as close to her as he could. "Your poor face," she said, seeing now the deep bruises colouring his palour, and the deep despair disturbing his eyes.

"Don't worry. It's just the guards having a go. I'm grand. Please, don't worry."

"Six months, Rory," she whispered.

"It'll be over before you know it," he promised.

"How can you think like that?"

"It's the only way I can think," he said. "If I didn't know you were out there waiting for me, I'd never make it. You're all I think about."

She started to softly cry.

"Don't cry, Maria. Please."

"I can't help it," she said, wiping her tears away. "I just wish I could help somehow."

"Just seeing you is a world of help."

"I wish there was more."

"There is, lass," he said.

"What is it?" she asked, her eyes hopeful.

His hefty chains clanged as Rory stiffly dropped to one knee. He gently slid a tiny shine of metal across the floor to her. It was a ring of intricately woven wires, fashioned into a rough band of Celtic knots of sorts, from the strands of metal he'd pulled from the netting fronting his cell.

Her pounding heart skipped a beat when she saw it.

"Promise you'll marry me when I get out."

Maria leaned her head against the cold bars and closed her eyes. "Of course."

Chapter Ten

And Then No More

The Sheehans next called in on the McCabe property, duty-bound as they were to announce the news to their future relations. Fiona heard Martin's knocking at the forge door and was out with the daughters in tow just as Liam and Conor emerged. Save for Rory, the whole of the immediate McCabe and Sheehan clans were suddenly assembled there in that narrow alley.

Martin put his hand out to Liam. "Congratulations, my good man."

Unsure what tribute the proffered handshake was marking, and deliberate as always, Liam glanced from Fiona to Mrs. Sheehan to Conor. But all their eyes were on Maria, sheepishly looking back at them with a thin, hopeful smile. Probably only Conor noticed how she unwittingly bit her lip when her eyes finally met his.

Of course, Fiona had it quickly sussed. "A bit of cop-on now, Liam," she said as she rushed up to hug Maria. "And shake the hand of Rory's father-in-law already."

She had the kettle on just as quickly and the two families sat down and discussed wedding plans, as soon as they first dispensed with all the obligatory talk on the weather. It was quickly agreed the day would be a simple enough affair, held soon after Rory came home. Conor would be best man and the McCabe girls would bear flowers and the ring, which had been passed around and noted by all, including Liam, as quite impressive handiwork, especially considering the circumstances under which it was crafted, though everyone also agreed that the present gathering wasn't the best occasion for such dismal thoughts.

Brigid and Katy were already climbing all over Maria, beside themselves with the promise of the prettiest girl in Clare suddenly becoming their big sister. It was all Conor could do to keep them hushed enough so the mothers could confabulate on Maria's wedding dress.

"Tell me now," Fiona asked. "Will it be lace or silk?"

Both mothers looked Maria over very carefully. Maria played with the girls and pretended not to notice and Mrs. Sheehan pretended she hadn't given it much thought. "Oh lace, I'd say."

"Lovely… but perhaps with a sash of satin?"

"Yes! - and a high neck, with a long back sweep."

"Oh yes," Fiona agreed. "I do like the sound of that."

The men left them to it, excusing themselves to escape outside for a smoke in the cold night air.

"This was a shocker to me as well, Liam," Martin said when they were in the privacy of the alley. "But I'll be straight with ya, I'm thrilled for her. You know I hold Rory in high esteem. There's no better lad I'd see her with."

"Sure," Liam replied. "Isn't Rory full of surprises these days?"

Martin stepped a little closer to him. "Regarding that, you might like to know we're looking into some ways of relieving him of his present accommodation, you might say. I can't promise ya anything, it's a tough nut to crack, but I wanted you to know we are looking at it. I'll let you know what way it goes."

Liam frowned and turned away from him, once again tamping down the pent-up emotions that rose in him any time he thought of Rory's circumstance, which was nearly always. "Leave him be."

"Leave him be?" Martin echoed. Incredulous, he was. "I'll have you know, man. I don't forget for a moment what put him in there."

Liam turned back to him. "I don't forget what put him in there either. And if he's going down that path with ye, best he learn now where it leads, before the consequences are more than a few months digging ditches."

Liam towered over Martin, as he did nearly everyone, but Martin didn't back away an inch. "I haven't led him down any path," he answered. "Fuck's sake, I've been putting gates in his way for years, all on account of you."

"And I'm grateful for that," Liam said, though the tension in his face certainly didn't agree with him.

"Well it's over when he gets out," Martin told him, deciding it only then and there. "He's a man now," he said with a nod toward the fiancée inside. "He can make his own decisions."

Liam didn't answer, but crossed over the alley to the door of the forge and opened it.

"It's happening, Liam," Martin continued. "Not soon. Now. The day has come, and we're prepared this time… organised. You can still be a part of it, no questions asked. I can see to that. We need every man we can get."

Liam just stared into the darkness inside, his jaw clenched. Martin moved close to his shoulder. "I know what you're capable of. There's no one I'd rather have by my side."

"Just leave Rory to serve his sentence in peace," Liam told him as he stepped into the forge. "T'wouldn't be much of a wedding for your daughter with the groom on the run."

He closed the door behind him.

Martin went back into the house to collect his family but the delighted McCabe girls begged him to let Maria stay longer. After his heated chat with Liam, he was sapped of his usual cool composure and had no patience to face their youthful pleadings. He asked Conor to see Maria home, said his pleasantries to Fiona, and had Mrs. Sheehan in their buggy and off down the lane in moments.

When hunger pangs finally overtook Katy and Brigid's elation for Maria, Conor tore her away to get her home before the early January night was fully down on them. An odd silence carried them out of Cloonlara, but Maria couldn't abide it for long. She held her left hand out, presenting her homespun ring for him. "Did you know about this?"

"The ring?" Conor asked, though he knew well that wasn't the question. "No. He did a fine job with it though. Trust me, that wasn't easy."

"No, not the ring," Maria chided. "That he was going to ask me. You convinced me to visit him. Was this the plan from the start?"

"I hadn't a notion of it," Conor replied. "But Rory isn't in the habit of asking my advice on much of anything, much less heeding it."

149

"And what if he had asked?" she pressed, her eyes seeking out his.

Conor couldn't resist. He looked right at her. "I'd have told him he could do far better for himself."

"Conor!" Maria cried. "How rude."

"I'm only messin'," he laughed, turning away. "I'd have told him to do it right then. On the spot."

They rode for another stretch in silence, passing into that eerie reach of road where the trees alongside it creep in to blanket the already darkening sky. Oscar hastened his gallop and Conor held the reins dead straight, barely able to discern the way in front of them with the sudden blackness. Even sitting side by side on the buggy, they couldn't see a hint of each other, but somehow Maria had no doubt that he was at his Trinity Knot again.

"It's so spooky here," Maria whispered.

Conor didn't dare tell her about the *púca*, though, as always, he had his eyes peeled in hopes of a glimpse.

"Can you even see?" she asked him.

"I don't know," he answered. "I'm too frightened to open my eyes."

"Conor!" she cried, playfully clouting him on the arm. But with the jostle in it, didn't they both edge their way just a bit closer together?

Out on the Ennis Road, sight of the very last of the fading light ahead served to brighten up their chat. "So what now of your plans for America?" she asked.

"Sure, I'm still going. Right after your wedding."

"Are you sure you can wait that long?"

"Waited this long," he shrugged. "A bit more can't hurt."

"Well, don't wait too long," she warned. "Or you might not ever get there."

"Can't have the best man missing your wedding…"

Maria didn't respond for a good while. For some reason she couldn't understand, her wedding was the last thing she wanted to talk about. But when they turned onto the lone road to the Sheehan farm, she realised their time together was almost over.

"And will you stay in America?" she asked him. "Or go on?"

"For a fair spell, I'd say... if I fancy it."

"You'll love it," Maria promised. "I know you will. There's just something so different about it. We barely left New York City, but still it always felt so vast. Not even the land so much, just the possibilities of it all."

"Why were you there so long, Maria?" he asked. "I mean, away from your da, like?"

"My father didn't want me to grow up here," she said. "He thought it would be too hard a life for me."

"So what changed his mind?"

"He says he could no longer bear being away from me and mother," she answered. "And he would never move to America."

Conor halted Oscar outside the door of the Sheehan home. Maria didn't move for a moment. She just looked off at the house.

"But," she decided. "I think maybe he just wanted to ensure I married an Irishman."

Conor laughed well at that. "Go 'way."

"That's what I think," she said. "I only realised it just now."

"Well, Mrs. McCabe," said Conor as he got out of the buggy. "You must've let on to Rory at some stage." He reached up a hand to help her off. "He sure didn't dally."

"I did not," Maria insisted, shunning his hand and getting out herself. "That would be just like giving the fox the key to the henhouse. I at least tried to keep him guessing a bit."

Conor just shook his head. "Rory's no man for guessing."

He walked her to her step. "C'mere to me, Maria," he said. "Weren't there plenty of eligible Paddy's roaming the States?"

"I'm afraid once you leave Ireland," she replied, "my father doesn't consider you Irish anymore." Then she regretted how it sounded. She put her hand on his shoulder. "I'm sorry. No offence meant."

There was a moment's pause. "None taken... fair play to him," he said, turning back for the buggy, though she could see it stung.

Maria walked back toward him. "I will take Rory to America someday though. We'll go and visit you."

"You might need me to come back over just to drag him away. Rory doesn't want to know of anything outside Ireland."

"Just think of all he could miss," she said, her eyes staring off into the night.

Conor's eyes were right on her. "Maybe if I was standing in his boots, I'd be set with that as well."

She turned her face to his for a long moment, then he turned away and climbed into the buggy.

"No Conor, you belong there."

"How do you know it's not here I belong?" he asked.

"Don't be foolish," Maria scoffed. "Your dreams are much too big for old Ireland."

Conor took up the reins. "They're sayin' Ireland has big dreams of its own."

She suddenly reached up for him, gripping his hand. "Please tell me you won't get caught up in all that."

"I won't," he said, a bit taken aback by her abrupt intensity. "Though you wouldn't want to be sayin' that too loud in yer parlour," he added, with a nod toward her house.

"Why not?"

"I do believe your da might have a strong opinion on all that," he answered, "… and your fiancé as well."

She let go of his hand. "And that's just fine. But those dreams don't matter for you."

"Why is that?" he asked.

"Because they're not yours," she said, turning again and walking up her steps.

Conor called after her in a hushed voice. "How is it you think you know so much about me and my dreams, Mrs. McCabe?"

Finally at her door, she whispered back to him. "You're not such a mystery to me, Mr. O'Neill." And with that she entered her house.

Conor slapped the reins and steered auld Oscar back down the long, dark road toward home. Somehow the night seemed to grow even blacker with their every stride closer to Cloonlara, but it hardly mattered. He could tell exactly where he was by the smells of the night alone… the sweet flour off the mills on the River Blackwater, or the turf smoke in the air from Annegrove House approaching the bridge.

He knew every inch of that ground like the back of his hand. He'd trod its paths and trampled its meadows since he could walk. It was all he'd ever known. Why then, he wondered, did he still feel like a wayward stranger?

Rory's sentence of hard labour kept a shovel in his hands most of his early days in the jail, which were usually spent in and about the stables and that suited him just fine. With well over some eighty horses kept at the barracks, there was good steady work in it and he got to join in with the other prisoners, though all chat was forbidden. The exertion of it was no real bother to him, and he certainly fancied the fresh air over the dank cell, even with the near constant winter rains down on them. Besides the quiet and boredom of it, it was really only the guards and the soldiers that left it wanting. You'd think a man could be left to shovel his shite in peace.

During the insipid drudgery of one particularly mucky session, Rory looked up at the low, grey sky lavishing sheets upon them. Sure, it hadn't moved an inch in days.

"Feckin' rain seems pushed to outlast us, lads," he griped aloud, to no one in particular.

"Keep that spade moving, Paddy," says one of the overseeing soldiers, while sipping on his hot tea under the roof of a nearby shed.

"Fuck up, ya ignorant git," Rory replied. Not so loudly, but then not so under his breath that yer man wouldn't have an ear on it.

Moments later, a shiny boot stepped upon his shovel just after he jammed it into the seemingly endless pile on the ground in front of him. He looked up to a smiling soldier, with four more standing behind him, and their rifles leveled steady at Rory. "Did you have something to say to me, Mick?" your man asks.

Rory stood up tall. He had several inches on every one of them. "I did," Rory answered. "Did ya not hear me, now?"

"Well, why don't you try saying it again?" the soldier dared.

Rory looked over at his fellow captives, all watching warily. Part of him hoped someone would offer some quick words to dissuade him, though he couldn't for the life of him think what they might be. He looked straight up at the pouring rain for a long moment, but it didn't do a thing to wash away the fierce urge in his gut. Then, he looked back to the soldier and winked at him. "Fuck up, you ignorant git."

The soldier forced a laugh to cover his hard swallow, and then looked back at the men behind him. They were egging him on for a bit of sport, and he was well in it now. With a nod he had them encircle Rory, guns still at the ready. When they did, he pointed at Rory's shovel. "Hand it over," he ordered.

Rory raised it up flat to the ground, plainly weighing it in his hands and gently twisting it as he stared hard at the man. Then he tossed it down on the pile just at the soldier's feet, splashing the well-sodden shite all over his boots.

The soldier picked it up, brandishing it in much the same manner Rory did. "What was it you had in mind there, Paddy?" he asked calmly, once again glancing around at his support. He went for the surprise on the turn back, quickly swinging the shovel up at Rory's head - but didn't Rory simply catch it clean and rip it free from his grip?

Then he dropped it right back onto the pile at his feet. "Have another go."

The butt of a rifle suddenly struck him low on the back of his skull. The blow drove him as much forward as down though, and he managed to grasp the lead soldier around the neck as he fell. Another man hit him on his back but he was still able to rise himself up to his knees - with a good push of your man's face straight into the shite. There was all manner of shouting and swearing, but he didn't hear it, his anger overwhelmed everything. The next blow struck him square on the temple. It didn't put him down, but did put any hope of getting to his feet right out. The next knocked him cold. The rest just came, courtesy of the ignorant git wielding Rory's shovel.

When yer man grew weary, he ordered the other prisoners back to their work, then washed his face and sat down for another cuppa with the other soldiers. They left Rory laying there in the filthy mud, the rain washing away the blood streaming from his head. When the day's dull light quit on them, four prisoners were told to carry him to the barracks hospital.

It took the prison doctor and his orderlies a few full weeks to get him on the mend, but they spared no care to ensure he'd be fit enough to endure a sufficient level of suffering during the solitary confinement that was next in line for him. That cell was nothing more than an old kennel, and with dog biscuits and water the main sustenance provided, save for the odd gray potato or pint of skilly, Rory lived like a mangled, mangy dog for his next six weeks.

And with Rory far from presentable, the barracks wasn't about to accommodate Maria's scheduled visits. When she arrived they'd give her any manner of excuse for the cancellation, from a temporary suspension of his visitation privileges to simple prisoner unavailability, but first they'd keep her waiting a good spell for their general ogling purposes.

It was on a darkening afternoon that followed yet another such disappointment, when Maria rode Brooklyn out to the McCabe forge straightaway. Nearly at her wit's end, she barely kept herself together well enough to apologise to Liam for the lack of information on Rory and to confirm with him that they'd heard nothing new themselves. When he told her she was just after missing Conor, who'd headed off only a while before with a big, thick book stuck under his arm, she knew right where he'd be going and took off at a full gallop. She caught up with him in no time, just on the old *boreen* approaching St. Senan's Well, nearly running him over with the speed they came in on.

Conor grabbed hold of the reins to settle Brooklyn, but he could see on first glance that Maria was the one who needed to be calmed. She was desperately shook up. "Are you after seein' him?" he asked.

"I wasn't allowed."

"Again?"

"Something's wrong, Conor," she said. "It's been three times now. Why won't they let me see him?"

"Don't go jumping to conclusions, Maria," he says. "I don't think they're generally in the habit of making kindly accommodations for prisoners, like - especially with everything going on lately."

"It's more than that."

A spittin' rain started as he pulled Brooklyn along the path. "They're just doing it to mess with him," he assured her. "It's nothing to do with you."

"There's something wrong with him," she insisted. "I know it."

"You don't know it," Conor says. "And you'll only drive yourself mad thinking that way."

"I think it's too late," she said. "I'm already so confused and worried I don't know what to do anymore."

Conor handed her back the reins. "Here's what you do," he says. "Go back to our house until the weather breaks. Play with the girls and have a cup of tea with my mam. Chat about yer wedding."

The drops started to come heavier, but Maria took no notice. "Do you miss him, Conor?"

"Ya know," he sighed. "Before he went in, I'd not gone a full day of my life without seein' him. I'm not sure which of us is unluckier."

"The pair of you," she laughed. "I remember at the crossroads dance that night. He swept us both off our feet, didn't he? He just burst right in to my life. Then he left, nearly as fast."

"It's not long now you'll have him all for yourself," Conor said. "And good luck to ya."

"Conor," she said, looking right at him. "I don't know if I'm ready for that."

He turned away. "That's just a dash of nerves."

"Is it?" she asked.

He looked at the sky. It was about to open up. "You better go, Maria."

"What are you going to do?" she asked.

"Get stuck into my book," he says, showing it to her, but then holding it over his head to block the rain. "But I gotta leg it."

She reached her hand down to him. "No. Get on. I'll take you."

"I'll be grand."

She kept her hand out for him, and sure, wasn't it bucketing down at that stage? He took it and jumped on behind her.

"You better hold on," she told him, and Conor draped an arm around her waist, gripping his book with the other. Then, and with quite a dramatic flourish, Maria impetuously pulled off her riding cap and tossed it aside. "Tighter!" she cried, and she kicked Brooklyn straight off on a dead rush. They bolted into the stretch of forest past the cemetery grounds by the old church ruin, right along the path the lads had trampled wide over the years. She pushed him hard, leaning and lunging into each turn as the rain pelted their faces, leaving Conor just that instant to dodge the branches zipping by. With the broad clearings near the Shannon's edge offering no cover from the weather, Maria dropped down her reins and let the stallion tear into a full gallop all the way clear to Fenian's Trace.

Sure, it was bold and altogether unnecessary, but it was pure exhilarating all the same and more *craic* then Maria'd had in months. Conor hopped off the first chance he got. "Jaysus, Maria," he says with a laugh. "I think I'm after losing my bollocks somewhere back by your poor hat."

"Conor!" she cried, getting off Brooklyn and rushing into the old entryway of the stone turret.

He ducked in out of the rain and sat across from her. They were both soaked to the skin. "Not so bad," he said, dumping a puddle of water from out the pocket of his jacket. "A bit dewy is all."

Maria shook the rain from her long locks. "I'm drenched," she said, pulling off her riding boots and draining the water out. She noticed Conor staring at her. "What?"

"No, not a thing," he stammered, twisting on his Trinity Knot. "Work away."

She nodded toward his nervous fidgeting. "No, Conor, tell me," she pressed. "What is it?"

He dropped the pendant with a roll of his eyes to Heaven and smiled at her. "Well, it's just the last time I seen you takin' off yer boots out here, ya just kept on going, like."

"Is that so?" she said, suddenly blushing and flustered. "Well, you can rest assured you won't be witnessing that again."

"Of course not," he apologised. "I was only messin'."

They sat for a long moment in silence, until Maria finally broke it. "Did you ever tell Rory about it?"

"No," he answered. "Should I have?"

"No. I wouldn't want him to know."

"I'd say he wouldn't fancy the idea."

"I don't care about that," Maria replied. "I like that it's just between us."

"I just wish your damn horse wasn't between us," he says.

Maria laughed out loud for the first time she could remember. "What were you even doing here? Reading your book, right?"

"I was."

She reached over and picked up the book he had beside him. "This book?"

"Not that book," he said. "History."

"What is this?"

"Poetry."

She read the cover. "*Selected Poems of James Clarence Mangan.* I've never even heard of him."

"He was Irish." Conor said. "But he's long dead. Of too much drink and opium they say."

"Sounds wonderful."

"He's one of Yeats's favourites."

"I've heard of *him* at least."

"Mr. Clancy loaned me it," Conor told her.

And indeed, I had. Though I don't believe it ever found its way back to me.

She opened it up, gently peeling apart the damp pages. "Would you read me one?"

"I will not."

She found an earmarked page and turned to it. "This one, *And Then No More.* You folded the corner." She tried to hand the book to him but he wouldn't take it. "Fine then. I'll read it." She cleared her throat, suddenly nervous for it. But she read aloud, her pace slowing as she considered a meaning in the words:

> *I saw her once, one little while, and then no more:*
> *'Twas Eden's light on Earth a while, and then no more.*
> *Amid the throng she passed along the meadow-floor:*
> *Spring seemed to smile on Earth awhile, and then no more;*
> *But whence she came, which way she went, what garb she wore*
> *I noted not; I gazed a while, and then no more!*

Her eyes left the page to find Conor's, but he had stood to look out the doorway and his back was turned to her. The rain had tired to a light mist and the sky was brightening.

"It's beautiful," she said.

Conor spoke softly, reciting from memory:

I saw her once, one little while, and then no more:
'Twas Paradise on Earth a while, and then no more.
Ah! what avail my vigils pale, my magic lore?
She shone before mine eyes awhile, and then no more.
The shallop of my peace is wrecked on Beauty's shore.
Near Hope's fair isle it rode awhile, and then no more!

He never saw the tears she quickly wiped away as he continued:

I saw her once, one little while, and then no more:
Earth looked like Heaven a little while, and then no more.
Her presence thrilled and lighted to its inner core
My desert breast a little while, and then no more...

"Stop," she had to whisper, nearly overcome by the feelings running through her. "I have to go now." She pushed right past him and climbed up onto her horse, my loaned Mangan collection still clutched in her hand. "I'll take you back."

Conor could see she was desperate to go. "I'm grand," he said.

And with that, she gave Brooklyn a kick and dashed off. Conor climbed the steps to the top of the old turret and watched her ride until she vanished into the mist. "And then no more," he said to himself.

I can only imagine the toll Rory's time in that dark, dank pit of solitary confinement took on him. The physical conditions were shocking. Given his height, the ceiling was just about a long foot too low for him to stand fully tall, same as the length and width. He had to lie diagonally to ever get straight. There was no bed at all, just a tattered blanket and with no source of heat to be found, the ill-fitting clothes they'd given him in the hospital never quite came dry.

The only light to reach him at all came from whatever spread the sky managed to push through two thick, dirty windows high at either end of the corridor containing his cell. With the sun scarce or gone missing altogether over those lengthy months of winter, Rory's days were dark in every way.

He was fed only enough to keep him ever hungry. Every midday a warder would slide some manner of food and a jar of water through a hatch low on the cell door, and every morning would empty the chamber pot and his small wash basin, but they never spoke a word to him.

Two or three times a day, though never on a regular routine, the metal slot in his cell door would slide open and eyes would peer in on him. The shriek of its long, slow scraping ran right through him and grew increasingly maddening with each day. The warders found every opportunity to jolt him awake from any deep slumber he managed to capture.

But when one morning the grinding rasp of the steel was followed with a gruff, old voice calling through it, it was music to his ears, and not only because the voice was Irish. "Keep away from the door now and stay yourself back at the wall," the warder told him.

Rory slid backwards as the lower hatch was opened. "I'll need your ankles just here," yer man said. Rory barely had to move, he just put his legs forward and the man fastened shackles onto his ankles. When he got chains on Rory's arms as well, he opened the full door and shuffled inside a bit. An old man, ruddy faced, portly and drooping, he could stand erect with inches to spare. "Square yer feet and I'll pull ya to a squat. Then ya can shuffle out yourself."

He strained to heave Rory up and had to steady him a good moment while he found his legs, but they managed to get him out of the dismal cell. "Cells not made for a man your size," the warder said. "Not made for any man actually. Used to keep the fox hounds in 'em."

He pointed down the corridor. "You'll follow me along there and I'll take ya down and get ya out of those rags." The man headed off, but Rory's step behind him was unsteady. "Take yer time, lad. Legs not used to walking."

In a musty supply room in the bowels of another barracks building, the old warder rummaged through shelves of clothing. "Not an easy lad to fit, are ya?" he said. "He didn't make many like you." The man finally selected some pieces and handed them to Rory. "You'll give these a go. Best I can do for ya."

As he led Rory outside to the building that housed the regular detention cells, he produced a naggin of whiskey from his coat for a good slug. "I do believe I recall a McCabe lad in with us here before. Big fella like yourself. Maybe all of twenty, thirty years ago."

The possibility hit Rory like a hammer.

"Some sort of rebel activity, I reckon. Memory's not what it used to be. Gun-running, maybe, or some sort of agitatin' at any rate," the old warder recalled. "Hadn't seen much of that sort of thing since yer man Parnell."

The man brought Rory back into the prison building and then up and along the hallway on the same floor he was kept before the shoveling work went all arseways. Rory noticed more men in the cells, some even wearing makeshift military uniforms. The old warder nodded in their direction. "I do believe the agitatin's coming 'round again."

When the warder put him into his old cell and locked the door, he looked up at Rory's face for the first time that morning. "Some'll do just about anything to keep what they've got," he says. "Others'll throw everything away without even knowing what it was they had."

As he tottered off, Rory tried to figure his meaning, but it was only a moment and he came shuffling back. He handed Rory a thick, freshly folded blanket and the first pillow he'd seen in months. "Now, Rory," he says, heading off down the hallway. "Get yerself some kip."

The cold, hard bed all of a sudden looked heavenly to him. He set the pillow over the wooden block at the head and began to spread out the blanket, though he stopped when he noticed something clunky within it. Wouldn't you know, there was yer man's naggin of whiskey, slipped into its warm fold.

It was in the time Rory spent in the hospital and solitary that the secret Brotherhood eventually marched out of the shadows as the Irish Republican Army and declared independence from England. All Crown forces in Ireland, both British Army and RIC - loyal representatives as they were of an illegal rule - were named as legitimate targets of the IRA's guns. And in the Limerick circle, Martin Sheehan was the centre responsible for choosing those targets. It was him in command of the men carrying the guns.

Martin was a brilliant organiser, sharp as a tack and a man who spoke and carried himself in such a way that other men naturally paid attention, even hard men like Crotty and O'Keefe. But Martin wasn't a military man and he didn't have much of a taste for blood. Not that he was afraid of the dirty work involved with his chosen pursuit, just that he recognised his own limitations when it came to some of the more physical chores required.

So, as the campaign began, the directive from the top of the IRB to utilise flying columns, as they came to be known, perfectly suited Martin's leadership approach. It would be small groups of men, tightly orchestrated, on the move and on the run, and acting against specific targets - none of this madness of battalions facing off in an open field for a mutual massacre.

He might have been content enough with formulating plans from the seat at his desk and staying right there to hear if they were carried out, but he couldn't stomach ordering lads to take on the risks of his design if he wasn't willing to also chance them, so he was resolved to participate and made no complaints on it.

Still, the challenge of leading inexperienced soldiers through battle plans was at least proving less dispiriting than listening to a rancorous and inconsolable daughter fret over a wedding she had to plan without her fiancé. He found no respite from hostilities, even under his own roof and was nearly as eager for Rory to be released as Maria was. She was constantly furious, and blamed him everytime she went to visit Rory only to find him 'unavailable'.

Of course, Martin had been told of Rory's rough treatment and the solitary confinement, and was only trying to spare Maria the anguish over it with his vague explanations of prison procedures and bad timing. He'd never considered that her imaginings might actually be even worse than the realities that Rory was suffering.

He'd also learned that Rory had held up soundly enough through it all and was on the mend. Martin was eager to finally welcome him into his unit when he did get out. They needed all the help they could get and he had no doubts that Rory was more a man for the action than he his ownself could ever hope to be.

But any hopes Martin had that Rory might leave his stay at the barracks fit for fighting would have been quickly extinguished had he heard the sound of Inspector Bowen's baton being run along Rory's cell bars on the night before his release. Two of the men behind him carried rifles and four brandished their own brutal batons.

"Congratulations, Mr. McCabe," Bowen said. "You are to be released in the morning. And, as I believe you may possibly have had some childish aspirations to rebellion upon your arrival, I want to ensure that we've sufficiently rectified any such delusions over the course of your time with us."

As he unlocked the cell door, the riflemen leveled their guns at Rory through the bars. "You see, you've been treated rather kindly here because you're only a common thief." He waved the baton gang inside. "But should you return to us as a rebel, I'm afraid we'll be far, far less genial."

Just then, and for the first time since his arrival, Rory was certain that he was going to get out of the barracks prison alive. Sure, if they intended to kill him, why bother with the baton brigade? He could see that he was about to take another hiding, but if that was the price of keeping vengeance alive, he was able for it. Hell, he almost welcomed it.

As they descended upon him, wildly thrashing and clubbing him, Rory still somehow heard Bowen's voice trailing off down the corridor. "Ireland does not belong to the Irish. Ireland belongs to His Majesty the King. You are simply guests at his pleasure and should be grateful for the Crown's hospitality."

Chapter Eleven

A Perfect Fumbling

Conor sat waiting on their wagon behind auld Oscar when the barracks gates slowly opened up for Rory's freedom. At first glance, he looked sound enough. He was back in his own clothes and standing tall, and his face was without the swelling and bruises Conor'd seen on him last. Of course, the soldiers had kept their beatings of Rory mostly below his head in order to avoid any accusations of cruelty, but as soon as Conor saw the unsteadiness of his first steps through the gates, he knew Rory was in fierce pain and suffering something terrible.

"Could ya stand a pint?" he asked him.

"Jaysus," Rory answered, ignoring Conor's helping hand up and climbing in next to him. "I thought ya'd never ask."

We had the welcome gathering set at Clancy's and as soon as the lads pushed in the door the whole pub erupted in cheers. Maria stood out front and center, looking absolutely stunning in a green velvet evening dress and matching cloche hat, but she was beside herself with nerves all the same. When a wide smile came to Rory's face, she rushed up and hugged him with all her strength, trying to make up for the full six months with one embrace. "Oh, Rory," she whispered to him. "I missed you so much."

Holding her there in his arms, it was all he could do to keep his battered legs under him. "And I you, Maria," he said.

Perhaps it was only due to the agonising effects of the farewell beating he'd endured just hours earlier, and I suppose Maria would never know either way, but Rory eased her arms off of him much more quickly than she had envisioned for so many days. He kissed her cheek as he did so, but his eyes were already searching the crowd. His sisters wrapped themselves around his legs and Fiona put him in a doting embrace, but still he swiftly edged himself forward. After a sturdy handshake and tender clap on his shoulder from Liam, Rory pushed right to Martin, there with Mrs. Sheehan, alongside Crotty and O'Keefe.

As Mrs. Sheehan welcomed him, Martin offered his hand. "Good to finally have you home, lad."

Rory shook it, but threw his other arm around Martin's shoulder and pulled him close in a broad hug. "I want in," Rory whispered. "Now."

Martin felt like every pair of eyes in the room was down upon him, most especially Liam's, but he just smiled, unflappable as always. "Not to worry, lad" he replied. "You are, indeed."

As he passed him off to the other relations and friends eagerly waiting with their greetings, he spotted Maria, still standing alone by the door where Rory left her. Staring daggers at him, she was.

Liam stoked their fire a little brighter that night, even though the March chill wasn't any worse than normal. It only felt as much. He and Fiona nestled in close to each other in an effort to hold it all at bay.

"He looks as though he's aged years," she said.

"He had a tough go of it. The more stubborn ya are, the harder it is."

"It'll pass with time," Fiona assured him. "Like all things."

"These things don't pass easy," Liam replied. "There'll be no keeping him now."

They watched the flames in silence for a long while.

"Would you ever have a chat with him?" Fiona asked, already knowing the answer. "It wouldn't go astray."

"He won't listen. To me or anyone. His mind is set."

Fiona burrowed in even closer to him. "Your mind was set once."

Liam just stared into the fire. "That it was," he said. "That it was."

Even with the late session he put in, Rory was knocking at the Sheehans' door early the next morning. "Maria's still sleeping, Rory," Mrs. Sheehan told him, though she was pleased that he was so eager to be again in her daughter's company so soon.

"Actually ma'am, it's Mr. Sheehan I was hoping to chat with."

"Oh," she says, slightly surprised. "Well, he's only getting started this morning as well. It might be better if you could come back -"

"He'll see me," Rory interrupted, just stepping right past her and into the house. "Please, tell him I'm waiting in his study."

"Good morning, Rory," Martin said when he came in a few moments later to find Rory sitting in one of the chairs at his desk. "What can I do for you?"

"I want to know what's being done."

"Lucia is fixing breakfast," Martin tells him, with a nod to his kitchen. "And your fiancée is still above, dreaming away."

"That's just grand," Rory says. "And where are my rifles?"

Martin shook his head. "This isn't the time, lad."

Rory nodded his. "Yes. This is the time. You said last night I was in."

"And I meant it," Martin assured him. "But this isn't the time. For fuck's sake, you're marrying Maria in a week."

Rory stood up. "I've waited six months," he said. "I'll not wait any longer."

Martin didn't give an inch. "Rory, we can't just rush into these matters. You yourself should at least have learned that. That's how men get caught, or worse."

"Me getting caught got you four fuckin' crates of rifles. Now, are ye gonna put 'em to use or are they going to rot?"

Martin just walked around him and sat down at his desk. "You don't understand, lad."

"No, *you* don't understand," Rory said, following and standing over him. "Something will be done, and it will be done this week. If I'm to work within the movement, then let's get to work. If not, hand over a crate of my rifles and I'll get to it myself."

"We've not the arms or the men to take any action that's not planned down to every last detail. I won't have you out there fucking with those plans."

Rory took off his coat and sat down across from him. "Then we better get to planning."

Martin stood up, but now he was smiling. "Will you give me the morning, lad?" Rory voiced no answer, but Martin picked up his coat and held it out for him. "Wait outside and I'll send Maria out for you. Take her for a long walk in the meadow and have a chat about your wedding. When you're back, I'll have some men here. We'll get to work."

Rory pulled on his coat and went outside to wait for Maria.

He did just as Martin advised, a long talk and stroll with his lovely bride-to-be. They walked up into the craggy, wooded hills behind the Sheehan demesne, along the horse trails with a broad view down to the fields below. Her tiny hand was nearly lost in his own gentle grip, but it felt safe and secure there, and she had not a doubt that he'd never let it go.

When Maria asked him of the jail, Rory quickly nixed any discussions of it. "Whatever about the jail now," he answered. "I'm out. I'm grand. Tell me of our wedding."

There was so much to consider. Maria reported on all the arrangements they'd had to make for everything - the church and the guests, the ceremony and the afters. She begged for his own opinions on it, or for any comment at all, but didn't Rory agree with her every plan and idea? "Whatever you like is grand, my dear," he said. "I know it will all be perfect. Just like you."

Maria didn't notice the black jaunting car that was approaching the farm, but Rory had marked it as soon as it turned in from way off on the Ennis Road. He tightened his grasp on her hand and led her back down the hill. "It will all be perfect."

Crotty and O'Keefe were already waiting in Martin's study when he led Rory in and sat down at his desk. "Rory'll be listening in on our plans here, and he'll be with us out there as well. He's a fine addition."

"How do we know that for sure?" O'Keefe asked.

"Because I'm tellin' ya," Martin barked at him. "It's him got us the Enfields you're all carryin' and he's after spending six months in a detention cell for it."

"His da spent some time in there as well," O'Keefe replied. "How'd that work out?"

Rory turned to him. "What are you goin' on about?"

O'Keefe just glared back at him but Martin cut into it. "Lads!" he shouted. "Are we here to plan an operation or bicker like fuckin' schoolboys?"

Rory turned back to him. "I want Bowen," he says.

"Jaysus!" O'Keefe moans. "Are ya fuckin' serious with this, Martin?"

Martin shot Rory a hard look. "Let's get something straight now, Rory. Revenge will not dictate our actions. Our first mission is to capture arms and ammunition."

"To use against anyone representing the Brit government," Crotty added, with a supportive nod to Rory.

"Bowen's the County fuckin' Inspector," Rory says. "Is there a better representative?"

"Sure, we want him, too," Martin said. "And we've someone tailing him whenever he leaves the barracks. Or they would tail him at least, if he ever did leave. But he doesn't. You'll just have to be patient, lad."

"I'll be patient," Rory promised, tapping Martin's desk for emphasis. "But I want to know the next time that man steps outside those gates."

"Will we get on with it then?" O'Keefe asked.

Martin unfolded a map and spread it out on his desk, then nodded at Crotty to begin. "We know they've an effort underway to bolster up their armaments at the local barracks. And the word from Dublin is a major shipment just came across from England and they've been sending full lorry loads out to the cities. Intelligence says Limerick's delivery is comin' in later this week. Two big motor lorries. One'll carry soldiers, ten or so armed men. The other'll carry the guns and ammunition." He looked back to Martin. "But it'll be fuckin' stuffed with it."

"Our orders from Dublin are to intercept it," Martin said. "And seize every weapon we can."

O'Keefe joined in. "So, we stop the one, we get the other."

Martin stood and looked at them. He shook his head. "This week is too soon."

Rory stood up as well, and put a finger down on the map. "They'll come by way of Nenagh?" he asked Crotty.

"They will," was the answer.

"Then the Killaloe road past O'Briensbridge?" Rory confirmed, tracking the way along the roads shown.

When Crotty nodded, Rory looked right at Martin. "I know the spot."

"That country's all flatland and bog for miles," Martin said. "Nowhere to conceal enough men... nowhere to gain an advantage. Even if we could get the guns off 'em, we'd be stuck right out there in the open, miles from any cover. It's all wrong."

"So why don't ya sit down and keep yer gob shut?" O'Keefe said to Rory.

Rory just ignored him. "I know the spot," he repeated to Martin. "They'll never see us coming. And they'll never see the guns going. Just give me a chance to explain it."

Martin sat back down, giving Rory his chance.

By the time the men walked out of Martin's study, a plan was made and agreed. Even Martin couldn't help but crack a smile. "A bit ambitious lads," he said. "But it just may work."

O'Keefe shrugged his begrudging approval. "It just might at that."

"It'll work," Rory vowed.

"Then we've a lot to do in a short time," Martin said, patting Rory on the back. "And you've a lot to learn, Rory." He looked at the others. "Get him ready, lads. Off ye go."

As the three men climbed into the jaunting car, Maria rushed out of the house calling to Rory. He stopped and went back to her. "Were you not even going to say goodbye?" she asked.

"I've things to do, lass," he answered.

"But we still have our wedding plans to decide."

"Whatever you decide is grand."

She looked at Martin, then back to Rory. "Do you not even care?" she asked him.

"Of course I do," Rory assured her, planting a kiss on the top of her head. But as she went to hold him, he pulled away.

"We have to meet with Father O'Dea at the church tomorrow evening," she told him.

"I'll be there," Rory promised, climbing in with the others. He gave them a nod. "Off we go, lads."

Late that same night, Rory ducked into the forge to find Conor alone, straightening up and tinkering a bit after a good full day at it.

"What are ya at?" he asked him.

"Feck all," Conor said.

Rory watched him continue to do feck all for a long few moments, then started tinkering a bit his ownself. Conor gave him his time with it, but eventually he just looked straight at him. "Go on, so," he says.

Rory still hesitated, and wouldn't meet his eyes, but he finally dove in. "I need your help."

"Now?" Conor asked.

"No. Not now."

Conor didn't really want to know anymore, but he asked all the same. "What sort of help?"

Rory looked at him now. "An ambush," he said, quite matter-of-factly. "On the Ballyglass road."

Conor slowly shook his head. "I'm not interested."

"No one knows that ground like us. I just need someone to back me up. Who can do that better than you?"

"You best hope someone can," Conor answered.

"I wouldn't even be askin' ya," Rory assured him. "But there's not a lot of time."

Conor shrugged. "I'm off just after your wedding."

"You can still do it," Rory says. "Then head off. And you'll never hear another word from me about it."

Conor didn't quite believe his ears. "When?" he asked.

"Two nights' time."

"Fuck's sake, Rory!" Conor says. "You're to marry Maria on Saturday. Can't ya leave it alone for a few days?"

"Leave it alone?" Rory barked at him, his voice echoing through the forge. "We've been leavin' it alone for seven hundred years. Our time is now. It's not just me, the whole country is ready. There's a whole organisation of lads ready to fight, finally ready to take some fuckin' action and not runnin' off to fuckin' America like we've been doing for fifty years."

Conor pushed past him for the door. "Then you don't need me."

As he walked down the alley, Rory shouted after him. "What's wrong with ya, Conor? Where is your heart?"

Liam stepped out of their house. "Leave him be."

Rory turned and faced his father. "Leave him be?" he roared back at him.

"It's not his fight."

"It's all our fight!" Rory cried out. "How can ya not see that? It's all our fight." He looked to Liam for some response but it didn't come. He moved closer to him, searching desperately for an understanding. "What happened to ya, Da?" he asked him. "I know you were involved before. Why did ya give up?" He reached out and put his hand on Liam's shoulder. "What did they do to ya?"

Liam just turned away from him and headed back inside. "Leave Conor be."

There'd be full days you couldn't count twenty men on that stretch of the Ballyglass road that gets one from Cloonlara to the Athlunkard Bridge. But on the first dusk after Rory asked Conor for his help, you might've counted twenty in the one spot - Rory's spot, that was - if only they could be seen, which they couldn't. The dark tunnel of old beeches swallowed everything that might be viewed by distant eyes and they had whistle men far at either end to sound a signal if anyone drew near to them on the road.

Martin and O'Keefe positioned the men of their brigade column in and among and behind the giant trees. Half were posted on the one side and the others lined opposite, but with a fair gap in between the rows to ensure no danger of crossfire. They ran through the plan, detailing each man's orders and responsibilities, and then ran through it all once again. It was a lot to learn and remember, and with nearly every lad among them distressingly near to his first taste of bloodshed, a lot to keep in his stomach. You wouldn't blame someone for forgetting other appointments.

When the drilling was complete, the unit left as they came, in small groups by different paths. Rory found himself walking alongside Martin, a good pace behind the rest. "Martin," he says. "Were you in the barrack's jail with Liam?"

Martin took a long while to answer. "I wasn't."

"Was it running guns he was in for?" Rory pressed.

"Not exactly, Rory," Martin answered, though he knew it wouldn't be accepted as one. "On one of my travels to America, I arranged for a small shipment of guns to come over on a steamer to Limerick. They were dropped over the rail and into the water at Carrigaholt Bay, and fished out by your da, and Conor's da Brendan with him."

Rory just walked, not betraying his reckonings on Liam's involvement, or his ignorance of Conor's father's.

"Evictions were rampant in them times, with farmers being put off their lands and nothing they could do about it. We were young and foolish, the three of us. Along with a few others, we had grand ideas to maybe stir something up, a bit of innocent sedition I might call it today. But there wasn't near the support for that sort of activity as there is now. Most were dead set against it. At some stage, word got out about the guns, and about the lads maybe having something to do with it, and they were taken in on suspicion. They had a tough go of it, but neither gave up the guns and eventually they were released. They had a good idea who'd informed on 'em though, and after confirming that, they took care of the man the next night."

With the dark, Martin couldn't see Rory's face or read his eyes, but he didn't have to to know that every word was thundering news to him.

"Turns out the Brits expected as much and were tailin' the man," Martin continued. "So they both went in on murder charges. Two weeks later Liam came out, and that day the guns were found. Brendan's body came out the next day."

Martin waited for the next question, but it never came. He figured Rory might rather not know the answer to it for a finish, but then he couldn't have given it to him even if he did. "He never told me what happened over those weeks and I never asked, but Liam never had anything to do with us again."

Rory had already parted ways with Martin and the others when he finally remembered his and Maria's mandatory pre-wedding audience with Father O'Dea at the church where they were holding the ceremony. There were very important questions to be asked and, of course, some delicate guidance to be dispensed before God would allow their union.

There wasn't a hope they'd still be there at the hour it was, but neither was there any doubt where they would be found. His fiancée at home giving out about him missing their meeting and his priest at Clancy's sitting on a high stool. Rory didn't struggle long with that decision.

He had a pint and a chat with the good Father and patched over any devotional vexations that may have been stirred by his truancy. Father O'Dea was a loyal patron from days even before the lads first ventured into Clancy's and he certainly knew Rory well enough by then to guess at the justifications for his absence. He gave him his full blessings for the marriage and then threw in his full sympathies for having to explain himself to Maria. She'd had some head on her leaving the church, he told him.

Rory gave a good thought to rushing out to the Sheehan home with an apology for Maria, but every explanation he could think to give her put his head right back onto the Ballyglass road. Anything away from that plan was only a distraction. Her hair in the moonlight and the touch of her hand on his face, it was all pushed away. He sipped his pints and rehearsed the ambush in his mind. He was ready, no doubt... could almost taste it, metallic and violent. Then Liam was in his head as well. Another distraction to push out. He couldn't have him in there. Right in there, holding a gun to a man's head.

He was ready though. He could almost taste it.

Conor came in for last orders and I chatted with the two of them... Rory's wedding, a bit of hurling. They headed off together and rode out to Cloonlara side by side, but any idle chat was left back with me. They spoke not a word, until Oscar picked up his pace at the darkness of the Ballyglass road.

"You'll want to be well clear of here before the day's done tomorrow," Rory said quietly.

"I'd say the same for you," Conor replied.

"I'll be grand," Rory said. "But I've a notion that shifty old *púca* of yours might be visitin' on some unlucky travelers passing this way."

"Fair play, Rory," Conor said to him. "You've got some bold days in front of ya."

"Ya know, Conor," he says. "Every night I was stuck in that black fuckin' pit, do ya know the one and only thought I kept in my head to get myself through it?"

Conor knew. "Maria."

It wasn't until they were nearly home that Rory corrected him. "It was payback, Conor," he said. "I knew if I didn't get through it, I'd have no hope of vengeance."

He slowly voiced the old lines:
Give them back blow for blow, Pay them back woe for woe,
Out and make way for the Bold Fenian Men!

Conor and Liam were at work in the forge the next day when Rory stuck his head in. They waited on words from him, but all he did was stare at Conor. He didn't need to say anything… Conor knew Rory was asking him one last time to change his mind. The look on him made Conor think of the day they heard Captain Dinny's horn, when Rory's eyes were asking him to bolt from the forge and run off to find adventure.

But they weren't boys anymore… and this time Rory knew exactly where he was headed. Conor barely shook his head, but it spoke loud and clear to Rory. He closed the door and walked off down the alley. Liam looked to Conor for an explanation, but the lad couldn't even meet his eyes. He just got back to the work at hand.

Rory arrived at the Sheehans' earlier than he'd arranged with Martin to allow time to talk with Maria. Even with the long ride to think on it, he still wasn't sure what he'd say to her, other than to relay the assurances Father O'Dea had given him. Of course he'd give them their day, that was never in doubt, but somehow Rory knew that message wouldn't go very far toward soothing her anger.

He was pleased to find her with her mother in the sitting room. He knew she wouldn't make a scene in front of her, and he was even more gratified when he learned from Mrs. Sheehan that Martin had already taken the blame for his absence at the church with a clever account of horse trouble and vital assistance. Martin had also covered him for the day's coming events. Still, as he offered his pleasantries and took a seat, Maria wouldn't even look at him. He thought up a question for Mrs. Sheehan on the wedding plans but he was far too distracted with the ambush plans to even hear her answer.

When Martin stuck his head in and asked Rory outside, Mrs. Sheehan tried to clarify a point with him. "Martin," she asked, "after the walk down the aisle, will you -"

"Not now, Lucia," Martin said sternly, and the strain in his voice immediately filled the room.

Maria noticed how her mother's eyes met Martin's. They didn't challenge him, but neither did they relent. It was more a silent acknowledgement of some accord between them, long ago struck and well practiced.

She stood up and put her hand out for Maria. "Come, Maria," she said, almost in a whisper, but Rory quickly knelt beside Maria and took hold of her hand. "Maria," he started… and she finally looked at him, but without a hint of understanding in her eyes, only a soft hope on the words to follow.

But just then he realised he hadn't a notion of what to say next. Martin wasn't allowing it anyway. "Rory!" he commanded.

Rory's eyes dropped from Maria's and he stood up and walked out with Martin. The two of them got into the waiting jaunting car with O'Keefe and Crotty, grim faces all around.

Maria came running straight out after them. "Rory, wait!" she cried. "What were you going to say?"

But she stopped when he turned back at her, off the look in his eyes alone, even before she heard the words. "Not now, Maria."

The men rode off toward their endeavours and Maria headed right for the barn. Mrs. Sheehan tried to stop her but she just climbed up onto her horse and tore off across the fields.

When Maria saw the turf fire smoke drifting in the dusky sky above Fenian's Trace, she knew she'd find Conor there, just as he knew it was her that was approaching at the first sound of Brooklyn's hoofbeats racing upon the muddy ground by the river's edge. He set down his book and rolled out of one of the hammocks he and Rory had rigged years earlier, but he'd barely reached the entryway when the horse charged up and she jumped down.

"They went off to fight, didn't they?" she shouted at him.

"Maria, slow down," he replied. "What happened?"

"Don't play dumb, Conor!" she cried, pushing past him to the inside of the ruin. "Rory, my father, the others, they've gone to carry out some kind of attack or robbery, I know it. How could you let him go again?"

"I don't even know where he is."

"Please Conor, don't you lie to me, too," she begged. "I couldn't face that."

He could see there was no point in disputing it, and even more, he was helpless against her pleas. "I couldn't stop him any more than you could."

"I knew it," she said. She hunched down, holding her head in her hands. "It's all he's thought about since he's got out. He's consumed with revenge."

Conor squatted down next to her. "He'd never let on to you, Maria," he said softly. "But he had a rough go of it in there. It'll take some time 'til he's himself again."

"No, I've lost him," she whispered. "I could see it in his eyes. Nothing else matters to him now. Just like my father."

"Maybe he will have to get it out of his system," Conor said, "but the fighting won't last forever."

She looked right at him, incredulous. "You said yourself that once it starts there won't be any end to it."

"Sure, Maria," he said. "I don't feckin' know what I'm talkin' about, like."

"You told Rory Ireland will have to be torn all apart before it can ever become whole again."

Conor could only shrug, because he still believed it. Maybe the lad did always know something of what was coming…

She hugged herself tightly and rubbed her arms, finally realising she was near freezing, having taken off from home without a proper coat. Conor stood and took off his heavy *geansai* and draped it over her shoulders, then moved her closer to the fire. "If Rory's going to be a part of that, he'll need you by his side," he said. "And he'll need to know you're there for him. It's the only way he'll ever get through it."

"But what about me, Conor?" she asked, "How will *I* get through it? What about *my* life? Do I have to give that up for the sake of Ireland, too?"

He placed another few sods of turf on the fire. "It's not for Ireland's sake, it's for Rory's. He needs you Maria, especially now. And you know you have his heart."

When he turned back, she was crying. "But I don't anymore, can't you see? His heart was always full of love, maybe more for Ireland than for me, but at least there was love in it. And he was so joyful." As she huddled in close to the fire, Conor watched the flames glistening off the tears on her face. She wiped them away. "All that's changed. There's no love left in his heart. It's so full of hate for the English and whatever they did to him, and to his beloved fucking Ireland."

"I know he loves you, Maria," Conor promised. "It's there underneath it all. He'll find it again."

"My mother once thought my father would find it again. She gave up on that a long time ago."

Conor sighed heavily. There was little he could say, for he agreed with her every word. "You're to be married this week."

"I know," she said, crying softly. "I spent every day Rory was in jail making myself accept that. I know it's what I have to do… even if it means giving up all I want for myself."

Conor kneeled down by the fire and warmed his hands. He couldn't face her.

SEAN P MAHONEY

Maria wiped her tears again and stood. "But there's one thing I won't give up," she said, softly placing her hands on his shoulders.

Conor bolted up with the shock and backed away from her. "Sure, what am I to do?"

"Show me what love is," she whispered.

"Jaysus!" he says. "What in hell makes ya think I'd know?"

"I can see it in your eyes," she said. "I see it every time you look at me."

"Feck's sake, have you finally gone daft, Maria?"

She moved towards him. "Are you telling me you're not in love with me?"

"Just leave it be," he answered, his right hand suddenly twisting up his pendant like there was no tomorrow.

She covered it with her own to settle him, pressing both against his chest. "Then tell me."

He shrugged and turned away. "I'm not in love with you."

She placed a hand on his shoulder again, but this time he didn't bolt. She pulled him around to face her. "Look me in the eyes and tell me."

Conor backed himself right up until he was hard against the craggy stone wall of the ruin. "What difference does it make?"

"All the difference in the world," she whispered.

You'll be marryin' Rory in four days!" he exclaimed. "And me his best man."

"Not without knowing," she insisted.

"Knowing what?"

She whirled away then, confused and frantic. "What love is," she cried. "What it's really about." She stared into the fire. "I love Rory and I always will, no matter what he's become. I know how much he needs me and that my life is with him. I'm ready to face that."

She went back at him. "But I can't give everything up, Conor. I can't give up my only chance of knowing all that love can be. And I can't live my life feeling empty inside and always wondering…" She couldn't get the words out for the tears and turned away again.

Conor moved close behind her and placed his hands on her shoulders. "Wondering what?"

178

Still she couldn't look at him. "If you love me anywhere as much as I love you."

He put his lips to her ear. "From the first I saw you," he whispered. "With every beat of my heart."

She spun and found his lips with her own and he pulled her against himself everywhere they could possibly touch. They fell into the cocoon of Conor's hammock and pulled the sides over them to shut out the entire world. Their bodies melded and floated together in a timeless suspension, their tender passions a perfect fumbling, explorations and discoveries momentarily free from the burdens and bounds of the cold, hard earth.

Chapter Twelve

The Ballyglass Road

Informers are the fuckin' scourge of Ireland's long history of rebellion and as good a reason as any that another uprising has always been needed. So when Martin learned from his contacts that the local Crown forces had somehow gotten wind that a plan for seditious activity was afoot, there was serious talk of scuttling the ambush altogether. The word was that the Brits had already sent random patrols out searching for a particular band of rebels rumoured to be setting up an ambush. Martin had his orders though, and he was confident enough of his men and the plan at hand to stick it out with both.

If the patrols were simply off on a slapdash hunt, then their specific location hadn't been betrayed. He'd take his chances with wandering patrols. The column would have to run up against some seriously hard luck for the operation to be foiled altogether, and the potential haul of weaponry was well worth the risks. This was a military campaign after all. Orders were orders, they were going ahead with it.

But the intelligence had to have come from somewhere. He was sure every lad in the brigade column was sound, but still breathed a sigh of relief when roll call came up full of all sixteen lads he'd organised. Suspicions would have settled immediately on anyone who didn't turn up, even though they'd already proven themselves under his command for a good long spell.

"Except for Rory McCabe," O'Keefe pointed out, just before they set out for the Ballyglass road.

"Rory's sound," Martin said. "I've no doubt of that."

"What's bred in the marrow…" O'Keefe pressed. "… comes out in the bone."

"He's sound," Martin repeated. "And his father has nothing to do with this."

"Sure, of course he doesn't," O'Keefe said. "So long as Rory didn't let him in on our little secret."

Martin took Rory aside, just to shut O'Keefe up on it.

"Have you spoken of this to anyone?" Martin asked him.

"Not a word," Rory lied.

The men staggered their arrival routes and times but had all assembled and taken up their assigned positions by late morning. They held them for a good five hours, hidden in amongst the tree line, huddled under their raincoats and caps, laying in wait. Each had his own weapon, be it a rifle, shotgun or revolver, and just enough ammunition to accomplish his specific task.

It was a long spell to keep any band of lads reasonably quiet and still, but with the nerves jumping with every tick of the clock closer to the operation, not to mention a ban on fags for fear of the light and smoke, it was nearly impossible. Martin knew there'd only be so many times he could tell them to check their weapons and run the job through in their heads, so he'd given them each a book to read if they started getting restless.

The roadside was quiet as a library and not a soul passing had a hint of their presence that day. They even observed two of the Brit patrols they'd been warned about passing by in open lorries, but they were traveling in the opposite direction of their intended targets, so they left them alone. The patrol forces rode by completely unawares that the rebel column they were searching for was only but feet away, guns trained right on them.

It was just before nightfall when their eastward scouts finally signaled the approach of two vehicles, an open lorry carrying ten or so soldiers trailed by a large cargo truck. They were along earlier than anticipated, but the timing couldn't have been better for the attack. Though the surrounding sky was still alight with the fading day, the tree shrouded stretch created an unexpectedly deeper darkness for anyone entering it. The men there aiming rifles already had their eyes well adjusted, if not necessarily their stomachs, which left the Crown forces at a sudden visibility disadvantage.

So it would be impossible for anyone in the trucks to see up into the canopy of branches overhead, where Crotty sat perched and nervous, a two-pound cocoa tin in one hand and a rosary in the other. In the can was a homemade bomb of four sticks of gelignite and a rake of shrapnel. In the rosary was his every prayer for bang-on timing, for his task was the trigger for the entire operation. The ten-second fuse had to be lit at just the right time to drop it amongst the men of the first lorry without leaving them time to throw it back out, but while still being sure not to cause it to explode just below himself, at least if he had any hopes to get out of the tree with all his limbs intact.

Crotty cupped a cigarette in his hand and smoked it slowly, ready for use to ignite the detonation cord. The minutes passed like hours as they waited, each man fighting to contain his doubts and fears.

Then, the signal came that the open lorry had rumbled into view, just after passing over the canal bridge at Cloonlara. The men re-checked their weapons, then crouched and took aim. Rory was with the first row, east of Crotty's position and charged with seizing the cargo truck and its supplies once the lorry was past them and immobilised. Sure, the soldiers in it wouldn't be much of a threat if Crotty hit his target.

Martin had purposely placed Rory just at his side and now put a hand on his shoulder in an effort to embolden him past any last rise of fear. "Yer alright, Rory," he whispered. "Stay calm and remember your drill and you'll be grand."

Rory flashed him back a wide smile, once again feeling that familiar flood of bold fortitude wash over him. Martin immediately realised he needn't have bothered with the bolstering. There wasn't a hint of trepidation on the lad as the roar of the first vehicle approached. He seemed invulnerable. Even Martin's own nerves were heartened by it.

Feckin' Crotty made a hames of the drop. He lit the fuse before time, got panicked hands, and landed it some twenty feet in front of the lorry. But he'd at least erred on the proper side and the crude bomb, far more powerful than expected, blew the lorry completely off track and straight into one of the great old beech trees bordering the road. Soldiers not crushed or crippled by the crash quickly spilled out when it erupted in flames, but they had no bearings and were immediately raked with gunfire from the westward row of the brigade column. About half of them ran ahead on the road and made it into the trees unscathed.

The large cargo truck was trailing by only a hundred yards and moving fast when Martin realised that the lorry's wreckage hadn't blocked the road as planned. He ordered the men to open fire on it, but when it didn't immediately crash or slow down, Rory knew it would get past them and all its cargo would be lost.

He broke position on a dead run and leapt onto the running board just before it cleared the crash ahead. He pulled open the driver's door and yanked the steering wheel to the side, sending the truck smashing into the back of the flaming lorry. Rory was thrown clear but managed to get back up in time to see O'Keefe rush forward and blast the driver with a shotgun as he was getting out. O'Keefe's job was to commandeer the cargo truck but while he was pulling the driver's body out of his way to get inside, another soldier in the cab fired a bullet into his leg. He fell to the ground and was about to get another in the face, when Rory shot the man dead.

He went to attend O'Keefe when Martin caught up and pointed him to the cargo truck. Its rear cover had caught fire and was threatening to engulf the crates underneath. Rory quickly climbed aboard and began tearing off the flaming tarpaulin. Martin dragged O'Keefe back into the trees and out of sight of the remaining enemy who were now returning fire. Even amidst the turmoil and crack of gunfire, he perceived the rumble of two more vehicles rolling toward them. Martin managed a silent curse of their intelligence as he shouted at his men. "Back to the trees! Take cover!"

The first approaching truck was another large supply vehicle, but with only the one driver. Upon sight of the action in front of him, which was still all alight from the flames, he took it straight through at top speed, leaving the surprised column with barely a chance to fire. When Martin saw it stop to let the other soldiers on and then speed away on the road ahead, he knew that their plan was suddenly short on time.

But there were more pressing matters. The open lorry that was trailing, and holding a mixed force of another ten or so British soldiers and RIC men, had drawn to a stop about a hundred feet away. A few of its force spilled out with guns firing, but Martin's men who'd reached the trees were able to pick them off. The rest were shooting from behind the cover of the lorry itself. For them, poor Rory was a sitting duck, alone and isolated on top of the burning cargo truck.

He managed to get the last of the tarpaulin clear of the crates, heedless of the bullets that flew past his head. Then he dropped down the front side of the truck and got in behind the steering wheel. His hands were scorched from the flaming canvas but still he jammed the gears into reverse and backed it straight toward the gunfire. The soldiers reacted too late and the impact knocked them and their guns all arseways, most of them completely thrown clear of the smashed lorry. Rory jumped out to find them sprawled and stunned, easy targets for himself and the column men rushing back out from the trees.

The black road was viscous with British blood, but finally all guns fell silent.

The stench of cordite and burning petrol hung in the air as the men moved from their positions. A few of them stood about, unsure what to do next, just staring in shock at what they had wrought.

"Take their weapons and ammo and clear the bodies off the road!" Rory commanded, as he climbed back into the truck.

"What about the wounded?" someone asked.

"Leave 'em be," Rory answered… but Crotty was of another opinion. He put bullets into the only two bodies still moving.

Martin ordered some men up onto the crates in the back and climbed inside next to Rory. "Move this fast," he said. "They'll be on us at any time."

Rory drove the truck straight through the same crossroads where he'd first danced with Maria and out to the wooden bridge that crossed the canal only a mile down from Cloonlara, just past the Newtown Lock. He jerked to a halt by the bridge and the men set to quickly unloading the scores of crates filled with rifles and ammunition.

And didn't they lower them right down over the side of the bridge, directly onto the narrow decks of Captain Dinny McGrath's waiting barge. Rory had enlisted the lads' trusty transporter for the night's secret navigation down the canal and out into the Shannon. The old sailor was only thrilled to finally sign on for that taste of adventure he'd been dreaming of since his youth, and with no sea legs required.

When the truck was emptied, Martin grabbed Rory and handed him a hand grenade they'd got hold of with the supplies. "Put that truck back at the crossroads and drop this in it." he ordered. "It might slow them down. Anyone tries to stop you, shoot 'em. Then stay off any roads and get yourself somewhere safe for the night."

Rory just smiled, calm as could be. Martin still wasn't quite sure what to make of him. "Keep yer head down, Rory," he said. "Patrols are out already and they'll be flooding this area with every man and gun they have once they hear what's after happening."

With that Martin and the others got aboard with Dinny to pilot their seizure to a safehouse only accessible by the river, and Rory drove off in the truck.

The grenade did the job quite well. Rory lingered to watch the explosion light up the darkness. The ensuing flames threw long shadows on the ground in front of him as he fled off into the night.

Conor heard the footsteps approaching before Maria did. He got quickly out of the hammock to see who was coming, without even a stitch to cover himself. "Be still," he whispered to her. "I'll come right back."

"What is it?" she asked quietly… but he was already away.

He silently moved to the entryway and peered out, just as the shine of a torchlight landed upon his face. It blinded his vision but it didn't block his ears, which heard the distinct cock of a rifle bolt. He froze.

"Don't move," a voice shouted. "Come out of there."

Conor slowly stepped out, only to see five British soldiers pointing rifles at him. Given his state of undress, the soldiers were as startled as Conor, but all he could do was stand there, arms up and willy out.

"What are you doing in there?" asked the old fella in charge of the patrol.

"Feck all," says Conor. "Just a bit of kip, like."

"A bit of fuckin' kip, is it?" said the old soldier, a sergeant by the name of Jones. "Anyone else in there?" he asked, with a chuckle. "For a bit of kip in the nip?"

"Only meself," Conor said.

Jones turned to two of his subordinates. "Take a look in there," he ordered.

As the soldiers started for the entryway, Conor called to Maria inside. "Yer alright now, Maria! Don't be afraid." They pushed past Conor and headed inside the old ruin.

"Now tell me, lad," says Jones. "Does Miss Maria kip in the nip as well?"

The soldiers pulled Maria out, but she was just after getting herself dressed. "She's the only one," a soldier said. "They're alone."

Jones shined his light on Maria's face for a long time. "You bloody Catholics can't get enough can you?" he said. "Like bloody rabbits, all of you." He ran the light over her body for a long lascivious look, then put it back on Conor. "Wouldn't blame you though."

One of the younger soldiers joined in with the laugh. "I wonder if this is the rebel activity we're looking for."

"Randy activity more like," Jones said.

"Can't carry on much of an ambush with only his pecker in hand," another joked.

Jones walked up right close to them. "Thought we might be onto a secret encampment when I smelled your peat fire, laddie. Was the shagging not keeping you warm enough?" He studied their faces with his torch again and gave Maria one more full look over. "No, I don't think you're at all what we're after, are you?" he said. "Now get your bloody pants on and go home."

The patrol turned and headed back to their lorry, which they'd left by the old Church ruin when they'd set off following the drifting smoke that led them out to Fenian's Trace. Of course, they had no way of knowing the ambush that was just after taking place only miles away had already left almost a dozen of their Limerick battalion mates dead.

And neither did Conor. "They wouldn't be out here if they didn't know something was going on," he said to Maria as he quickly dressed. "I've got to warn Rory."

"You know where he is?" she asked.

"I've a good idea of it."

She hopped up on Brooklyn. "Get on then," she said. "I'll take you."

Conor climbed up behind her and she raced Brooklyn through the woodlands and across the flats out toward the Ballyglass road. When they were near enough, Conor had her stop and he jumped off. "Get home as fast as you can," he told her. "Don't stop for anything."

"Please be careful," she cried.

"I'll be grand," he said, and he tore off running through the fields. He emerged to cross the canal at the same wooden bridge where Captain Dinny's barge had been laden with weaponry not long before, and ran on toward the crossroads to get near the stretch at Ballyglass where he thought he'd find Rory. Of course, Rory was only off on a dash through the fields himself, heading for the trusty sanctuary of Fenian's Trace. In fact, I do believe there was a moment in that dark night when the two lads and Maria were all quite near to one another, yet still heading fast in completely different directions, and totally unawares of what was coming their way.

What came Conor's way was ten British lorries that had roared out of Limerick as soon as the one that'd gotten through the ambush had delivered its news. It was the quare blaze at the crossroads that kept him from seeing their headlights speeding toward him and by the time he did, he'd been spotted. He cut back off the road to evade them but there's precious little cover in the flats there. When he heard the dogs barking behind him, he knew he was fucked.

Rory made his way out to the Sheehan home early the next morning. He was eager to make sure the haul of guns had been secured and to find out if there had yet been any response following on from their evening's activities. The audacity of their attack was something the Crown forces around Limerick hadn't seen for a long, long time.

There would be consequences of course, but if everyone had gotten away safely there wouldn't be much the Brits could rightly do about it. They'd no doubt suspect the involvement of Martin and his men, as well as a number of local lads, probably including Rory himself - and they might even haul them all in - but sure they wouldn't have the proof of anything, or the evidence even, at least if that bollocks O'Keefe could stay out of sight until his leg was healed.

From what Rory had seen with his own eyes, that lone injury had been the only real hitch of the entire operation, even with the shock of the second lorry full of soldiers, and their arrival had only gotten them more guns in the end. With each step, he grew more confident that his plan had been a brilliant success. They'd seized a truckload of weapons without losing a man, and they'd taken down plenty of Brits in doing it.

He'd wondered many times what it would feel like to kill a man. What it would mean to have blood on his hands. He'd certainly imagined the act of it, but how could one ever grasp the reality beforehand? In doing it, he'd paid no heed. He'd just done it, like being on the pitch and suddenly leaping for a catch of the *sliotar*. If it's high, you leap for it, you don't stand there ponderin' yer feet.

Now on his morning walk, with the deed done, and a few times over at that, there was time for pondering. And he didn't feel any different at all… satisfied with a job well done, but otherwise just the same in every way. He'd guessed that maybe it would serve to lessen the fierceness of the fury he held inside, but that hadn't been touched. That was gripped tightly and closely guarded. He knew now it would take more than a few bodies at his feet to get to it. He wasn't entirely distressed by that either. He was keen to keep it as long as was needed.

Rory took a roundabout way to Cratloe Wood, skirting clear of Ballyglass, even though it took a strong will to resist his curiosity for a peek back around the ambush site. Instead he kept to the fields, watching the morning mist lift off their bright verdure, and bounding over the stiles of the endless stone walls delineating the maze of farm plots that stretched on to the outskirts of Limerick City. He kept his head down to quickly get through it, then started to head straight out the Ennis Road. But, he quickly noticed the area was thick with patrols in the wake of the ambush, so he ducked right back into the fields. It made for a far longer walk, but all things considered he found it a fine morning altogether and quite enjoyed himself. He whistled nearly the entire way.

His good cheer didn't last him long past his destination. Maria's face was wet with tears when she opened the door to him. "They have Conor!" she cried.

"Conor?" Rory said. "Who does?" He went to comfort her, but she only pushed him away.

"The Brits," Martin said to him over Maria's shoulder. "A lorry full of police and soldiers picked him up by the crossroads near Ballyglass last night."

Rory gently pulled Maria into his arms, trying to calm her hysterics. It was clear she hardly knew what to do with herself, but he was sure the confusion was all a mix-up. "At the crossroads?" he asked, with a sidelong glance to Martin. "Conor wasn't at the crossroads last night."

"He *was!*" Maria wailed, pounding her fists against his chest. "He was trying to warn you."

"Warn me?" Rory repeated. "Warn me of what?"

"British soldiers, Rory!" she shouted at him. "Out on patrol, searching for rebels!"

"Pull yourself together, Maria," he said sternly. "Yer not making any sense."

"Oh God, Rory," she cried. "Do you really think I don't know what you were up to? It was all over your face yesterday."

He looked to Martin but got no guidance.

"After you left I rode out to find Conor," Maria continued. "I wanted him to stop you, but he said it was no use, he'd already tried.

Then the soldiers appeared and he knew they had to be looking for you." She turned away from him and pointed at Martin. "For all of you!" she screamed at him. "You dragged Rory into this and you don't even care if I'm dragged in with him!"

"That's enough, Maria!" Martin shouted, and Mrs. Sheehan quickly moved to pull her away. Maria held firm, quickly composing herself.

"Now you have Conor in, too," she said quietly, speaking to neither man in particular as she headed inside their house. "Where does it all end?"

For Conor it was all just beginning.

For the beating he took after the hounds finally ran him down, he'd hardly have considered himself lucky, but the soldiers that caught him hadn't yet been to the Ballyglass road. Had they already laid eyes on that bloodbath, Conor would never have been brought straight back to the New Barracks for questioning. He'd be rotting in a bog. Instead he'd been thrown into a detention cell in the same prison building where he'd visited Rory only months before.

The aftermath of the ambush had the British Government in turmoil. Incidents of *disaffection,* as they were after terming it, were beginning to crop up here and there across Ireland, but they were mostly isolated attacks and assassinations. The bold attack at Ballyglass was on a scale yet unseen and the Brits quickly declared the entire surrounding region a Special Military Area under their ignominious Defense of the Realm Act - that blanket justification for whatever cruelties they deemed necessary to preserve their empire.

In Limerick, the administration of those cruelties was falling on none other than the County Inspector, who was directed to use any means at his disposal to find those responsible, as well as anyone lending them support, and to maintain order at all costs. Bowen was thrilled to have due cause to develop a robust program of retaliation - which he would eventually inflict on any general locality where seditious acts were carried out - but he was still finding it somehow unsatisfying. The Ballyglass ambush had caught him completely unawares, which he took as a direct and personal affront to his authority over Limerick, an insult he knew only a direct and personal dose of revenge could remedy.

It was a culprit he needed, so when he was told that the man who'd been captured near the scene of the ambush wasn't likely one of its perpetrators, it was all he could do to maintain his composure. Sure, he was only a poncey prick of a man on a good day and now the ambush had him in a right tizzy.

"Please correct me here, if I've misunderstood," Bowen said to the small contingent of soldiers and warders he'd called in to his office. "A band of Irish rebels ambushed and murdered a dozen British soldiers - soldiers not very unlike yourselves I note - and we caught a man less than a mile from the slaughter, an Irishman no less, who absconded upon being spotted. Yet, you men submit that he had not a thing at all to do with it."

"There just isn't any evidence that he did, sir," came the answer from the most senior of the group of soldiers that had caught Conor. "And to his credit, he was actually running toward the site when he was first seen. And he was unarmed."

"Rest assured, sir," added one of the prison warders. "If he had any part in it, he'd have owned up to it by now." He grinned at his fellow warders. "Especially after our chat with him."

Bowen stood and moved nose-to-nose with the senior soldier. "Perhaps it is you that has misunderstood me," he hissed, repeatedly poking him on the chest with each word. "It is not evidence that concerns me. It is punishment... punishment of a severity sufficient to deliver an unmistakable message to these filthy peasants that the British Government will not tolerate any of this so-called rebel activity."

The soldier knew to his heart that they had the wrong man, but he knew even better that any further dispute was useless. "But, we've no grounds," he offered meekly.

"But of course, we shan't punish the poor lad without grounds. That would be indecent and bloody well uncivilised." He opened his door and ordered the men out. "We will simply have to wait until his confession yields them. And indeed it will."

Martin led Rory into his study for a similar line of questioning once Maria had gone inside. Crotty was there from the night before, waiting with O'Keefe, who was laying prone on a settee after having his wounded leg already treated and dressed overnight by a doctor sympathetic to the cause.

But Rory only nodded to them. He was still trying to get his head around the news on Conor. And they only nodded back.

"We have to get him out of there," Rory declared.

"Impossible," O'Keefe says.

Rory glared at him. "And wasn't it you O'Keefe, said the ambush was impossible?"

"He's right though, Rory," Crotty said. "We've looked at it enough now to know. Fuck's sake, we looked at it for you."

"Then we'll look again," Rory replied. "I'm not leaving him in there."

Martin sat down at his desk. "Let's not get ahead of ourselves, lads," he said. "He wasn't a part of it and he never has been. They've no credible evidence against him and no justification for holding him. We'll demand a hearing and put every bit of pressure upon them to either present a case on him or release him."

"After last night, who says they'll even bother with a hearing?" Crotty asked. "They could just let him rot."

"This government is still doing whatever it can to maintain its facade of legitimacy," Martin answered. "They won't hold him forever without charges."

"Not forever," O'Keefe countered. "Just long enough to beat every bit of information they can get from him."

"He'll not say a fuckin' word!" Rory barked. "I know him like I know myself. I didn't talk and he won't either."

"You didn't know anything to tell, lad," Martin reminded him.

"But we can't say the same now for Conor," O'Keefe says. "Isn't that so, Rory?"

Martin stood back up, eye to eye with Rory. "You told me you hadn't spoken to anyone of the ambush, Rory," he said. "Then how did Conor know where to go to warn you?"

"Are ya fuckin' serious with this?" Rory asked him. "Of course I told Conor. I was tryin' to get him to help. I didn't tell ye so I wouldn't have to listen to yer moaning. What of it?"

"And here we were, lads," O'Keefe says. "Wrecking our poor heads wondering who tipped the Brits onto us."

Rory reached down, grabbed O'Keefe's collar and yanked him clear off the settee. "I should have let that fucker put a bullet in yer head last night," he roared at him, while O'Keefe howled with the pain off his leg. Martin and Crotty struggled to pry him loose of Rory's grip until finally he let him go and they set him back down.

"Don't lose the head, Rory," Martin ordered, tying to calm everything down, himself included. "He's not saying Conor betrayed us himself, but there's no doubting they got information. Could he have said it to anyone else that may have passed it on?"

"Not a fuckin' chance," Rory said.

"Maybe he had a chat with yer auld fella?" snarled O'Keefe, still reeling from Rory's thrashing but not backing down from him either.

"Enough outta you!" Martin hollered at him.

Rory managed to ignore him, for that moment at least. "What is it yer so troubled about anyhow?" he asked them. "That the Brits'll find out you've joined up with the IRA? Well, so what? We are an army and this is a war. And last night was just the start. The days of coming home and sleeping in our own beds at night are over."

"Says him about to be married on Saturday," Crotty mumbled.

Rory glared at him. "And what fuckin' concern is that of yours, Crotty?"

"I'm only sayin' like," he answered, wishing he'd said nothing at all.

But his comment did get Rory to thinking about Maria and their impending wedding for what seemed like the first time in days. He looked to Martin. "How much does she know?"

"She knows enough," was the reply. "There was no way around that."

"Maybe it's for the best," Rory said. "I'm not one for all these fuckin' secrets anyhow."

He moved to leave, suddenly overcome with a desperate urge to speak with Maria, but Martin got in front of him. "You'll have to be,

Rory," he said. "The longer we operate in secret, the more effective we can be."

"Whatever about him," O'Keefe says. "Ye best hope Conor's one for the secrets."

"I already told ya," Rory said. "They won't hear your secrets from Conor. Ye can all be sure of that."

"They won't go easy on him," Martin said.

"Then get him the fuck out," Rory said, pushing past him toward the door. But first he stopped and leaned down close to O'Keefe's ear. "I ever hear you speak another cross word about my father and I'll put that bullet in yer head meself."

He found Maria alone in the barn grooming her horse and wasn't he only relieved to see the ring he'd given her still there on her finger? He watched her for a good long spell before approaching, first trying to figure out how to go about explaining himself, then giving up on it and just staring at her. He could well see the temper still on her, but the longer he lingered, just appreciating the grace of her movements, he started to notice for the first time a certain air of intimate detachment about her.

When he caught himself worrying that just maybe she couldn't be arsed if she ever saw him again, he suddenly knew he couldn't dally another moment or he might lose her forever.

"It's some Saturday we have coming, Maria," he announced, startling her from her reverie.

"Oh, Rory," she said, still with a cheerless smile for him. "I can't even think about it."

He took the curry comb from her hand and started brushing down the big horse. "It's no bother, lass," he said. "Just hold my hand, let me kiss you when they say to and remember to keep one foot on the floor when we're dancin' so the fairies can't steal you away."

"What about Conor?" she asked.

"Your da thinks he might be let out in short enough order," he said, though they both knew he didn't believe it. "Even if not, he'd never forgive himself if we put it off on account of him, and I might never forgive him either."

"But he's your best man."

"Nothing changes that, Maria."

"We should wait," she said. "So he can be there."

"I don't need him standing next to me to know he's by my side," Rory told her. "And sure, Father O'Dea'll crucify me if I miss another appointment in his church. I'm afraid it's Saturday or never, lass."

She looked straight at him. "Why does that sound to me like a warning?"

He just chuckled and handed her back the comb. He grabbed a dandy brush and ran it along the length of the horse in smooth strokes. "I want a big brood of children, Maria," he said.

She couldn't help but laugh out loud at that. "Is that so?"

"I want them to help me at the forge," he continued, mostly staying to the opposite side of the horse from her. "And I want you to show them how to handle a horse, all proper and haughty, like."

"I do not ride haughtily," she protested.

"I want us to ride with them. All together we'll be, tramping across the meadows and out to the seaside, like an army of McCabes, on a grand hunt for periwinkles."

Maria smiled at his dream. "You have it all figured out."

"And I don't ever want to have to send them away because life is too difficult here," he said. "Or too dangerous. Or too unjust."

She tried to catch his eye but he wouldn't look at her. He just continued his brushing. "I'm going to do whatever it takes to make that so," he promised. "And it's going to take killing. And it's going to put me on the run. And it could even put you in danger." He finally came around to her side and handed the brush to her, looking right at her. "But that's what I'm going to do."

They shared a long silent moment as the tears misted in her eyes. "Do I not have any say in the matter?" she asked.

Rory turned away to find a rag and then began a final polish of the horse's coat. "Do you remember the day we met?" he asked.

"Of course," she whispered.

"You were exercising auld Brooklyn here in your ring and you asked me to open the gate for ya."

"I remember," she said.

"Then you'll remember me sayin' only if you'll go to the *céilí* with me," he continued. "And you said you were busy, though you weren't, and I wouldn't have even minded, but sure we both knew you were only burstin' to go."

"Is that so?" she says.

"T'is, of course," he replied. "Then you jumped this big beast right over the gate, nearly landin' on top of me, and ya said to me, and I'll never forget it now, 'I'll expect you Saturday then.'"

She managed a sad smile at the memory. It must have seemed a hundred years ago to her.

Rory smiled as well. "I knew right then I'd have to marry you," he said. "But do ya know why, Maria?"

She shook her head.

"Any other girl would have had me open the gate and then played it cute like she was only goin' because she owed me, even if she was burstin' as well."

"Is that so?" Maria asked again.

"T'is, of course," didn't he answer again. "But you're not any girl, are ya Maria? You wanted to leave no doubts that you were only going because you yourself wanted to go and not because I wanted you to. I knew you weren't one to play games and I knew you would never do anything just to please someone else."

She looked at him, but her smile was gone.

"Even meself," he said, sweeping a few finishing strokes across Brooklyn's gleaming black coat. "So, c'mere to me, Maria," he said, handing the rag to her. "Will I expect you Saturday… or not?"

Chapter Thirteen

A Chlann Dhílis Dé

Conor was sure he had at least a rib or two busted from the kickin' he'd got when the soldiers had caught up with him. Deep inhalations hurt like holy Hell, and God save him if he let go a cough. But after some rather excruciating contortions, he'd eventually discovered a way of positioning himself in the corner of the detention cell that alleviated some of the worst pain if he stayed mostly motionless, a state his shackles and leg irons helped to buttress. But even that couldn't help ease the thumping pain coming from the deep gash in his head courtesy of a Brit boot.

Still, he managed to maintain that exact posture during the hours between visits from the jail warders. The coldness of the concrete gave it a soothing and, besides, it was one of those quare tantalising types of pains where the pleasure one gets from relieving it is almost worth its agony. When he wasn't slippin' into unconsciousness and couldn't fall into a sleep, he just lay there with his eyes closed tight and incessantly pressed the wound against the wall with more and more force. He'd ratchet up the intensity in it to the most he could take and then finally back off on it and savor the momentary relief.

It didn't allow for much rest or healing, but for a good while it kept his mind from thinking of just about anything at all - and Maria or Rory in particular - and that served to stave off the worst waves of guilt that were threatening to crash down on him with the cold light of day. Broken and bloody as he was, the poor lad was still more torn up inside than out.

When the warders did come in to him, he didn't need worry about creating any of his own pains. From what he could gather, they'd been at him every four or five hours since he was brought in to the barracks. Conor no longer had any real feel for when that was, but from the questions they kept putting to him he had managed to glean some ideas of what had likely happened on the Ballyglass road. If Rory's ambush hadn't met with at least some success, they wouldn't be battering him for IRA names and information and, if they had either already, they'd probably be using it to try and get more from him. With no sign of any other lads being brought in, he held onto his hopes that Rory and the rest had gotten away with it.

Initially, they asked him everything and all at once with it. All the who's, what's, where's, when's, and why's they could think of. They got back nothing more than just some culchie Conor O'Neill from Cloonlara who spent his afternoon at Clancy's gettin' pissed, and wasn't he only makin' his way home when he saw a fire blazing away in the dark of night and went off for a look? When he saw it was a British Army lorry after burning, and then suddenly a slew of ten more came racing at him, he decided he'd seen quite enough and legged it. End of story.

"And now here I am with ye pricks beating the head off me for no good reason," he added.

For a finish the only questions put to him, albeit repeatedly for hours on end, were who done it and who does he know that's involved. Eventually, he could see they were even abandoning their hopes of obtaining any useful answers to those either.

"You can't get blood from a stone," Conor heard the men say more than once.

From the outset, or at least after a bit of logical consideration, most of the warders didn't believe it was even likely he'd been involved at all. No one who'd taken part in such an ambitious and deadly a raid would have stayed around long enough to have been caught out there, especially alone and unarmed. The rest of the forces who'd been sent out in response didn't find a soul for miles, only dead soldiers and burning lorries.

County Inspector Tyler Bowen didn't give a fish's tit what the warders believed. Indeed, neither did he care in any regard for what the facts may or may not have suggested about their sole prisoner's likely role in the incident. His trusted well of patience was being well drained by their apparent lack of capacity to appreciate that indifference.

It was quite clear to him that he still may not have under his command men with the type of pluck necessary for fruitful interrogation work. Of course, some of the warders at the barrack's prison were Irishmen and he knew that their hearts were not usually in with any of the rough stuff. He'd been evaluating Catholic constables in the RIC since he arrived on Ireland's grass and had found them unacceptably sympathetic on most occasions and always incompetent. He'd rooted out plenty of the lazy drunkards already, and now that there was excellent cause to be spilling Irish blood, his intolerance was total.

And, it was even more apparent to him that he had to get directly involved with this Conor O'Neill. By the time the worthless warders came back into his office with another report of one more failure to wrest any useful information from him, he had already fetched his dependable old whisky box out of safekeeping.

"I can assure you, sir," one of the warders offered futilely, "… that man wasn't involved. If he was, he'd have confessed by now."

"And how is it you can arrive so confidently at that conclusion?" Bowen asked.

"We've put him under all sorts of pressure. If there was a drop of information in him, we would surely have wrung it out."

Bowen abruptly stood up from his desk for an air of the dramatics. "Gentlemen, we are entering a dangerous time here. These filthy Micks are beginning to believe that they are entitled to some sort of rights to this godforsaken island. Now, I have neither the mandate nor the inclination to entertain such treasonous theories. Therefore, it is our duty to clearly demonstrate beyond any possible misconstruction that any undertakings of insurrection will be immediately and unmercifully crushed."

He pointed off toward the detention cells with a flourish. "That man is our demonstration." He then took up his tin box and tucked it in under his arm. "I think it is time I make his acquaintance."

Conor was slouched against the wall asleep when four warders walked in ahead of Bowen and hoisted him onto his feet. It wasn't his rude awakening under the rough handling by the guards that sent the chill down his spine. It was the voice he heard giving them their orders. "Hang him up."

The men lifted him higher against the wall, setting his feet onto a small stool. Then, with the help of a handy ladder, they managed to hitch the chain connecting his arm shackles onto a metal hook that was long ago cemented into the wall at some nine-feet high. As they did so, Bowen introduced himself. "Mr. O'Neill, I am County Inspector Tyler Bowen of the Royal Irish Constabulary, and I am charged with maintaining order here in Limerick and its surrounds."

But sure, Conor already knew just who he was. Same as Rory, he'd never forgotten Bowen's face or even his voice since the day the bastard had struck Liam with Rory's rooftop brick. He was also well aware of Bowen's reputation at the RIC, as there'd been more than a few stories told over the years about his exploits inside the walls of the barracks' prison, recounted mostly by men who'd been left scarred, maimed or crippled after making his acquaintance. The poor lad was already terrified at just the thought of the man, whatever about meeting him in a detention cell.

The warders' work with the ladder left Conor hanging there once they removed the stool from under his feet. His back was against the wall and his shackled ankles dangled a good foot or so above the floor. His arms were extended straight up above him, which stretched his torso and forced out his thrashed ribcage. The breaks were visible right there on the bones pressing tight against his skin.

"You may feel some discomfort on your wrists situated there as you are," Bowen said. "But don't be distressed, in short order you'll hardly remember it's even there." With his head almost forced to slump forward by his shoulders, Bowen could get in close to Conor and look right up at his face. "You are aware by now, I'm sure, that a very serious incident recently occurred in this district, in fact not at all far from your family residence in Cloonlara - site of the McCabe blacksmith shop, a crude but serviceable forge, if I recall my visit correctly."

A flash of dismay lit Conor's eyes as he realised that the Inspector possibly knew exactly who he was as well. And Bowen didn't miss it. "Yes, of course," he smiled. "I've been reviewing our records. It's an interesting clan living under your roof. I believe both Liam McCabe and his son Rory have also been our guests here on previous occasions, after playing at a bit of petty disaffection."

He set his whisky box on a step of the nearby ladder and opened it. "I suspect you fancy yourself a rebel as well." Conor shut his eyes when he saw its contents. "But you're not a McCabe, you're an O'Neill. Maybe you aim your sights higher?"

Originally the rectangular case held a quart of White Horse Scotch whisky that Bowen's fellow officers had gifted to him years earlier upon his first posting to Ireland. It was intended for the occasional noble stiffener against the squalor and boredom they'd predicted for him here, but fine chaps they were, they proceeded to assist him in emptying the bottle there and then. But Bowen admired the fancy casing it came in, and with an aching head on him the next morning, he cheerily found that it perfectly accommodated a favored set of small implements that he was hoping to put to more frequent use in his new position. He was quite satisfied with the number of opportunities he'd realised over the years.

"You see, the theft of our guns is one concern," Bowen said to Conor. "Their use on His Majesty's army however, is quite another affair altogether."

He removed a pliers from the tin and set it on a lower rung. "Due to your reluctance thus far to aid our investigation, some of my subordinates have come to believe that you were not involved in their use, but I don't believe that for a moment." He removed a pincers as well. "Now, rather than make an unnecessary mess here, it would be most expedient for you to simply confess to your participation now, make a clean breast of it, and we can both be finished with all this inconvenience."

Bowen raised his hand up and lifted Conor's chin. His eyes opened from reflex, but they showed nothing. He was making every effort to gird himself against the coming pain, trying to will his entire existence to another place, abandoning everything of reality.

"No, of course not," Bowen whispered to him. "Not yet. Where would be the fun in that?"

He took out a small hammer and then a glass jar containing several long, thin nails. "Now, we shall spend some time chatting," he told Conor, "and you will tell me all that you know about what happened out on the Ballyglass road." He took out a pair of white, rubber gloves and pulled them onto his bony hands. "I daresay, if I haven't lost my delicate touch, that you may even wax effusive."

He pulled the short stool over and set it at Conor's feet. "It is names I'm after, Mr. O'Neill," he said. "I don't particularly care whose names you give me - your own, your comrades, even your enemies - but names will be given." He took the pliers in hand and sat down on the stool. "These I will use to crush your toes, which I concede does sound somewhat less painful than it actually is."

Conor's mind went out to the vast oceans he'd dreamed of crossing since his earliest memories. He put himself at the bow of a vessel, with nothing but water stretching before him, leaving all his past behind. He focused his imagination with every energy his brain could muster, nearly tasting the salt of the sea on his tongue, nearly feeling its swells in his gut.

He didn't even feel Bowen stick the jaws of the pliers onto his smallest toe before posing his first query. "Did you take part in the ambush on the Ballyglass road?"

Conor didn't even hear him, and so offered no response. Nor did he feel the two warders take hold of the chains binding his leg shackles to prevent him from kicking. He was far, far off, lost amid the rolling waves - until the excruciating crunch of the pliers plunged him into a depth of agony that immediately overtook his watery imaginings.

Conor's ambition at the outset of his capture was to speak not a word in reply to any questions. He'd managed such thus far when the warders were having a go at him, and upon Bowen's arrival he was initially hopeful he could maintain the policy. But the hurt off his toe was unbearable like nothing before, a stabbing of fire shot up his leg from it, and he knew musings of the Seven Seas hadn't a hope in Hell of getting him past it.

Bowen set down the pliers and took up the hammer. He showed Conor one of the nails. "This I will drive in under your toenail."

The lad's thoughts fled to the sanctuary of Fenian's Trace, lying back on the sun warmed rocks and dipping a foot into the Shannon's cool waters. A collection of Yeats read by the muddled light off a turf fire. Havin' the *craic* with Rory up in the turret, just out of the drizzle's reach on a grand soft day.

Bowen asked another question about the ambush, but still Conor didn't register the sound of his voice - or the strike of the hammer upon the skewering nail. The slicing sear of it prying up his toenail tore a terrible scream out from deep within him. The Inspector's suspicions regarding his soldiers' stomach for a bit of fierceness were confirmed when two of his warders left the cell upon the sight of the damage.

He set down the hammer and took up the pincers. "With these I will tear the nail from its root."

Conor finally put his mind to Maria. He hadn't allowed himself to think of her since they'd parted just before his capture, but now he was back in the hammock with her, shutting out the world, his desire enveloping her, his lustful longings upon her body, her skin, her breath, all of her. Maria.

Bowen ignored the pool of blood soaking his own boots and continued his questioning. "Did Rory McCabe take part in the ambush?"

It was only the utterance of the name that got through to his ears, and from there it burst right in on his memory of Maria. For wasn't she indeed his? Rory's Maria. Rory's fiancée. Rory's future.

Fuck's sake, what had he done?

And the overwhelming wave of guilt he'd been staving off for days crashed down on him. Its shame flowed over and through every inch of his body. It washed away all the mad fever of memory and imaginings clambering to numb his torment and left him with only the purity of the pain.

And didn't he now welcome it?

For as he heard the abrupt rip of his toenail coming out of his skin, and felt its jolting agony consume his being, a comfort instead was delivered him. A hint of anguish was lifted, the torture a sudden and improbable offer of penance for his sin. From that moment forward, every twinge of suffering eased his conscience something more. He opened his eyes and looked down at Bowen, the rabid mongrel mucking about there at his bloody feet, and he nodded his thanks to him.

Bowen nearly shat himself.

Through all his merry endeavors interrogating criminals and gathering intelligence over the years, his vicious toe tools had pulled every manner of stunners from his subjects, from prayers and pleas to apologies and confessions. He'd never before extracted gratitude. It took the wind right from his sails. More questions were asked and more toes were assaulted and bashed and mangled, but Conor cried out no more and still said not a word. Inspector Bowen's famous persistence was quickly poisoned.

He peeled off his gloves and told the warders to take Conor down from the wall. "Bandage his feet and give him a day to heal," he ordered as he quickly packed up his whisky tin and stormed out of the cell. "That boy has no bloody information to give."

On Conor's day of healing, Fiona got her girls into their dresses and set them up in their jaunting cart for the ride into town. Then she ducked back inside their house to fetch Liam. "We'd want to be getting to it or sure we'll be late for our own son's wedding!"

"We've plenty of time, love," he said as he pulled on his best and only suit coat. He held the door open for her but she stopped in front of him and straightened his tie. "Don't fuss," he said. "It was fine as it was."

She took a step back and gave him a good long look over, her eyes full with an unshakeable adoration. "Jaysus, Liam," she said to her husband. "All these years, and ya can still make me weak in the knees." She planted a tender kiss on him, then took his hand and led him outside to get on with their day. She knew well enough that he was doubting if he was even able for it.

As usual, the good priest Stephen O'Dea ducked into me for his whisky before donning his vestments to perform the early Mass. On this day, he'd also be conducting the McCabe marriage ceremony, so I had one meself and then closed up to share the short walk with him over to St. Michael's - the giant limestone house of worship on Denmark Street with the golden angel on its top - just around the corner and a spit from Clancy's.

I was only delighted to arrive in time to see the Sheehans' polished jaunting cart roll up to the church steps, guided by Martin himself and pulled along by Maria's fine stallion, Brooklyn. Maria and her mother were seated back to back and facing outward over its high wheels, their stylish dresses tucked under on its foot boards. They made quite an entrance, as stunningly handsome a trio as Limerick has ever seen.

As Martin helped the women out, I noticed Maria carrying a horseshoe in her hand for the good luck in it. Still hangs on her wall today, sure it does. But I later learned it was one of Brooklyn's own and even that much more special a charm as it was made of iron heated in the McCabe forge and put to her horse's hoof only weeks earlier by none other than Conor himself.

It was his glaring absence of course that held a somber cloud heavy over the proceedings. Maria was all glowing beauty and Rory a rock of beaming pride, but sure, weren't there still more tears than smiles on the day?

At Rory's request in respect of such, Father O'Dea kept the service short. His words I can give you here, but the page can't do justice to his voicing of them. That's an elegance that only can be heard in the sweet poetics of our Irish language. "*A chlann dhílis Dé,*" he began…

"Beloved children of God, you have come to this church for God to put His holy seal on your love in the presence of this congregation. Marriage is a sacred union which enriches natural love. It binds those who enter it to be faithful to each other forever; it creates between them a bond that endures for life and cannot be broken; it demands that they love and honour each other, that they accept from God the children He may give them, and bring them up in His love. To help them in their marriage, the husband and wife receive the life-long grace of the sacrament."

Martin walked Maria down the aisle to where Rory stood waiting, with Liam there beside him. The two old rebels shook hands and moved off to join their wives in pews on the opposite sides of the aisle.

Father O'Dea bade Rory and Maria to join hands and then little Brigid was summoned up to wrap a binding ribbon around them in the old Celtic tradition of handfasting.

"Maria and Rory, you are about to celebrate this sacrament," announced the priest with a lovely dash of magnificence. "Have you come here of your own free will and choice and without compulsion to marry each other?"

And didn't Rory give her the wink with that one? "We have," they both answered.

"Will you love and honour each other in marriage all the days of your life?" he asked.

"We will."

"Are you willing to accept with love the children God may send you, and bring them up in accordance with the law of Christ and his Church?"

"We are," they answered together, though neither had given much thought at all to God's plans for them, whatever about what He might send.

Katy was summoned to wrap a second ribbon and, after she secured a knot in the two, Father O'Dea says, "And so the bond is made. May you have a long life and days of sunshine, and may you not leave this life until your child falls in love."

When Rory lifted Maria's veil for the wedded kiss, he first had to wipe away the tears streaming down her cheeks. There was joy in them he knew, and love he hoped, but still a sadness he hated. "Tugaim mo chroí duit go deo," he whispered in his well practiced Irish. I give my heart to you forever.

I quickly left St. Michael's and got back over to Clancy's to get it opened again for the afters, as a fast thirst is the most common affliction of a wedding congregation. Maria and Rory walked out short moments after me, only with Rory now helping Maria up onto the Sheehans' jaunting car. With her and her dress safely in and on the seat next to him, he surprised more than a few when he then helped none other than the good Captain Dinny McGrath up onto the side seat. The plan as stated was to head right over to me, but didn't Rory steer Brooklyn in the wrong direction altogether at George's Street, heading south instead and leaving their trailing guests quite confused on just where to go with their congratulations.

They proceeded straight along until the turn at Roden Street, the narrow lane that took them directly up to the wide entrance gates of the New Barracks. They were closed at the time but nevertheless afforded the nearest spot to the detention cells that was still outside the perimeter.

The sight of the bride and the groom with the ginger auld sailor immediately caught the curiosities of the gate post guards and a few other soldiers that spied them from inside, but it was when Dinny produced his trusty horn and began to trumpet the tune of *Dublin Daisies* out over the barrack's wall that they gained the full attention of every member of the Crown forces within earshot.

Several gate-post guards rushed out toward them to put a stop to it, but weren't they swiftly shouted down by the near full brigade of men that hurried to the gates to view the odd spectacle? They pressed their faces against the iron bars and listened to the Captain's bouncy song, temporarily welcoming a bit of Irish mirth into the dreary isolation of Limerick's British command post. Of course, the lovely sight of Maria was another attraction in itself, and one Rory hadn't figured into his musical tribute for Conor, but a wedding gown naturally demands a certain respect from even the roughest characters, and the men kept themselves uncommonly quiet and courtly throughout Dinny's rendition.

One old soldier watching among them took a particularly keen interest in the young bride, and it took him nearly the full song to suss out just where he recognised her from. It was pitch dark when Sergeant Jones and his patrol had stumbled upon Conor and Maria at Fenian's Trace, but he'd regarded her beautiful face a good long while with the light of his torch that night, and he was beyond doubt that she was the same girl, only now alongside a husband he didn't recognise at all.

One soul who I don't believe ever heard Dinny's tune was Conor himself, at least not with heedful ears, for he was then still in the unconscious stupor of suffering that followed his interrogation. But still, I do like to imagine that the sounds somehow carried over the steel and through the stone to perhaps penetrate his oblivion and reach into his spirit. I like to think that maybe it even sparked a dream there. One where he was off on the high meadow when Dinny's call came, that had him dashing down through Cloonlara to the canal, and saw him hopping aboard Dinny's barge for the slow and splendid ride into Limerick to deliver the black stuff once again.

The Guinness flowed freely in Clancy's that evening, with many other bottles unburdened as well. There was music and dancing and good *craic* all around, led by Rory himself, I suppose on a bit of a much-needed respite from all the distress and heartache on account of the week's events.

But before they were too deep into the night, he did interrupt the celebrations and quietened everyone down. "I don't mean to throw a blanket on things," he announced, "but I have a few words to say." The room took to a full hush, for everyone knew what was coming. "It's tradition that the best man speak now, but as ye all know, my best man can't be with us today, though I know he still is, as always, and I know he will be again only shortly." He saw Maria's tears and took her hand in his. "But I'm sure if he was here, he'd only have some smart-arse comment to make about me and maybe even the new wife."

I put a fresh pint up for him and he lifted it to the room. "So, as he's not available to give me a toast, I'd like to take a moment to drink one to him." The room lifted their's likewise. "To Conor…" he said, his voice cracking with the emotion in it, "… who I miss today with all my heart. My best man and my best friend: To Conor!"

The crowd cheered him and took a long, silent drink in his honor. In the quiet, Rory sang out a song they all knew well.

High upon the gallows tree swung the noble-hearted three.
By the vengeful tyrant stricken in their bloom;
But they met him face to face, with the courage of their race,
And they went with souls undaunted to their doom.

The whole crowd joined in on the chorus.

"God save Ireland!" said the heroes;
"God save Ireland" said they all.
Whether on the scaffold high
Or the battlefield we die,
Oh, what matter when for Ireland dear we fall!

Conor's feet had been treated to cut the pain down and bandaged up for mending, but he was still out cold when Sergeant Jones shuffled into the barrack's prison building and found his way up to his detention cell. He spoke to the soldier on guard there. "I need to have a look at that prisoner."

"Have a look if you like," the guard said as he unlocked the cell for him, "but he's not looking so pretty."

Conor was facedown on the stone floor. He didn't move at all from the nudge off the guard's boot, so the sergeant bent down and gently rolled him over. His face was bruised and battered, but the old soldier still had no trouble recognising it.

"By God," he whispered. "That's him."

Chapter Fourteen

One Way or the Other

It was all Sergeant Jones could do to keep pace with the County Inspector on his hurried jaunt back to the detention cells once the old soldier had informed him of his discovery there the previous evening. Although Bowen had told the warders to do their best to hide any evidence of Conor's suffering before discharging him, he'd already given his official approval for his release and was quite concerned that some of his more sympathetic warders might have taken pity on Conor and let him go earlier. He didn't want to chance losing this new opportunity that had fallen right into his mean and bony hands. The bastard was almost skipping his way there.

And he arrived just in time. Conor was awake and up on his feet with the help of crutches, and only waiting outside of the cell he'd been held in, as word had already been sent to the McCabe home that he was to be getting out that morning. Indeed, he'd even been given a proper cup of tea and was having a chat with a few of the warders who'd been guarding him over the past days. It wasn't that they were so much sympathetic toward him, as they were simply well impressed with his keeping silent throughout Bowen's brutal mutilations. They'd never seen a man endure as much. They'd also never seen Bowen fail to pull a confession or some other vital piece of information out of his victims, and to a man they were quietly glad for it. Nearly every soldier in the New Barracks was convinced the man in charge of intelligence for Limerick was mad as the March Hare.

But when Conor caught sight of Bowen marching in on his spry step and heading right for him, his heart sank. He suspected he just might be in for a new spot of trouble. He didn't immediately recognise Jones when he trailed in behind, but somehow he knew his fate was tied to the old soldier shuffling slowly toward him. Somehow he knew he was fucked.

"I believe I owe you a grave apology, Paddy," Bowen said as he offered Conor his hand, like they were only two gentlemen meeting unexpectedly along the promenade. Conor didn't take it. He didn't move at all.

"See, it's been brought to my attention that there is no way you could have been personally involved in the incident that we were only just recently discussing. Indeed, all my bothersome questioning really was for naught. New information clearly indicates that you were otherwise occupied at the time."

Conor looked closely at the old sergeant, but still couldn't place him. He'd had a light shining in his eyes the whole time the patrol was upon them at Fenian's Trace, so he never got a clear view of the man's features. And he wasn't getting much of one now anyway.

The sergeant could only hang his head. He'd been well chuffed with himself for making the connection but he was suddenly regretting ever reporting it to Bowen. He, too, knew of his reputation and just hearing the menace in the Inspector's voice left him fearful for the poor bloke in front of him with the bandaged feet. He'd only laughed when his patrol had stumbled across the two young lovers and their secret tryst out at the old ruin. A part of him had found it charming… but he knew now that nothing charming would come from his disclosure of it.

"Right then," Bowen continued. "It seems instead that you were engaged in a rather awkward situation with one Mrs. Rory McCabe, whose name, albeit taken up only yesterday, I'm sure you recognise."

Conor felt it hit deep in his gut. He would have fallen if not for the crutches, but he only dropped his head.

And Bowen knew he had him. "Yes, it seems my good man Sergeant Jones here identified the lovely bride as - how shall I put this delicately - your personal companion on the evening in question."

Bowen put his face very close to Conor's and circled around him for a bit of extra dramatics. "Now of course, you and I have been over these details before," he hissed. "But this new development has once again piqued my curiosity regarding the whereabouts of Mr. Rory McCabe that night. And to think that you've been subject to so much unpleasantness here, when maybe I should have instead been chatting with him, for I'm sure he and I and Sergeant Jones here would find plenty to discuss."

Conor finally looked up at him. "What do you want?"

Bowen laughed, then took Conor's hair in his hand and yanked his head well forward and even closer. The poor lad had to lean hard on his crutches to keep his balance. "What I want, you filthy, ignorant swine, is Irish blood." He kicked away the supports, sending Conor sprawling to the floor. "What I'll get is a statement naming every man involved in that ambush."

Bowen pulled a sheet of paper and pen from his coat and dropped them down on Conor. "And feel free to include the inconvenient husband. That way, once we round him up, you can slip right into his wedding bed while it's still nice and warm."

With his toes mangled to bits it was a struggle for Conor to regain his feet, but he slowly managed to get himself back standing. "You'll not get a statement from me," he said. "We both know that. But if it's blood you're after, I can give ya yer man."

Liam knew the family of the soldier who'd arrived to inform him that Conor was to be released. His two older brothers had thrown in with the British Army at the start of the Great War, even over the fierce Republican objections of their father, whom Liam had been friendly with years earlier. They'd been sent to the Somme Valley together, but neither had come back and the da wasn't friendly with anyone after that. Liam still saw him on occasion, a drunkard now, living rough in Limerick.

The youngest brother, there at his forge door with a message from the New Barracks, was almost the same age as Rory and Conor, and therefore too young to enlist when the war was on. Still, with the weight of two brothers buried in British uniforms forever on his loyalties, he'd joined up the first chance he got, only to get posted right here at home where he wasn't finding many opportunities to follow in their footsteps. Unfortunately, the next few years would see many heading his way.

Brotherly loyalty was heavy on Liam's own mind as he steered their wagon through Limerick on his way to fetch Conor. Just after the ambush, Rory had assured him that Conor hadn't had any role in it. Martin, too, had promised him that there was no evidence that could connect Conor with it, as well as no just cause for holding him, and it turned out both were right. Of course, both were also quite cagey in explaining their certainties and somehow managed to avoid any mention of the actual ambush. We Irish can say plenty about something without ever speaking a word of it. But sure there was no point, by then everyone had heard every rumour going about what had happened, and Liam himself had no doubts that Rory and Martin had their hands deep in it.

He knew Conor would've known the same as well, and that sort of information would have put him under serious pressure. His last days would have been rough, but Liam wouldn't let his thoughts go anywhere near there. All he wanted was to get him home. He couldn't face the prospect of losing both his lads.

There was all manner of confusion at the gate post, but eventually a guard checked back at the barracks prison and the message came down as final. Conor O'Neill was no longer being released. There would be no explanation forthcoming.

Liam rode back to Cloonlara alone.

Had he instead lingered in the city centre through the afternoon, he would have eventually heard the headline shouts of the newsboys, out peddling that evening's edition of the Limerick Leader -

Ambush Confession!

O'Neill To Be Executed!

Having convinced himself that only the most public display of the Crown's authority would quell any budding Republican sentiments, Bowen had immediately provided the newspaper offices with the official Order of the Special Military Court that he'd established for the trial of anyone involved in the ambush on the Ballyglass road.

But Conor received no trial. His confession alone was enough to render a sentence of death. Bowen even included a copy of it for publication. He himself had swiftly prepared the statement for Conor's signature in triplicate following their brief parley with Sergeant Jones.

The news spread like plague, and it wasn't long after that O'Keefe and Crotty were rushing out to the Sheehan farm with it. Rory and Maria were staying under her parent's fine roof until they could build one of their own on a dowry property Martin had bestowed to the marriage. It was well across the meadow but still in view and Rory already had his stakes into the ground of it. It was from there he saw the men approaching, and he could tell by their pace that they weren't on a social call.

Martin was staring at the newspaper his men had just delivered to him when Rory came into the study. No one said a word as he picked it up, but they all saw his knees buckle with the headline. He nearly fell into the chair where he sat and read the account in full.

Tears were streaming down his cheeks when he looked up at Martin. "It says in two days," he whispered. "We haven't much time."

"Slow down Rory," Martin pleaded. "There's a lot to consider."

Rory's rage quickly overtook the shock of it. "The only thing to consider is how we're getting him out of there."

"It's not that easy," Crotty offered gently.

"I don't give a fuck if it's easy," Rory answered. "It'll be done."

"Rory, if there was any way in there, I'd go with you right fuckin' now," O'Keefe told him. "But it's impossible. We'd never even get around the gate soldiers."

"Then we go through them," Rory said. "The whole lot of us... every man we have."

Martin just shook his head. "And they'll kill him with their first bullet, the very last of us with the rest. We don't have the men or the arms for that. You know it yourself."

Rory moved to stand toe to toe with Martin. "What are ya sayin' then, Martin?" he asked him. "Just leave him to be shot?"

Martin wasn't saying that and nor was anyone else. But they weren't saying anything different either.

"Well you're all fuckin' daft if you think I'm to just stand by and let him be killed for something I done... something we all done."

"But something he's confessed to," says O'Keefe.

And Rory jumped at him, slamming him hard against the wall. "And what choice did he have?" he shouted into his face. "Give 'em your fuckin' name?"

Martin and Crotty pulled him off, but he was raging over it. "Or any of your names? I told ya he'd never fuckin' do that." He collapsed back into a seat, desperate and shaking with the fury and confusion.

Just then Maria pushed the door open on account of all the clatter. She looked straight at Rory and he at her. She saw him trying to keep himself together, but then his tears came back at him and he was helpless to hold them off. And she knew then that Conor was done for, even before she glanced at the headline there on her father's mahogany desk.

She just turned away to walk outside, but then something within stopped her. Instead she went to Rory. She knelt down and pulled his head to hers. "It will be alright," she whispered to him.

"Oh, Maria," Rory cried. "What have they done to him?"

The newly married couple rode together out to Cloonlara with the news. Neither spoke as they passed the ambush site on the Ballyglass road. Of course, the sun had well finished its day at that stage and it was far too dark under the trees to discern anything, but still Rory half expected to see bloodstains under their wheels. There hadn't been the rain to wet your cap since the evening of it... nothing to wash it away.

He felt an odd twinge of pride from it all. The plan of it was mostly his from the start and they'd carried it off with nary a hitch, even after the second two lorries took them by surprise. It had almost been easy, all things considered, and when he thought back on it, wasn't it great *craic*? He'd actually enjoyed every part of it, from the planning and training to the ambush itself.

He thought back to the Fianna of ancient Ireland, the great warriors I'd told him about over our bottling afternoons at Clancy's, many years earlier. The namesake of our modern Fenian's lived only for warfare, living apart from normal society in times of peace but forever ready to defend their people at the behest of their king. It took only the potent call of his battle horn and they set upon the enemy. That was the life for Rory. He'd never forgot their three mottoes - 'Purity of our hearts, strength of our limbs, action to match our speech.' He still hadn't found a want for much else.

If only for this bollocks with Conor… they'd have to get him out and that's all there was to it. He pulled Maria in close to him for the rest of their ride.

Liam came out the door within moments of their reaching the McCabe house and Rory instantly knew he'd already learned of Conor's confession.

It was Fiona who'd told him. While Liam was long outside the barracks awaiting Conor's release, Bowen had already dispatched a soldier out to Cloonlara to notify the McCabes and arrange for a final visit. She'd offered your man tea when he arrived, but he politely declined. His was news not to be conveyed inside. He left her standing just outside her door and that's exactly where Liam found her when he made it home some half hour later. She hadn't stirred. She didn't think she could carry the weight of it for even one step, at least until she'd given some to Liam. He took it, just as he always did. Solid and silent… but inside, he was near crumbling.

They talked it over for a long while and listed out everyone they knew who might be able to help, but Liam felt in his heart it would be all in vain. The solicitors and clergy he knew that wielded any influence in Limerick were all viewed as the enemy by the Brits. Their good standing amongst the Irish meant nothing.

But that wasn't what had him so disheartened. He just couldn't seem to stop himself thinking of all these past years of avoiding the frays. All the days that he'd managed to keep his emotions in check, keeping his head down, keeping his family from jeopardy, keeping his world from peril. But wasn't it all right here at his door anyway? Suddenly… finally, he was ready and willing to take action, and he knew there wasn't a thing he could do. All the strength he had put into his restraint had ultimately left him with none, and now he was simply powerless.

Of course Rory wanted to take the visit with Conor, but Fiona told them the officer she'd spoken to had been clear that he wouldn't be allowed to on account of his recent stay at the barracks himself.

"What will you do then?" Rory asked Liam.

"I can't say as I know, Rory," he answered. "Say our goodbyes, I suppose."

"Goodbyes?" Rory repeated. "Yer fuckin' jokin' like."

Liam knew what Rory was after but had no intention of abiding it. "What do ya propose I do instead, Rory?" he asked him. "Throw him over my shoulder and bust him out?"

"Well we can't fuckin' leave him in there," Rory answered. "We have to do something."

Liam just walked away from him, heading for his forge. "Haven't you already done enough?"

Rory knew then the blame was forever on him, and that hurt, atop everything else, was almost too much to bear. The fury rose from his gut like fire. He shouted for Maria inside and got back onto their cart.

"Where's your father?" she asked when she came out.

"Let's go!" he demanded.

"Let me speak to him," she said.

"It's fuckin' useless, Maria. He couldn't be arsed anyway."

"You go," she said. "I have to try."

Rory snapped the reins on Brooklyn and tore off into the night. Maria watched him go until he disappeared, and then knocked softly on the door of the forge.

Liam made it about halfway down the laneway leading to the New Barracks before he stopped. He kept his distance from the guard posts for a good spell, just standing in the morning shadows thrown from the high walls and watching the bustling activity around the entrance gates. Through their iron bars he had a straight view onto a group of soldiers building some sort of new structure. They were nailing wide planks horizontally up onto a wooden frame that had clearly only just been erected. It looked to be sized about ten feet by ten but was being built in a rather strange location, just there in the middle of the parade ground.

Then he copped on to why. It would only be temporary. An execution wall, plainly positioned to allow for a good viewing by spectators on the outside, from just about where he was standing. He walked to the guard post and gave his name to a soldier.

Two warders brought Conor into the cell used for visits. They hitched his shackles to the floor and left. A warm smile came to his face when he saw Liam standing on the other side of the bars. "Hello, Da," he said.

"How ya keepin' lad?" Liam asked him.

Conor only shrugged. There was no point in hiding the truth. "How's Mam?" he asked.

"Keepin' together," Liam answered. "A lot of praying for ya."

Conor looked around the cell and through the bars to the long hallway. Liam's eyes followed his. "I didn't expect I'd be seein' ya here," Conor said. "Ya didn't have to come. I'd have understood."

"There's something I need to tell ya," Liam said. "Perhaps I should have told ya years ago, I don't know. But I'm to tell ya now." He looked down at the floor, then to the chains around Conor's ankles and the bloodstained bandages on his feet. "I was in here once before, with your da. We were both in the Brotherhood then, at least what there was of it at the time, but we were taken in for shooting a man. Caught in the act."

He looked back up at Conor. "He was after informing on us for collecting a load of guns we'd had shipped over from America, and I shot him in the head over it. Your da was there, but it was me that killed the man. You should know that."

Conor nodded his understanding and Liam held silent for a long moment so to collect himself. "This was just a spell after Rory'd been born, when your mam was still carryin' you. We were both to be executed, both knew it, but first the Brits were after the guns we'd hidden away. We had a rough go of it for a week or so, but neither of us let on to anything." Liam shook his head and let go a pained smile at the memory. "Jaysus lad, your da was the toughest man I've ever known. They took to holdin' guns to our heads, set facin' each other, and tellin' us that the first to give up the guns could go free. The other'd be shot. We weren't havin' any of it. We'd known the risks when we joined up and we weren't afraid to die if we had to."

He paused with those words and studied Conor's eyes. When he didn't see any fear of dying there either, his hopes for him began slowly melting away. "Then word came in to us that you'd been born... and that your mam had died birthin' ya. Your da took it hard, as any man would, but somethin' changed deep inside him as well. He'd not been afraid a dyin' before, and still he wasn't, but now he welcomed it. He hadn't a will to live without your mam."

The tears were welled up high in Liam's eyes, but he was smiling once again. "You never knew her, Conor, but your mam was something else. The sweetest girl in Ireland by all accounts, but she was always messin' with your da. And she could get him laughing 'til he couldn't stand up. T'was great *craic* we all had together - the best days of my life."

Conor smiled too, and with the tears wet on him as well.

"Your da tried to get me to talk," Liam continued, "so I'd be let out and he'd be shot, but I couldn't do it. He was my best friend. One night he made me promise, if I ever did get out, to take care of you and raise ya as my own. I agreed and made him promise the same, if anything'd happen to Fiona. Next morning, the Brits took me out to the spot where we'd hidden the guns. And then they let me go."

Liam dropped his head and wiped his cheeks dry. "Your da was shot that same day. He'd made a deal for my life, against his own, so I could get out to look after you, and my own family." He looked back up at Conor. "Your da didn't die for Ireland, lad. He died for me."

Conor had to wipe away his own tears before he could speak. "It was a sound decision."

"He didn't feel he had a choice," Liam said.

They shared the silence for a long moment, each thinking on the past - Liam on those few fiery days that suddenly bent his entire life in a way he would never have imagined, leaving him cold and hardened like so many hunks of iron he'd shaped over his years; Conor on so much he never knew about, a life lived without any past at all.

The warders interrupted the silence as they approached the cell to take Conor out.

"You do have a choice, Conor," Liam whispered to him. "I spoke with Maria."

Conor took a long read of his face. There wasn't a hint of anger or condemnation in it, but he could see for certain that she'd told him everything. "That's no choice," he said.

"It is for her," Liam said. "And I'd say it's your only way out of this."

"No," Conor protested. "That's no way at all. Ya gotta make her see that."

His chains were unhitched, but as he was being led out of the cell he grabbed a bar on the door to stop. "Liam," he called back, not realising he'd just used the given name of the man that raised him for the first time in his whole life. "I'll need your help."

Liam moved as near as he could get as the warders struggled to pull Conor's hands free of the doorway. "If ya understand why my da did what he did," Conor shouted, "you'll see it the same as I do."

As Liam was led from the prison building back toward the entrance gates, he saw that the soldiers were gone from the parade ground. Their job was complete. The execution wall was ready, looking solid and strong now in the last of the day's dull sunlight.

Liam had passed outside the prison gates, and was making his way back along Lord Edward Street to where he'd left his horse and wagon, when he saw Maria standing next to it, holding Brooklyn's reins. "Did you see him, Mr. McCabe?" she asked.

"I did," Liam answered as he climbed onto his seat.

"Well?" Maria pressed. "What did he say?"

Liam looked down at her. "What's done is done, Maria. His mind is set." And he started auld Oscar off toward home.

She quickly climbed onto Brooklyn and caught up to ride alongside him. "But why?" she asked. "Why is he doing this?"

"Because he's protecting the people he loves. That's all."

"But he wasn't even there," she cried. "He didn't do anything."

"But Rory was there," Liam snapped back at her, "and all the others with him, too. But they're not the ones got caught out on that road." He softened his tone after seeing the hurt in her eyes. "Someone has to pay the price for what happened, Maria. That's for certain. And Conor's takin' that on himself, though they couldn't be bothered with who it is anyway."

They rode side by side awhile until Liam halted his horse when they reached the point on Sarsfield Street where Maria would turn off for the bridge. She stopped Brooklyn as well. "There must be something else we can do," she said. "What if I just go in and tell them what really happened."

"That's just it, Maria," Liam replied. "They don't care what really happened. Now you're just going to have to let it go. He signed a confession. There's nothing anyone can do about that."

"What will I tell Rory?" she asked, almost to herself. "He won't see it like that."

"He'll have to," Liam answered as he prompted Oscar to head off. "One way or the other."

It was before the next dawn that Conor finally mustered up the nerve to pull boots onto his feet. He hadn't dared yet to remove the bandages someone had put on them after Bowen had gone at him with his pincers, but a warder had placed a pair in his cell overnight and told him he'd need them on for walking out to the parade ground in the morning. They didn't want him looking as if he was after suffering any mistreatment. He didn't much want to be limping along shoeless either, so he gingerly slipped them on. The pain was brutal when he stood up, but thank Christ they were more than a size too big and his butchered toes barely met the leather.

He was only back off his feet and laying in the darkness when a familiar voice softly spoke to him. "Hello, Conor," said Father O'Dea.

Conor didn't get up, but he smiled and said hello as a warder let our good priest into the lad's cell. He was cupping the draft off a lit candle and had a satchel hanging from his shoulder. "How ya keeping, son?" he asked.

"I can't sleep, Father." Conor says to him. "I'm exhausted but I keep thinking it's wrong to be wastin' my last hours on kip, like." He patted the proper mattress that the warders had brought in to him for his last night. "Instead I'm only wastin' this fine bed they gave me."

Father O'Dea took a Bible from his satchel and set it by him. "Comfort yourself the best you can, Conor." He slipped out a naggin of whiskey and set that next to the Bible. "I'm here to help with that."

"Cheers, Father," Conor said, but his eyes were on the long hallway outside the cell. "I don't suppose there's any chance of anyone else being let in?"

"I'm sorry, lad," says Father O'Dea. "I'm afraid you'll have to make do with just meself."

"Ah sure, Father, I didn't mean it like that. It's very good of ya to come."

Father O'Dea winked at him. "I'm only teasing," he says. He produced a writing pad and pen and handed that to him as well. "But I'll be sure any letters are delivered safely."

Conor thanked him again and closed his eyes.

"Please don't lose hope, Conor," the good priest urged. "There's a petition for mercy going around as we speak, from the Bishop of Limerick himself. I'd say thousands have signed on. And there's a gathering now right outside the gates, demanding they give you a reprieve. All is not lost."

Conor arranged the holy book, the spirits and the pad in front of him and stared at them for a while. A smile slowly came to his face.

"What is it?" Father O'Dea asked.

"I guess that right there is all anyone needs," Conor said.

"How do ya mean?"

"One helps ya know what to do, one helps ya tell what ya done, and one helps ya do it."

"He works in mysterious ways," the priest assured him.

"I've no question His ways are mysterious," Conor says. "I'm just not sure if they're workin', like."

Father O'Dea removed a gold pyx from his satchel. "I'll give you Communion and hear your confession, lad."

"I'd appreciate Communion, Father, but it's confessin' that's put me in this mess." Conor took up the whiskey and opened it. "No offence, but I'd just as soon leave that be." He took a slug, then passed over the bottle.

"The Lord understands some sins more than others," promised the priest.

"I'm well countin' on that, Father."

The gathering that Father O'Dea mentioned was stuffed into the laneway that led to the entrance gates of the barracks. There was no hope of a lorry or anything else getting in or out, but no effort for it either. Inspector Bowen purposely had that wall built in plain view of the gates. His demonstration needed an audience and even the pissing rain on the morning hadn't kept what seemed like half of Limerick from turning up.

There was hardly the room to move, but I managed my way to the front where the anger was surging right up toward the gates. Armed soldiers lined them on the inside, sometimes striking out with the butts of their rifles but mostly keeping a few steps off and just watching the crowd. Folks were waving protest signs and Irish flags and it wasn't long until they took to the singing.

Oh! Paddy, dear, and did you hear the news that's going round,
The shamrock is forbid by law to grow on Irish ground.
Saint Patrick's Day no more we'll keep, His color can't be seen
For there's a bloody law agin' the wearing of the green.

I met with Napper Tandy and he took me by the hand
And he said "How's poor old Ireland? And how does she stand?"
She's the most distressful country that ever you have seen,
They're hanging men and women there, for the wearing of the green.

Conor was penning a letter to the soothing murmur of Father O'Dea's prayers when he heard the clang of a heavy door several floors below. It was only faint, but his ears that morn were keenly attentive to even the slightest rustle. When he heard the footsteps of several men climbing the stairs, he hurried to find a finish for his words.

It was six soldiers that came for him. None could even look in his direction. They only spoke quietly to the warders lingering outside the cell. A fair group of them who'd done duty since Conor was brought in had taken to keeping an impromptu vigil in the hallway. To a man they knew the lad was innocent, and though not one voiced it they all were wishing for his last-minute rescue from the evil looming beyond the walls. But each man had already been poisoned by it, and their futile hopes for a late stay did little to spare them their shame. Seeing it to the very end was their self-imposed punishment.

The six soldiers in the hall had not arrived to deliver a stay. A young warder unlocked the cell door. "It's time," he announced.

Conor scrawled out a few final words, put down his pen and tore a page from the pad he'd been writing in. He rolled it up tight, then pulled the Trinity Knot pendant off his neck and wound it securely around the paper by its leather cord. He handed it to Father O'Dea. "Could ya see that Rory gets this, Father?"

"I will of course," promised the priest, struggling hard to keep his emotions together.

Two of the soldiers stepped into the cell and locked the lad's wrists into chained shackles. One pointed forward and down the hallway. "Follow there now," he told him.

As Conor walked out, the warders formed a line to shake his hand and wish him luck. When he shook the last, Father O'Dea filed in behind him... but he was halted. "Sorry sir," the soldier said. "You're not allowed any further with the prisoner. You'll have to view from outside."

The priest was loath to break off from him, but Conor extended his hand as far as the shackles allowed. "Thanks for everything, Father Stephen," he smiled. "I won't forget it."

The priest embraced him. "God will be with you, lad," he whispered through his tears. "But hold tight to His sleeve."

Martin, O'Keefe and Crotty had positioned themselves at such intervals along the laneway leading to the barrack's gates that they could still see one another, even amongst the huge crowd that had assembled. No one had seen Rory since he left Maria at the McCabe house on the day before, but there wasn't a notion that he would stay away. When O'Keefe caught sight of him approaching on a horse and cart by way of O'Connell Avenue, he signaled the others. As they closed in on him, they watched him get off and furtively pull a rifle out from under some blankets. He slipped it under the long topcoat he wore just before Martin put a hand on his shoulder. Rory jerked around off the unexpected touch.

"Do you know how many men are inside those gates?" Martin asked him. "How many guns?"

Rory didn't answer. He was angling on his chances against the three of them.

"What are you aiming to do, Rory?" Martin pressed. "You can't save him. You've no chance. You might get a few of them but you're only gettin' yourself killed."

"And others with ya," O'Keefe added.

"I'll get Bowen," Rory said.

"I won't let you do it, lad," says Martin. "We've got too much work to do."

Rory's face was delirious with anguish as he pulled a small revolver from his coat pocket. He pointed it at Martin. "I'm sorry, Martin," he cried.

Martin wasn't about to back off, but just then a heavy hand landed on his shoulder. Liam stepped in front of him, facing Rory and the gun. "This is the life you've chosen, Rory," he said to him. "I can no longer keep you from it, so the sooner you can take responsibility for the deaths of others the better. But you best know this. Conor's is one death you are not responsible for. This is a decision he's made, not you."

Rory's hand on the gun was shaking. "But he's dyin' 'cause of somethin' I done, Da."

"No, Rory," Liam says. "He's giving his life so you can have yours. Not so you can throw it away."

Rory just stared beyond them, out toward the parade ground, as tears filled his eyes.

"Think of Maria," Liam pleaded, "and your mam and the girls." He wiped away tears of his own. "Christ, Rory," he said, "think of me. Please, I can't lose you both, lad."

Finally, he just stepped aside, leaving Rory a clear path forward down the laneway and to the gates beyond. "If all that means nothin' to you, then do what you will, but there's more than one way to be brave, son."

Rory lowered the gun and just stood there, shaking and crying. Liam put a hand on his shoulder and pulled him into an embrace. Rory whispered in his ear. "Tell me what to do, Da."

"Find Maria," Liam told him. "She'll be at the gates."

Rory handed the gun to Martin and rushed off into the raucous crowd.

Chapter Fifteen

Make Ready

Conor heard the din of our song the moment the soldiers pushed open the exit doors of the prison building. From his angle there just outside it, he couldn't yet see the entrance gates or the huge mob behind them, but the sound drifted over and around the high stone walls in between. Even the cold morning downpour couldn't dampen the pluck that was in our voices there and maybe it heartened his walk across the muddy grounds of the prison yard. But there was fuck all to block his view of the execution wall. It was dead ahead of him.

When the lead soldiers he was following turned the corner in sight of the entrance point, even they were shocked by the scene. Those among us that weren't pushing the gates in hard against the authority of the barrack's chains and soldiers, were waving up signs and flags in the pelting rain:

FREE CONOR O'NEILL!
BRITAIN OUT!
UP THE IRA!

And when Conor came into view, our volume rose to near deafening.

Still, he did perceive one particular voice screaming out to him from among the throng. Maria was right there at the front of the gates, her hands gripping the iron bars as she tried to brace herself against the forward impetus of the crowd. The crush was becoming dangerous, but everything within her was focused on Conor as she frantically screamed his name.

When he heard it, he instinctively broke off running toward her, but with his legs shackled in irons the soldiers caught him after his first few steps and tackled him hard. They yanked him up and dragged him across the yard toward the wall. Upon reaching it, they momentarily freed his wrists before switching them behind his back and relocking them. Then they clasped the chains to a hitch they'd positioned on the wall especially for the occasion. They'd even measured the height needed for it to ensure he wouldn't be left in any sort of awkward stance when the fuckers were measuring him up in their sights.

The laneway was packed thick and unruly, but Rory was still able to force his way through to the front. He would have moved a mountain to get himself there and when he put his hands to the gates he felt he just might tear them down. But on sight of Conor, fastened up to a shoddy, temporary wall constructed only to oblige a murder, he directed every strength he had to him. "Be strong, Conor!" he shouted again and again. "Be strong!"

Conor heard his voice as well and could see him at the gate, pushing against it in a frenzied rage, completely oblivious to the soldiers bashing batons and rifle butts against him. From his vantage point he could see both Rory and Maria, both right up front but separated by the many others stretched along the full length of the gates. He couldn't point with his arms bound up, but when his eyes met Rory's he put him right at Maria and then watched as Rory made his way to her, hand by hand along the black iron bars, shouting out his support to him with every step.

He only looked away when Bowen approached, with six soldiers trailing him, each carrying a rifle. The County Inspector stood himself about dead center, between the wall he'd ordered built and the gates he hid behind. He unfurled a paper scroll and read aloud from it. He shouted out every word with all the aplomb he could muster, but was still barely heard over our singing.

"Under the laws of Great Britain, His Majesty the King, and the laws of God, Conor O'Neill has been sentenced to death by firing squad for his crimes committed against the Empire, and to which he duly and willingly confessed. His execution serves as the only just and rightful punishment." He took a step toward the gates and pointed out his bony finger. "And be it known, all other participants in those treasonous acts, no matter how minimal their involvement, await the same fate!"

He rolled the scroll and tucked it inside his long topcoat. He then pulled a small white cloth from his belt and approached Conor with it, pinning the small target to his coat, right over his heart. As Bowen wouldn't meet his gaze, Conor looked past him to the soldiers. Three dropped down to one knee, while the others stood directly behind to form their very tidy and contemptible firing line. Then Bowen asked if the poor lad had any last words.

Conor stepped forward as far as possible given the chains, and when he looked out toward our roaring crowd we cut the singing and fell perfectly silent. For a moment, I could even hear the tinny clink of the rain hitting the metal roofs over the guard posts.

"I don't deny that I've confessed to these crimes," he shouted, still watching Rory clutch his way along the gates, frantic to reach Maria. His eyes settled on her as he continued. "But the only crime I've committed is against the truth that lies within my heart. I do so without regret and I accept my fate without fear. When I die, that truth will die with me, but the love in my heart will live on forever."

When he stepped back, we burst back into song.

Bowen turned to his firing squad. "Make ready!" he ordered.

Conor stared straight at Maria as the soldiers raised up their rifles. She had fallen to her knees and her face was pressed against the bars, crying desperately.

"Take aim!" Bowen shouted.

Finally, Rory reached her. He pulled her up and into his arms, hiding her eyes from the sight.

And Conor closed his.

"Fire!"

Chapter Sixteen

A Treasure

Liam McCabe never heard the gunshots. He was nearly back to Cloonlara by then. When he did arrive, he got off his wagon and looked toward his doorway, but his feet wouldn't make the steps and suddenly he had to turn and brace himself against auld Oscar to keep from falling down.

Fiona came outside to him a moment later and placed a hand on his mighty back. "Yer alright there, love," she whispered. "Yer alright."

Liam turned to her and fell to his knees. He clutched her waist and sobbed for all of Ireland, and she gently stroked his hair in the rain.

It was several days before Rory opened the letter Father O'Dea had given to him from Conor. He waited until the sun shined again on Fenian's Trace and he climbed to the top of the turret where he could see the rapids running on the Shannon. He unwound the leather cord holding Conor's pendant and set the letter upon the flat stone top of the parapet there that faced the river. It covered the letters they'd carved into it the first day they'd found the old ruin - Conor and Rory.

Dear Rory,

> *Seems now I won't be leaving Ireland after all. I've no regret though, it's a grand country. And I know you'll help in bringing it all the greatness it deserves. I know what that means to you. I only wish I could see it with you.*

Yet as the last hours of my life fall away, I'm troubled by how ready you are to give up your own. For there is so much to live for Rory, so much that makes life precious. Most of all, you have Maria. I hope one day you realise, every step you take with her is a step in heaven.

I don't fear that I'll die soon, for I'll go with love in my heart. I only hope I have even half the courage you do when I face the rifles. You've never been afraid of anything.

I ask only one thing of you. Please don't waste your life hating England. Live it loving Ireland and all that it can be.

I think my time is almost here.

I once told Maria I'd try to write a poem for her, but it doesn't look like I'll be getting to it now. Maybe you'll read these next lines for her. They're from Mangan, though I've trampled on 'em a bit.

Death soon will heal my griefs! This heart, now sad and sore,
Did beat anew a little while, and then no more.

Take care of her, Rory, and love her with all your great strength. She's a treasure.

May God watch over you.
All my best,
Conor O'Neill.

They buried Conor at Fenian's Trace, just down the path from the entryway, with a headstone Rory pulled from the Shannon himself.

Still there to this day.

Chapter Seventeen

Kind and Knowing

Rory fought in the War of Independence for Ireland and was responsible for the deaths of many men after the hostilities around Limerick escalated following Conor's execution. He was quickly promoted to lead a flying column of his own and spent most of the conflict on the run, though he always managed to steal moments with Maria, tending to their children in the home they built near her father's horse farm. She hadn't known it at the time Conor passed, but she was already carrying then. He wouldn't have been the first wedding night baby in Ireland... and they followed him up with several more.

When the Treaty was signed at the end of 1921, Rory went back to working with Liam at their forge and helped Martin in his horse trading. He had no stomach for the horrible civil war that followed and swears he never had the use for violence again. I take him at his word of course, but I also know of a curious incident that occurred in Dublin, shortly after the Union Jack came down for the Tricolour at the New Barracks and the Crown forces posted there marched back to England.

The Brits went off in ships from Dublin Port and I'd say most were thrilled to be leaving. Some even took to celebrating in the local pubs while awaiting their departure. Even Tyler Bowen, who hadn't been to a pub outside his barracks walls in over three years, enjoyed a few tipples himself. His favoured White Horse Scotch Whisky I understand, but he never did make his scheduled departure to England.

The former County Inspector of Limerick somehow went missing and was only found several days later all the way back in Limerick's People's Park, missing most of his head. It was obvious he had suffered a gunshot at very close range, possibly even with the rifle's barrel stuffed into his mouth. Curiously enough, one of his feet was also missing several toe nails. But the detail most interesting to me was the report that he was holding half of a brick in one hand when his body was discovered. Of course, I didn't need to lay my eyes on it to know that it was probably a right close match to those of me own chimney.

I'm delighted to say that Rory and Maria still call into Clancy's now and again, where they still enjoy the best pint of Guinness in Ireland, though they usually have a trail of children nipping at their heels. Four or maybe five to them now, I believe.

I'm told they're all avid horse riders, often to be glimpsed galloping fast out to the River Shannon to watch its great waters run, and all the boats atop it. Maybe waiting on their own clarion call to adventure. I suspect Rory's shown them the ruin of Fenian's Trace, but sure, if he hasn't, they'll eventually discover it themselves, if not its every secret.

T'was their eldest - name of Conor, of course - who sat up at my bar not long ago. We were only after chatting a bit when I chanced my arm asking him about the leather cord hanging around his neck that looked familiar to me. He pulled it from under his shirt and explained me that it was a Trinity Knot that had belonged to his uncle, who he was right quick to proclaim his namesake. He told me he wasn't sure what it had symbolised for him, but as it was now his own, it represented his mam and his da and himself, as he was their first born and therefore always of special regard.

I thanked him for this fine lesson and then, being a bit of an amateur *shenachie*, albeit one with a flair for the occasional embellishment when it suits, I just couldn't help meself from launching into a grand auld story of ancient Ireland. Young Conor latched right on to my tale, and as I blathered on I caught the smiles on Maria and Rory as they watched us.

But it was another look that left me gobsmacked. The lad seemed to be quite keen to nearly everything I was telling him. Like he already knew it all, but just didn't have the heart to let on.

And sure, in all my days, I'd only ever seen a look like that once before.

An críoch.